THE
TWIST AND SHOUT
MURDER

THE
TWIST AND SHOUT
MURDER

A
SWINGING SIXTIES
MYSTERY

Teresa Trent

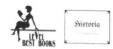

LEVEL
BEST BOOKS

Historia

Author Photo Credit: M. K. Higginbotham

First edition

ISBN: 978-1-68512-070-2

Cover art by Level Best Designs

This book was professionally typeset on Reedsy.
Find out more at reedsy.com

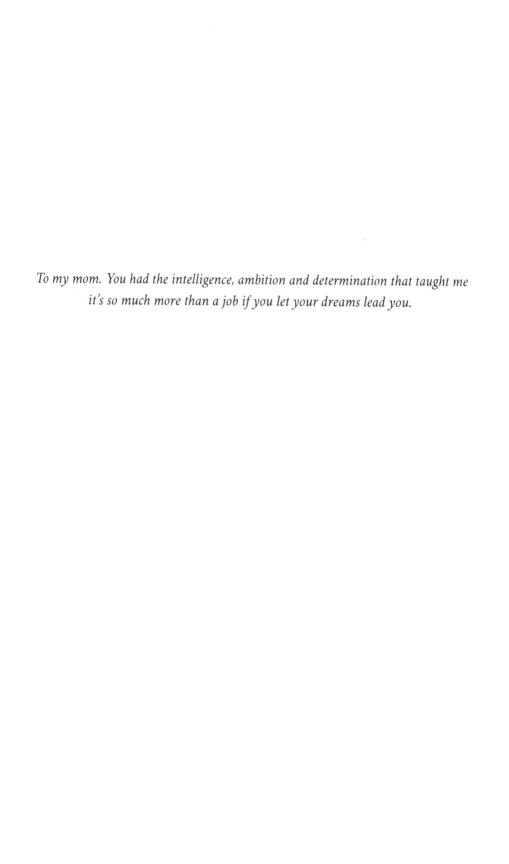

To my mom. You had the intelligence, ambition and determination that taught me it's so much more than a job if you let your dreams lead you.

Chapter One

1962 Camden, Texas

A shiny turquoise Cadillac parked at the curb.

Barb Manning nearly took my breath away as she stepped out of the car in a crisp blue linen suit. Some people simply get out of a car, but others make an unforgettable entrance. She was in the unforgettable group. Her hair, cut in an elegant style, framed her cheekbones and accented her deep blue eyes. She was slender, and the heels she wore made her look even more regal. She was as glamorous as a Pan Am stewardess or maybe Liz Taylor. I pulled on the hem of the yellow cotton dress I had worn on the night of my high school graduation. It was a little less crisp than it was on that day but still dressy enough to meet with her. This woman was the wife of the town's district attorney and a resident of the prestigious King's Hill neighborhood on the other side of town. Mrs. Manning was the president of the Camden Ladies' Club, and the rumor was she ruled with an iron fist. The civic group was well known for raising money and hosting social occasions regularly featured in the *Camden Courier* .

I was nothing like her. I was single and not a lady of local society and shared an apartment with my cousin Ellie on the top floor of Arlene Clark's modest home. A lifelong resident of Camden, I lived in a different world than Barb. She had probably traveled all around the world on luxurious vacations. I went to the movies. I loved sitting there in the dark as the world unfolded before me. When I was a child, my parents took me to the movies weekly, that being one of the chief entertainments in a small town. Now that I was older, outside of an occasional date, I would get my cousin Ellie to go with me or go alone. Romance, mystery, westerns, I went to see it all. My parents were still a big part of my life and they were helping me with tuition for a local secretarial school and on the rent. I was fortunate I could attend a school right here in Camden. We didn't have the glamor of Dallas, but some families had lived here for generations. We had a public library and a movie theater where my cousin Ellie and I had just seen *The Music Man.* I was happy with my station in life and would never have attempted to approach Barb Manning and her set if I didn't have to.

Why would I do this?

It all started when my father, Mike Morgan, would come home and tell me about the trials he witnessed during his twenty years as a clerk at the courthouse.

Dad loved watching the wheels of justice grind and how our system could work to help victims. Many nights he and Mom would discuss his job at Columbo's Diner, Camden's favorite restaurant, and I would listen as he talked about the people whose lives had changed because of the courts. I guess that was where we first came up with the idea of his running for city council after poor Phil Boggs died unexpectedly. "You know, Dot," my dad would say, "our court system is a place where a man, any man, can have his voice heard. It's what America is all about."

I corrected him. "Don't you mean a man or a woman?"

"Of course," he said. "How could I forget the better half of humanity?"

Twirling a string of spaghetti on my fork, I asked, "Who do you think will run for his seat?"

"I don't know, but I hope whoever it is will be more effective than Phil was." Phil Boggs had been a heavy eater and often fell asleep at evening city council meetings. When it came time to vote, someone would have to jostle him awake and then, no matter what the issue, he always voted the same way.

Yes.

More taxes?

Yes.

A cheaper trash pickup company?

Yes. Yes. Yes.

That was when the idea hit me. My father had always been a champion of the common man, and this was an area where he could actually make a difference. "Why don't you run for the job?"

My father looked surprised. "Me?"

"Sure." Mom patted him on the shoulder. "You care about this town more than Phil Boggs ever did. I think you'd be good at it. I think Dot might be on to something. Besides, I like the idea of being a city councilman's wife."

"I don't know. I'm not much of a politician. I don't think I'd be good at giving speeches and convincing people to vote for me."

"Politician?" When he said it like that, he made it sound like a despicable profession. It wouldn't be long before he shut the whole idea down. "I hardly think this is the presidency. Come on, Dad. It's Camden city council, a little town whose biggest problem is crabgrass. You'd be helping people. That's what you like to do, right? The election is just a small part of the job. A precursor. As desperately as they need an immediate replacement, there might not even be one. I haven't heard about anyone pining to sit through those meetings. Working on the city council is your chance to help our community."

He took off his glasses and cleaned them with a corner of his shirt. I'd seen him do this before and it usually meant he was taking time to think about something. "I don't know. I never thought of myself working in city government."

My mother leaned over, the chain on her glasses clunking on the table. "You already do. You work at the courthouse. Isn't that city government involvement enough?"

After that evening and an overabundance of badgering on our part, Dad put in his name for Phil Boggs' position. He never stopped being nervous about the process he would have to go through to get elected, but this was a small town in Texas with a low crime rate, and people who had known each other all their lives. Anyone who had ever gotten a ticket, had a will probated, or lived through a divorce case, knew my dad. They knew he was fair and honest. A seat on the city council was a simple yet vital job that needed to be done. In the last few years, Camden's population had been rising because of the expansion of Dallas. Who knew what the future would bring to our city? Dad would now be on the cutting edge of all of it and a sure winner for the council seat. Just in case he wasn't I came up with the idea of joining the Camden Ladies' Club. These women were married to the most influential men in town, and it wouldn't hurt to have the name Morgan in front of them. I know, normally a candidate's wife would have filled this role, but my mother swore off mixing with the upper crust years ago.

"I'm a librarian, not a debutante," she said when I suggested it to her. "If you want to hobnob with those women, then do it. I'd rather spend my days with the books in the library."

I wanted my father to win. I wanted someone with his moral code in government, and if he would have any chance, I wanted to help him. It's not what you know, but who you know.

Barb's heels clicked on the sidewalk as she approached the porch of Arlene's white two-story frame home. The orange and yellow marigolds looked a little droopy this morning, and I regretted not offering to water them. The Texas summer heat had settled into the low 90s, and it was taking its toll on everything including Arlene's marigolds.

She turned on a smile fit for a beauty queen. "Hello. You must be Dot Morgan." Barb Manning fanned herself with long slender fingers, "It's getting warm for it to be only June."

"Come on inside." I opened the door, and she stepped into Arlene's front room, her glance taking in her surroundings. She pursed her lips, looking as if she were trying to be diplomatic as she eyed the furnishings. Arlene had chosen tones of yellow and burnt orange, including a pair of throw pillows with owls she needle pointed to pick up the colors in the wallpaper. The room had always felt cozy to me. Some nights Ellie and I sat in this room watching television with Arlene. Now I couldn't escape the feeling it looked like a bad day at the thrift shop. Maybe those handmade owls looked tacky to someone like Barb. Maybe the people of her set considered orange and yellow too folksy and brash.

"I'm glad you had time to meet with me today." She glanced around the room again, but this time she looked closer to the floor. "You can imagine it surprised us when you approached us about joining our little group. We have so few single girls."

"I know, but I thought it might be fun." I hoped that sounded convincing, hiding my true motive of promoting my father's campaign in their influential circles.

"Well, even though it is unusual to have an unmarried member of the club, I figured you were just the woman for the job we need to have done. Your new membership couldn't have come at a better time."

It was wonderful they wanted me in their club, but there was something about her evaluation of my availability that worried me. Being single didn't mean I had nothing to do. "What kind of job did you have in mind, Mrs. Manning?"

"Oh, please, darling. Don't call me Mrs. Manning. Call me Barb." She wrinkled her nose playfully like we were old buddies from the country club. "We're friends now, aren't we?"

"Barb," I repeated obediently if not awkwardly.

"From looking at your lovely outfit, I can see you have an eye for color." Her eyes shone as her eyebrows went up.

A compliment? Maybe the dress still looked good after two years? I began to feel better about our meeting. Could it be I misread her signals all along? I began to embrace the possibility that just because somebody lived in a nicer neighborhood didn't mean that they couldn't be a friend.

"That's why I know you'll be the perfect club member to make the flower arrangements for the Founder's Day Banquet."

The banquet was only two days away. When I attended the last meeting at the Camden Ladies' Club, they were planning food, speakers, a guest list, and decorations. It was much more involved than I would have ever imagined. Assuming I would play a minor role at the banquet, I had thought little about it. I was in my fourth and final semester of a two-year program at the Hudson Secretarial School and was hoping the ladies' club wouldn't take from the time I needed to devote to finishing up my classes. Volunteering was important for my dad's brand-new campaign, but school was my top priority, and I was looking forward to graduating, and beginning to apply for secretarial positions.

Barb squinted at me and then questioned. "You've made flower arrangements before, right? I'm sure it's a part of the Home Ec course they teach at Camden High."

"I guess so, but I'm not a florist. I've put flowers in a vase, if that's what you mean."

Her eyelids lowered as if hiding her disappointment. Maybe I could fit it in around studying for my next test.

"How many flower arrangements were you thinking of?" I was almost afraid of her answer, but how bad could it be?

She clapped her hands together, taking my question as a "yes." "Not too many. Thirty would do it."

"Thirty? You want me to make thirty flower arrangements?" I tried to hide my shock at this last-minute request, but I could feel my cheeks heating, not something I could hide with my fair skin. "As I said before, I'm a full-time student. As much as I would like to help you out, I have a big test coming up, and don't have time to create thirty flower arrangements."

Barb Manning tapped her deep red fingernails on the coffee table and licked her teeth behind a coat of matching red matte lipstick. Her expression was one of pity. "I guess I'm the one who's sorry. I thought you wanted to be a part of our civic organization. I must have been wrong."

Being in this club could give Dad that extra push he needed, and I didn't intend to get booted out before I took part in my first event. I had to think of something. "Is there someone else I can work with to make these flower arrangements? Maybe if there were two of us, the task wouldn't seem so monumental."

Barb slowly shook her head as she smiled. "Out of the question. All our ladies are busy doing their own assigned tasks. Even though your contribution to the group was well, untested, we just assumed you could handle something as mindless as this."

I stared at the floor, feeling her disappointment in me. "You have to admit making that many flower arrangements is a lot to ask at this short notice."

Perhaps I had been unrealistic thinking I could juggle a club membership and my studies. For people like Barb, volunteering was a full-time job.

She picked up her clutch bag and held it close to her body with her fingernails curled to the front. "By the way, congratulations on your father running for city council. So sad about Phil Boggs choking on that chicken bone. He always was the overindulgent type. I think it's wonderful we have another fine citizen stepping up to the plate."

"You know about his campaign?" My spirits lifted. She already knew about the city council race. Maybe, even if I did have to drop out of the club, she could be helpful anyway. Having the wife of the town's D.A. happy to hear Dad would be running for the city council seat had to be good news.

"Of course, if you're no longer a part of the Camden Ladies' Club, attending the function would be slightly awkward. It will not do much for your father's political career, either. We're all pretty tight-knit around here. I might also mention other factors that could destroy the voters' perception of him."

Other factors? What other factors? "Just what exactly are you saying?"

She raised her chin. Her red fingernails clamped onto the bag. "I didn't want to have to bring this up," she tilted an eyebrow, "but you should be aware we know about your father's...arrest record."

I paled. This was like something out of a bad radio drama. I half expected to hear distant organ music. "I'm a little confused."

"Your father was caught in a raid over at Miss Daisy's last year. He might not have been charged, but his name is a part of the record."

Miss Daisy's was a brothel between Camden and the next town. I didn't understand how Barb had gotten hold of this information, but if she were to dig deeper, she would have found out he was there to retrieve an old friend who had imbibed a little too much that night and was about to ruin a 25-year marriage. He told me about it one night at dinner.

"Dot," he said. "I think I should tell you that I was taken down to the station by the police last night."

I almost choked on my spaghetti. "Why?"

"They raided Miss Daisy's. You know what that place is, right?"

"Oh, that's the place where they..."

"She knows," my mother interrupted.

"Yes, but why were you there?" It was a strange question to have to ask my father, but if my dad was visiting prostitutes, I wanted to know.

"It's not what you think. I got a call from a friend who was in trouble. He'd had too much to drink and was in their lobby. He called me to take him home, because if he called his wife, well, you know. I had just entered Miss Daisy's and found my friend sprawled out in the waiting room when the police broke in. It looked bad, but I was innocent. I just thought you should know in case anyone else finds out."

Listening to Barb talk, my father's fears had come true. "It's so interesting what I find out because my husband is the district attorney. If the city council were to find out about your father's deviant behavior, it could be the end of his little campaign." Barb was silent a calculated five seconds and then came back hard. "Now about these flower arrangements?"

She had me. "I'll throw something together."

"Good girl." She reached into her bag and pulled out a slip of paper. "Here's the address where you can pick up supplies so generously donated by the city." She patted me on the shoulder. I almost expected her to say, *good dog.* "I can see we're going to get along just fine."

Even though I would have rather been studying my dictation notes, which sounds boring, even to me, I plunged ahead with the dreaded floral arrangements. I dutifully picked up supplies from the florist and had them spread out across our apartment when Ellie arrived home from work, her hair straggling around her face. She was somewhere between being a seamstress and a dress designer, and I could still see the red mark on her neck where she wore her tape measure.

"What's going on here?" Ellie asked.

We had a small landing at the top of the stairs between our bedrooms, and we furnished it with a small couch, chair, and coffee table. We used it as our "sitting room" and shared the space. For me, it was for watching cop shows on our little black and white TV while Ellie was always hand stitching something. There were flowers strewn over both pieces of furniture, and I had scattered vases on any flat surface I could find.

"Um, I'm making flower arrangements for the Camden Ladies' Club."

A wrinkle formed above her eyes. "Seriously? You actually joined the ladies' club? I knew you were talking about it, but I didn't think you'd go through with it."

One thing about Ellie, she knew me. She also knew joining social clubs and working on flower arrangements when I needed to study wasn't me. Even though she was eight years older than I was, we had grown up together. When she was sixteen, and I was eight, I trailed after her whenever we were together. Amazingly, she let me. She was never a popular girl with her gangly figure and plain features. Maybe if she had been prom queen with boyfriends and admirers, things would have been different. For the last five years, Ellie had a longtime boyfriend, Al the electrician. I always wondered why they never married, but she and Al seemed comfortable with the situation. She had Bluebonnet Fashions, and he ran his own electrical repair company. They were busy with their own careers.

She cast me a sidelong glance, and it didn't look like she approved of my industrious efforts to mass create the centerpieces.

"I know what you're thinking, Ellie, but I'm willing to put up with them, for a while at least. I think they can help with Dad's campaign. You know what they say. It's who you know, not what you know that gets you into public office."

"I can't believe you're doing this for Uncle Mike. What a sacrifice." She picked up a vase. "Don't you have a test tomorrow?"

"I do, but…" Barb's threat played around in the back of my head. "It's no problem. The centerpieces are for the Founder's Day Banquet. It will be a great way for Dad to make his entrance onto the political stage."

"Oh, yeah. Is that coming up already? Your dad only announced a week ago. He can't have any campaign materials ready to hand out."

It was awfully soon to go into campaign mode, but I couldn't let my father be absent at the Founder's Day Banquet, especially with the threat Barb had made to expose his accidental arrest at Miss Daisy's. If he knew what was going on, he would tell me to quit the club. He wouldn't understand my motivation. Dad might like to help people, but sometimes he was oblivious to how the world worked.

"Does he know he's going to the banquet?"

With all the fuss about the flowers, telling him had escaped my mind. "No, but he will."

When I called him a few minutes later, he quickly tried to get out of attending the banquet. "Honey, that is nice of you to think of this, but I was going to go about this whole campaign thing pretty low-key."

"I don't know if you'll be able to wait. Barb Manning already knows you are planning to run."

"That's because I had to file with the city, and her husband works there. Still, I'm skipping this one."

I had to find a way to convince him to go to the banquet. Not only would skipping the event harm his campaign, but it would also be humiliating when Barb let the whole town find out he was visiting a house of ill repute for a reason he couldn't disclose.

"Being unprepared could do me more harm than good. The people in this town have already put up with years of Phil Boggs barely paying attention. I need to show I'm qualified and competent. Right now, I'm not ready for anything."

"I don't think it'll be that bad. You just have to show up. These people need to see you as a candidate."

"And it would be nice if I was a prepared candidate."

"Promise me you'll think about it."

"Well, you certainly are going to a lot of trouble for your old man. I promise I'll think about it."

The next morning, after a tedious evening of sticking flowers in vases, I stepped out into the morning sunshine. Luckily, my green shirtwaist dress was ironed, so I pulled my hair back in a ponytail and had just enough time to drop off my night's work before school. My shorthand class was at ten, and I was loading up the flowers in my car at 8:30 sharp. Most of the women who lived in single-family modest homes around me were married and didn't work. They spent their time raising their children and providing clean homes for their families. I wanted children someday, but not yet. I wanted to have a job. I loved business and the idea of owning one of my own someday. I could see myself as a corporate executive, but business school was tough to get into as a woman, so I chose the only easily available option and enrolled in secretarial courses.

I struggled to carry the vases and fit them into my 1958 Plymouth Fury, a car that had once been a snazzy red but had faded to a sickly pink. If I planned to deliver these to the banquet hall and get to the secretarial school in time for my class, it would be cutting it close. I was squeezing in the last vase when Barb Manning parked her car on the street and popped out holding a small bag. Today she wore bright yellow linen slacks tapering at her ankles and a white sleeveless top with multicolored polka dots. "Glad I caught you, darling. I want you to attach these cards to the vases." Barb pulled out a hand-lettered card that read *Flowers Provided by Barb Manning for Your Pleasure.*

"You want me to put these with the vases?" I asked, confused. Barb had nothing to do with creating these floral arrangements but seemed determined to take credit for it. Funny, I didn't remember her being elbow to elbow with me last night as I threw together the flower arrangements.

She looked at me as if I was a distracted child. "I thought I made that clear. Now, of course, you and your sweet father will be attending? He is a local candidate, after all." Barb glanced at the arrangements sitting on the backseat of my car. "I see you've completed them." She reached out and straightened one of the vases I had wedged onto the crowded backseat. "Oh, this will never do."

I held my tongue, wanting to lash out, then with all the control I could muster asked, "Is something wrong?"

"They look too thin. You need at least three more carnations in each arrangement. I'm sure the florist must've given you more than what I'm seeing here." Barb clucked her tongue and shook her head at me as if I was a careless child. "This is really too bad because time is running out. Be a dear and fix them, won't you?"

I had used every flower the florist gave me, and if she wanted me to add more, I would have to go by and beg the florist. I hated to tell her I didn't

THE TWIST AND SHOUT MURDER

have time to redo the flowers but plunged in any way. If I was going to be a part of her club, I needed to set some boundaries. Ellie expressed concerns that I was letting her take advantage of me, and this could be my way of showing I could hold my own with the DA's wife. "I wish I could, but I have a class this morning. I need time to study. Remember, I'm in secretarial school."

Her head bobbed back and she grinned. "Oh, I see you're in the market for a husband. Well, I've never been one to shoot down ambition. With your looks, you should be able to land quite a catch." She paused a moment and then zeroed in on me with those blue eyes. "Just make sure he's not married to someone else first."

I didn't know how to explain to Barb why I wanted to learn about business for myself and had no evil plans to snare some unsuspecting Gig Young type. Before I could open my mouth to attempt it, Barb dumped the bag of cards in my arms. "Oh, well. To each his own, as they say. Now I know how pressed for time you are, and I won't take up another minute. The Camden Ladies' Club so appreciates your help. We want everything to be perfect for the banquet. I'm sure you understand." She surveyed my green cotton shirtwaist, and her lips drew into a thin line. "I do hope you have something nice to wear to the banquet." There was that nose-wrinkling again. This time, I knew it meant she was about to strike. "Something nicer than a day-to-day housedress."

I fingered the collar of my dress. Ellie had made it for me, and I thought it looked fine to wear both at home and out in public. It wasn't as glamorous as what she had on, but it didn't look bad. Deciding to ignore her comment, I made one last attempt to reason with her about my father and his reluctance to attend the banquet. "By the way, I don't think my father is comfortable with the idea of going. He needs a little more time to prepare his campaign."

She stiffened as if being told "no" never happened to her. "Not going? You can't be serious. Of course, he's going. I insist. Besides, if you want to be a part of our little group, attendance is mandatory. Sorry to cut this short, but I'm in an awful hurry. Don't forget to add the cards. Ciao, darling."

That night, exhausted from my added floral arrangement duties as well as school, I was in my mother's kitchen helping her prepare dinner. We had the radio turned up and one of my favorite songs, "Twist and Shout" by The Isley Brothers, came on. Some songs are impossible to resist and tired as I was, I couldn't help but do a few dance steps in the kitchen. What I hadn't realized was my father had walked in and was standing in the doorway. Upon seeing him, I gave him a smirk and then extended my hand. "Dance with me, Daddy."

With an infectious grin on his face, he reached out and took me by the waist, and we fell into the familiar steps of the jitterbug. It wasn't the newest dance craze, but he taught me this dance when I was a little girl, and we did it together so well.

"I'm going to have to call the police. There's a wild party going on in my kitchen," my mother said behind us.

"Call away. A man can dance with his daughter, can't he?"

"Watch your back, dear. You're no spring chicken anymore," my mother said as we twirled around.

We danced until the song ended and then laughed as my father bent over, catching his breath. "You just may be right about that. Where does she get all that energy?"

"I just love that song," I said.

"It sounds like some sort of grizzly accident to me," my mother said. She was always about finding the true meaning of words. "Think about it. 'Twist and shout' sounds like something you say when something is falling on top of your head. These songs today just make no sense."

I laughed at her description. "It makes plenty of sense. You just have to understand today's culture. It's rock-and-roll."

She patted me on the shoulder. "Aha. Let's eat."

We served meatloaf and creamy mashed potatoes with a side salad. My mother was a wonderful cook, and she wanted me to learn recipes for when as she said, "I have a husband of my own to feed." I wanted to learn them for myself with or without a husband.

As Dad unfolded his napkin, I casually mentioned, "I hope you thought more about going to the banquet."

He picked up his fork. "Not really."

I tightened my shoulders and squeezed my eyes shut, preparing for his reaction. "I told Barb you were thinking about it. I think she is expecting you there now."

He pushed the potatoes around the plate, mixing them in with the meatloaf. "This is exactly the kind of thing I was worried about when you told me you wanted to join this group. These women are a throwback to the forties and fifties, and you aren't like them. They see you as a vulnerable young girl they can push around."

I held up both hands to explain, "I know it seems that way, but Barb means well." I bit my lower lip. "At least I think she does. Although she did dump a bunch of cards on me today, she wanted to add to the flowers. She's taking credit for the flower arrangements."

My mom stopped her fork midair. "She's what? Are you kidding?"

Why did I tell them that part? There was nothing worse than bringing out my mother's protective instinct when it came to me. I knew what Barb was doing wasn't fair, but in the end, I didn't care who took credit for the flowers. I made those flower arrangements for my father, not some club. "I know, but I'm willing to put up with her if it helps you. I think we should all go to the banquet."

Dad looked confused and laid down his fork. "Aren't you going a little far in the martyr department? I appreciate you wanting to help, but this is ridiculous. It's not 1912. It's 1962. First the flower arrangements and now we are told to attend this thing before I'm even ready? It's almost as if she has something on you."

His deduction was close, but it wasn't about me. "Of course not," I replied a little too quickly. I couldn't stand to look him in the eyes and instead focused on the edge of the tablecloth. The threat of revealing the night at Miss Daisy's hung over me like a dark cloud. If he found out she was willing to fight that dirty he might drop out of the campaign altogether.

"I thought we already discussed this. I'm not ready to be at a city function yet. I'm still putting together my platform."

My mother rose from the table and brought back a little white cardboard box, pulled out a card, and held it up. "Look, I picked up the postcard from the printer. I designed it myself." The card featured a picture of my handsome father and below it the words "Mike Morgan. He's Your Man." My mother had come up with the slogan, and I just loved the sound of it.

"These look great," I said. "Exactly what you need for people to get to know you. Anyone running against you couldn't beat that handsome face."

"I'm running against Anson Manning," Dad said offhandedly as he returned to his dinner.

"Manning?" I asked.

The knife squeaked on the plate as he procured a piece of meatloaf." Sure. He's the district attorney's brother." That would also mean he was Barb Manning's brother-in-law.

"Barb didn't tell me that," I said. Why didn't Barb tell me her brother-in-law was the other candidate? This was the kind of thing I would consider important to share. What is it they say about keeping your enemies close to you? She had to have known my father was unprepared for a function as soon as the Founder's Day Banquet.

"Sounds about right," my mother said. "Barb Manning might be setting us up to fail, which gives us another reason going to the Founder's Day Banquet is not a good idea."

My parents were dead set against going. If Barb hadn't threatened to reveal his trip to Miss Daisy's, I would have agreed, but I knew I couldn't let my father take this chance. "I know, but she said if I want to stay in the club, I have to attend this banquet."

"And how much of a loss is that, really?" My mother asked.

"I know you don't believe this, but I think the group will help, but if I go without you, it won't look good. Please, will you reconsider? I think I'm learning Barb has a way of backing people into a corner. If you don't do it for me, think about your reason for running. This is how we end up with ineffective city council members."

Dad sighed and gazing into my pleading eyes, nodded. "Okay, but only because you are willing to sacrifice so much for me by being in the Camden

Ladies' Club. I guess I'll have to get to work tonight on the campaign. I'm not as ready as I'd like to be, but I could at least make an appearance and fake it, I guess."

"Isn't that what all politicians do?" I said, with a twinkle in my eye. The surrounding tension was melting, and even though we disagreed, we came to a compromise. Okay, he compromised.

Chapter Two

A day later, I straightened the hem of my plaid skirt, my parents and I walked into the location for the Founder's Day Banquet. The room we would be using had a sedate wallpaper that featured strands of ivy on the top, with dark wood paneling on the bottom skirting the room. The tables that now held my flower arrangements were lined up in neat rows and bore freshly ironed tablecloths. Barb stood in the corner giving directions to another woman I recognized as Jane, one of the many members of the Camden Ladies' Club and the wife of a local accountant. She had come along with him when he had lectured at my school. Jane wore a bright pink sleeveless dress, and although pregnant with her third child was still trying to keep up with the demands of the club.

My mother came up behind us and stuck a couple of postcards in my father's coat pocket. "Looks like a full house."

She pulled a speck off Dad's gray jacket. I had wanted him to wear his navy jacket with a red tie, but he preferred the less noticeable gray. He still wasn't ready to stand out in the crowd even if he was running for office. He was a humble guy which made him a perfect servant of the people but a lousy politician.

The sound of tires squealed outside, and as my focus drifted to the window, a lime green Camaro weaved through the parking lot, finally skidding onto the line between two parking spaces. Most of the people at this event looked conservative. Certainly, there was no one here I would suspect of driving such a flashy car.

I turned back to my father, who was wearing out the corner of one of his cards as he turned it in his hand nervously. I attempted to calm him down with small talk.

"I'm sure you know some of the people here, Dad. I think you're going to do great." There was more noise from the street as loud rock music drifted up from the Camaro.

"What was that?" He asked, his focus still on the card.

"Don't worry about it—some idiot in a Camaro. I'm surprised there are so many people here. I didn't even know this banquet existed until a couple of weeks ago."

A tall man with his suit jacket sleeves pushed slightly up towards the elbow, and a fedora that reminded me of Frank Sinatra came up to my dad with a pad of paper in his hand. "I'm Ben Dalton from the *Camden Courier*. I was told you're running for the vacancy on the council. Did you want to tell us about your platform today?"

Dad froze up at the reporter's questions. It didn't help that Ben Dalton was about an inch taller and leaned forward when he spoke, making Dad step back. I pushed between the two men.

"This is Mr. Morgan's first public appearance. I'm sure he will be giving you a statement later that will outline his plans for our beautiful city."

The pushy reporter's eyes met mine, corners crinkling as he smiled. Even though the windows were open letting in a breeze, the humid June weather was making the room quite stuffy. "And are you his campaign manager?"

My mother, who had returned from visiting with friends in the room, tapped him on the shoulder. "She's his daughter, and as she said, he'll be glad to fill you in at a later time. We're just here to enjoy the fun and fellowship as we celebrate Founder's Day."

He grinned. "Well, darn. I was looking forward to working with you," he said to me, the grin still in place. Before he left us to go across the room, he winked at me.

My attention drifted from the reporter to Barb, who looked to be in full command mode as she continued to direct a list of tasks to Jane. "I should probably go over and make sure there isn't anything else Barb wants me to do."

"Make sure we set my husband and his brother near the front, and myself, of course," Barb said as Jane nodded with the speed of a hamster chewing a kernel of corn. Barb turned to me. "Good, you're here," she glanced at my parents, "And you convinced your parents to attend the event. Excellent. I knew you had it in you." My mother waved at us from across the room. It reminded me of the time I was dressed up like a turkey in the Thanksgiving play at school, and she waved at me when I was on stage gobbling away. At the time, I had been embarrassed, but now I thought it was sweet. My father may have been reluctant to show up as a candidate, but my mother was full-on-board as the candidate's wife. Barb returned the gesture flapping her hand up and down.

"Oh, they're adorable," she said. I had never heard my parents called anything like that and suddenly felt as if she were looking at a puppy in the window.

"Where do you want us to sit?" I asked.

Barb glanced toward the empty tables. "Why not right behind us?"

"Are you sure? I almost think my father would be more comfortable sitting near the back," I suggested, hoping for his sake we could play it slightly offstage for this occasion.

She shrugged me off and gave a knowing glance to Jane, seemingly sharing an inside joke. "Nonsense. It's our little way of welcoming you into our community. I insist you sit near the front. After all, we wouldn't want anyone missing out on seeing one of our wonderful candidates, would we?"

"Barbara." A man in a crisp tan tailored suit stood behind us. His sandy hair reminded me of an actor, the way it was naturally pushed back in a slight pompadour. Not too much, but enough to make him look boyish. There was an upper-class air about him like he would have been comfortable tossing around the football with the Kennedys at Hyannis Port.

A scowl crossed Barb's face as she turned around. Then as if it had never happened, her expression disappeared, and she opened her arms to him like she was welcoming him home after a long journey.

"Anson, you're here." Her lips drew into a straight line, and she gave him a look that only could be translated as *You Naughty Boy*. He had to be the brother-in-law who was running against my father for the city council seat.

"You almost act as if you're not glad to see me. Now how do you think that makes me feel?" His full lips curved into an artificial pout. He looked at Jane. "Are you still directing your troops, Barb? I'll bet you arranged this whole thing. I told old Morty you were too on-the-ball for him." He gave a mock salute. "Private Manning, reporting for duty." The newcomer wobbled on his feet, and the smell of alcohol hung about him. It was barely three in the afternoon, but it seemed Mr. Anson Manning had started drinking way before the rest of the Founder's Day crowd.

"Jane," Barb signaled. "Why don't you get my brother-in-law a cup of coffee?" Jane nodded and tried to take him by the arm.

"Coffee? This late in the day? Not my beverage of choice, m' lady. Point me to the bar." As Anson spoke, a cloud of hot alcohol breath hit me. I shot a glance at Dad. Maybe nobody would notice him if his opponent received all the attention for being drunk. He was watching us but looked confused by Anson's behavior.

Barb drew closer to Anson and lowered her voice, "I don't know why you think you needed to drink before the banquet but try to keep it together."

"Keep it together? Aren't I together?" He turned to me, and his eyes drifted from my face to other strategic parts of my body, making me feel uncomfortable. "Hello, beautiful. You are much too fresh-faced to be with these old hags." He slung an arm around me and lowered his face to mine. "Don't I look together to you?"

Before I could think of something to say back, Barb jerked him away with surprising force. "Listen, Anson. I won't tolerate any problems from you today. Do you understand me?"

Anson looked confused and then dutifully scorned. His mouth curved downward, "Ah, Barbie Barb. I'll be a good boy for you and Morton." His sickly sweet tone had succeeded in making Barb Manning look like a scolding schoolmarm. Even Jane giggled, but then returned to a straight face when Barb looked around to see how much of this scene the crowd was observing. She was a pot about to bubble over, and yet she attempted to at least look calm.

Anson pulled Barb's constricting grasp from his arm and returned to me. "I'll let you take me to get a drink. What do you say? Want to have a little drinkypoo with me?"

Barb stepped between us. "She's the daughter of your political competitor. You might want to think about that."

Anson's eyebrows rose as his gaze raked over me again. "Ah, even better." He lowered his head with a wicked smile. "And so lovely. How about I check out your polls, and you check out mine?"

Barb reclaimed her grasp on his elbow, attempting to pull him away from the potential voters engaged in conversation around us. "Anson, why don't we get you a cup of coffee?"

"Why would I do that, especially in the company of such a beautiful woman?" His gaze lingered on the part of me that wasn't my face. Is this how he treated all women or was I just the lucky one? Before I could tell him, my eyes were nowhere near my chest, the reporter, Ben Dalton, came up behind me.

"How do you do. I'm with the *Camden Courier*. Do you have a statement for the press at your first official junket?" He was giving the same treatment to him as he had my father. I quietly said thanks as he inserted himself between us. Maybe he was on the trail of a hot story, but it felt more like he was coming to my rescue.

Anson stumbled a bit. "Why, yes. You see that poor sucker my brother has running against me?" He pointed across the room at my father. "I have some shocking news for him, sport. Here's your story. He's going up against the Manning machine, solely responsible for getting my big brother the esteemed position of D.A. in this town. Just look around. Barb, here, is in charge of everything." He spread out his arms, nearly knocking down a vase, and attempted to straighten it. He picked up the card with Barb's name that had been carefully placed by the flowers, read it, and laughed. "She even made the flowers. Nothing left to chance, right, Barb? She runs everything, does everything, even controls me. Even you. I'll bet especially you." He flung out an arm and pointed to me. "Even her. If I wanted her, all I'd have to do is ask Barb."

He turned to Barb, "Hey Barbie, can I have…"

Ben scowled at Anson's request to acquire me. "I'm no expert at manners, but I think you owe this lady an apology…"

"Anson." Barb regained her grip on his arm. "Off we go to the refreshment table. Let's not monopolize the press. I'm sure the other candidate would like to talk with him."

Morton Manning, the district attorney, and a heavier version of his brother rushed over to help Barb with the stumbling Anson. He put a hand around his waist, attempting to steady him.

"He's drunk, "she said under her breath.

"I can see that," he grumbled back in a whisper trying not to alert the crowd.

"I can hear both of you saying I'm drunk. I'm not drunk. I'm stupidly happy," Anson blurted out.

Barb and Morton finally got Anson settled at the table right behind us, and Jane returned with a cup of black coffee. I couldn't help but notice Barb didn't choose to set him at her table. Earlier it had sounded like she wanted him right in front. Especially in front of us.

"If that's your competition, your dad just might be Camden's newest member of the city council," the reporter whispered in my ear.

When I returned to my table, my father gritted his teeth and cast an unfriendly gaze back at Anson Manning. "I don't like the way he was talking to you."

"I'm okay. He's just drunk. No harm was done," I assured him.

"Attention everybody," Barb said from the microphone resting in a tall silver stand in front of the room. "You won't believe this, but we have two candidates running for Phil Boggs' recently vacated city council seat with us today. What do you say we ask each one of them to tell us a little about themselves after our meal? I'm sure our city's forefathers would highly approve of the political process in action." A round of polite applause rose from the room.

"Great," Dad said under his breath. "I knew something like this would happen. I wouldn't put any money on me being the next city councilman.

Even though he's highly intoxicated, I think my opponent was right. They are a machine. They had to know I wouldn't be ready this early in the campaign."

"Don't be silly. A political machine in Camden, Texas? I don't think we're big enough for that." My mother put her hand over his fingers as he nervously drummed them on the table.

"Isn't that sweet!" My landlady, Arlene Clark, came bustling over. "Still holding hands after all these years." She pulled out a chair next to my mother. "Mind if I join you?"

"Please do," I said, happy for her presence at our table. "It's nice to have an actual friend here."

Arlene looked around. "I thought Ellie was coming to this."

"That's what she told me, but I think she was waiting on Al to finish up a job."

A girl with a slight figure barely filling out a light blue jumper with a crisp white cotton blouse and an embroidered collar stood behind my landlady.

Arlene took her by the shoulders and thrust the teenager slightly forward. "You know my niece, Clara? Doesn't she look lovely in baby blue? Clara's going to be singing for us today."

Clara blushed and gave us a quiet smile then tapped her aunt on the shoulder. "Aunt Arlene, Bertram was supposed to be here."

Arlene looked around. "Well, it seems he isn't. It's your lucky day. This is turning out to be your very own event to entertain the people of Camden. At least we won't have to put up with that boy and his pushy mother."

Bertram, our newspaper boy, would often come to events like this with his ventriloquist dummy, Mr. Sammy who seemed to have all the rights of real people. Bertram would set Mr. Sammy in an empty seat next to him and on occasion converse with him about the day's events. His mother, Constance Benedict, loved to slick back Bertram's hair with much more than a dollop of Brylcreem to match the hard plastic hair the dummy possessed. She was as much of a promoter of her son as Arlene was of Clara. If Bertram's ventriloquism act was more remembered than Clara's singing, Arlene sulked about it for days.

Arlene gave a little grunt. "Thank goodness Constance didn't weasel

Bertram and that doll he carries around to this function. Thinks he's a regular Edgar Bergen with his dummy Charlie McCarthy. Bertram's lips move so much you would think he was standing with his mouth open in front of a fan at full speed." Arlene's cheerful mood had turned. She didn't like Bertram and his mother. Was competition for local talent that intense?

No one spoke, and she became aware we were all staring at her and her little break from pleasant landlady to vicious amateur talent agent, Arlene backtracked a bit. "Of course, I do feel sorry for him, with his sister being so sick, and all, but Clara's abilities to provide beautiful music are so much better than that kid slurring his words." She turned her attention to Clara. "Don't worry, sweetheart. You just get up there and sing your little heart out." Arlene turned back to me, "You know she won the Kiwanis talent show last year? I expect we'll be hearing from her for years to come. Who knows? She might end up on television someday. If she only had a couple of sisters to sing with her, she could be on Lawrence Welk or any of those variety shows. Fame is hers for the taking."

"Yes, it is," I responded, causing Clara to blush.

Ellie walked over and pulled out the last empty chair at the table. "Is this the winning candidate's table?" She squeezed my father's shoulder. "You look great, Uncle Mike." Ellie was in a floral print dress with a gathered skirt at the bottom. It fit her thin frame perfectly, and I was sure she had created it herself.

"You think so? Opal thought I should wear the blue," he said.

"Save it for the next function. I can't believe it. My uncle on the political circuit. The Morgan family is certainly coming up in this town."

"And you look lovely today, too, dear. Where's Al?" Mother asked, looking around.

She touched her shoulders. "This old thing?" She leaned closer. "It took me half the night to make these pleats. The next time I say silk is easy to sew, slap me. As for Al, he said the job was too big this time. I don't think he's going to make it."

"Too bad. I think your outfit looks great. Even with using silk, you did a wonderful job with the dress anyway," Arlene said and then turned her focus to Dad. "What about you? Political waters a bit choppy?" Arlene began to remove her gloves.

"Did you see that scene with Anson Manning?" he clipped, casting a glance at his opponent. Anson had settled into his coffee but grinned at our table when he caught us looking at him. He had pulled the extra chair from the table next to him and now had his feet propped up on it. Dad was nervous about speaking on this occasion, but Anson looked relaxed. Being in front of all these people didn't seem to have any effect on him whatsoever. Of course, it might have been the alcohol he had consumed before arriving. I could feel Dad bobbing his knee up and down under the table in a staccato rhythm.

"We all did," Arlene said. "That's what took me so long to come over here. People are talking, my dear, and it's all about you, Dot. Well, about you and the lewd looks he was giving you. Anson Manning never did amount to much, and now his family is trying to make him a politician." She sighed. "Well, I guess that's not the first time something like that has happened."

"I'm glad it's not just us noticing the way he's acting," I said.

Arlene gazed in a different direction and then let out a little gasp. "Well, somebody in this room has taken a shine to him. Will you look at that Maureen Johnson over there?"

Arlene signaled to a buxom redhead in a white silk blouse. She dangled a wineglass in her hand and was taking in Anson Manning like a cat surveying its kill. She dripped sex appeal with her top button unbuttoned showing ample cleavage.

"Did she just lick her lips...that way?" Arlene attempted to cover Clara's eyes, but the teenager batted her away.

I squinted my eyes, trying to see how she was moving her mouth. "No. At least I don't think so."

Ellie stared at Maureen, who was her exact opposite. Where Maureen was evocative and forward, Ellie was someone you'd miss in a crowd if you didn't know her already. "You think she's setting her cap for Barb's brother-in-law?"

"I'd bet money on it," my mother said. "That's Maureen Adams Simpson Morales Johnson. Maureen's in the market for a new husband, and Anson Manning fills the bill. Money, social standing, and too drunk to say no."

"She's getting another new husband?" Ellie asked. "I should have done more bust exercises when I was younger." Ellie was in the b-cup for life crowd.

"Stop," I whispered, trying not to laugh. "Whatever happened to her last husband?"

"Now, that's a mystery. Nobody's sure. Some say he ran off, while others think he was pushed off a cliff somewhere," Arlene whispered.

As interesting as all of this was, Dad was oblivious to it as he continued to bounce his knee under the table.

My mother quietly set a hand on his knee. "Are you okay?" I had never seen him this nervous.

"Yes...no. I'm just not good at giving speeches and talking in front of people," he answered. I reached for his hand. It was ice cold.

"You can do this, Dad."

"Go ahead and try out your 'vote for me' speech, Mike," Arlene suggested. "I want to know why I should choose you over the other guy."

He cleared his throat and reached into his pocket. "Okay. My name is Mike Morgan, and I'm the man for the job." He handed her a freshly printed postcard.

Arlene waited for him to say more and after a couple of seconds, leaned forward, egging him on like she was teaching a child a Bible verse. "And?"

He gave her a blank stare and then he started to take on the look of a frightened animal backed into a corner. He was freezing up. I never realized how nervous speaking in public made him. His fear of being thrust into the spotlight could be a genuine problem for his campaign. I remembered how badly Richard Nixon did in the presidential debates in 1960. Nixon looked like a cardboard doll attempting to speak, where John Kennedy spoke with passion and conviction. I vowed we would practice his public speaking skills after this. Mom attempted to explain Dad's lack of persuasion. "He's still working on his platform. This banquet came a little early in his campaign efforts."

Ellie nodded. "You've got to be a little bit of a salesman to pull this off, Uncle Mike."

"A salesman, huh? I'm a court clerk, not someone who could sell you a used car."

Arlene glanced at the card that Dad had pressed into her hand. "Your postcard looks nice. Very colorful." She pointed to the red, white, and blue border. "I think I'll vote for you even before I know what you stand for. Very convincing, young man."

Dad gave her a weak smile. "I'm pretty sure everyone else is going to expect a whole lot more from me. I didn't realize this sort of thing could be so uncomfortable. You're an easy mark, Arlene."

"That's what you think. It takes a lot to get to a tough old bird like me," Arlene said.

Clara, who had been quiet at the table, nodded her head. "Nobody says no to my Aunt Arlene."

"Now, now. That's not always true," Arlene said.

"That's not what Pastor Farnham said," Clara replied.

"I'm sure he was going to give you the solo, anyway. I just had to make sure he didn't forget. It's important to make your case known, right, Mike?" Arlene asked.

Instead of responding, Dad's focus had returned to Anson Manning.

I followed his gaze and realized Anson was still staring in our direction. He mouthed silently, "She could be mine." Was he referring to me?

Dad stood up abruptly, causing his chair to scrape against the floor and echo through the hall. The nervousness of a moment earlier had vanished, and the rage of a protective father now replaced it at Anson's suggestion.

I touched his arm. "Dad?"

"Be right back." He strode over to Manning's table. "You've got a lot of nerve."

He pointed at himself. "Born with it. I was born with everything, whereas you look like you have to fight for everything. I suppose that makes you the better man, but honestly, I don't care."

The reporter who had saved me earlier was instantly in the fray. Was he going to try to cover a potential fight between candidates?

Anson picked up the card next to the flowers. "See this name? Manning.

You might as well face it. This is an unwinnable race. Your name on the ballot is just a formality to make it look like they won fair and square. Go home, old man. You're out of your league."

Dad squared his shoulders and closed in the distance between himself and Anson. The nervous man who couldn't stop bouncing his foot under the table had vanished. "I'll have you know my daughter made those floral arrangements, and your sister-in-law took the credit."

Manning laughed. "Really? Oh, even better." He looked across the room to Barb and gave a golf clap. "Brava, Barb! You've done it again. Taken credit for something you didn't do."

My father's tone took on a menacing note. "If you're going to congratulate anyone, it will be my daughter. She worked all night to finish those vases." Dad gestured to me, and then a disgusting leer came over Anson's face.

"Ab-so-lute-ly. Let me go and personally congratulate her. Your daughter would probably welcome some attention from me if you know what I mean…"

Just as I was about to set him straight, Ben Dalton grabbed Anson by the collar of his shirt, pulled him up out of the chair, and slammed him against the wall. "Don't you think you've said enough?" Who knew a member of the press could be so noble?

Dad gave Ben an acknowledging grin and then faced Anson. "You will apologize to my daughter for your rudeness." He bumped Anson's coffee cup sending it crashing to the floor completely silencing the chatter going on around them. If the crowd gathered at the banquet weren't watching before, they were now. Anson pulled away from Ben and did a two-handed push on Dad's shoulders, knocking his postcards out of his jacket pocket. Ben grabbed at his arm, attempting to stop his attack, but he pulled free, and before he could throw a punch, my father got in a left jab, busting his lip. Morton Manning, who had been busy talking to the members of Camden's society crowd started over after the coffee cup hit the floor.

"Unhand him," he shouted, struggling to push away my father and the reporter. Barb drew closer, her hand across her mouth, looking shocked. She grabbed a napkin and gave it to Anson to press on his bleeding lip. I ran to my father's side and started picking up cards. With the men successfully divided, I tried to get Dad back to the table and out of the situation. Ben, catching my cue, also returned to his table.

Anson's voice rose above the whispers as he pointed to us retreating to our table. "And this man is running for city council, everybody. Obviously, he has the press in his pocket. Do you want this hothead in charge of your town? I wouldn't count on him solving your problems, especially if he doesn't like you. I could be one in a long line of victims, who knows?" The last part of Anson's speech was slurred, and even though he made an excellent argument, he seemed to be having trouble standing.

"That's enough," Morton Manning said to his brother, his voice gruff and unyielding. Was he as upset with his brother as the rest of us? Barb ran to the microphone frantically switching it on, causing high-pitched feedback.

Maureen Johnson took this moment to move across the room toward Anson. She slinked around Morton and put her hand on Anson's arm. Anson looked up at her touch, and then his eyes focused on her revealing cleavage. It was like a dog who had just spotted a squirrel.

Once the feedback from the sound system stopped, Barb began speaking. "Thank you all for coming. It's so wonderful to get the chance to celebrate the glorious beginnings of Camden and remember our brave founders." Barb was carrying on as if the fight had never happened. Her composure was an amazing feat of acting worthy of an Academy Award. "We want to thank the kitchen staff, who made this all possible." The crowd gave a polite clap. "I'm happy to announce we are going to be entertained by one of Camden's most talented youngsters today. We have little Cindy Clark to sing for us. It's so wonderful to have such an accomplished little entertainer, and now, I'm happy to present our precious Cindy Clark."

Arlene cringed, her shoulders tensing. She raised a hand and waved it at Barb. "Excuse me." Barb ignored her, so she repeated, "Excuse me. Mrs. Manning? Her name is Clara, not Cindy…"

"Yes, of course. Thank you so much for keeping me on my toes. Clara, darling. Come on up…" As Clara neared the stage, Morton tried to steer his brother out of the room, but Anson easily pulled from his grasp and stood next to Maureen, slipping his arm around her waist. As forward as his gesture was, she didn't seem to mind one bit and proved it by leaning back enough to put her head on his shoulder.

The crowd clapped as Barb handed Clara the microphone. Suddenly being thrust center stage, Clara's hand began to shake. As she stood in front of Camden's social elite, she looked smaller than she had at the table. A fight between two candidates for city council had to be a tough act to follow. Was I worried this banquet might be dull? At this rate, people wouldn't stop talking about it until the election.

With Anson settled, Barb scooted off, crisis averted. Morton huffed and returned to his table. Maureen and Anson pulled out chairs and sat at his table as if they had been sitting there together all along. The smile on his face, happy with the unexpected attention of such a beautiful woman, said everything. Barb gave Maureen a thankful look, but Maureen didn't seem to notice. She didn't seem to be keeping Anson occupied for Barb, but herself.

Clara gave a shy smile to the crowd and began to warble Blue Moon. Nerves began to shake into her voice, and she skidded off to a flat tone.

Anson's voice rose. "Oh my God, get that cow away from the microphone. Spare us this agony." Maureen giggled at his heckling. Arlene jerked her head around to the loudmouth.

Clara gasped, and her face turned pale. Like radar in a submarine, Arlene zeroed in on Anson.

"Why has this man not been removed?" She shouted to anyone who would listen. Arlene stomped over and placed her hands on her ample hips. "You will apologize to my niece."

"Oh, she's your niece. That explains the remarkable resemblance to a cow. Moooo."

Maureen placed a hand over her mouth, ineffectively hiding a smile at Anson's remarks, spurring him on even more. "Blue Moooooon."

Barb Manning re-emerged from the kitchen and made her way to Anson. Clara laid the microphone on a table and ran from the room in tears.

"You are a despicable man, Anson Manning. You need to watch who you cross. Not everyone in town is willing to put up with you like your rich family. We all know you're a loser who can't do anything else, so now you're trying politics," Arlene said.

"Yes, I suppose I am despicable, but I'm a Manning which makes me untouchable, even from old cows like you." Maureen put her pink lacquered fingernails on his arm, content as if they were about to take a walk in the park.

"I wish you had never come back to this town. Do you realize what you just did to my niece? She's just a child. Mark my words, you will be sorry for humiliating her. No one gets away with insulting my family."

"And that is an unnecessary, cruel thing to say to my brother-in-law, Mrs. Clark," Morton said. "He is a Manning, don't forget."

"How could I? You people make sure you lord yourselves over everyone in town. You'd better watch out throwing around that name. I don't think it carries the cache you think it does. I'm a Clark. Put that in your pipe and smoke it." Arlene grabbed her pocketbook and left through the door her niece had run out of earlier.

"Wow, that guy is a real piece of work," Dad whispered. "He shouldn't be allowed to get away with insulting a kid."

"As the D.A. said, he's a Manning. I guess they operate by a different set of rules," I said.

"Rules they make up themselves as they go along," Ellie said. "The only problem is the rest of us have to live with them. It's amazing how many people that man affected in such a short time."

"Quite a contrast to Phil Boggs who never bothered anyone," I whispered.

Barb snapped her arm in the air signaling the waiters to serve dinner and then came over to our table.

"I'm so very sorry for what happened here tonight. Please accept our apologies, and well, I guess this is the best time to tell you that I have a surprise for you. I've planned a debate between you and Anson on Friday night at the town hall."

My dad's eyes grew large. "A debate?"

"Certainly. It seems like the only voice heard today was my brother-in-law. So unfair to you, don't you think? I had already planned it, but now after this whole ugly scene hanging over your head, you need a chance to speak for yourself."

"Are you sure?" I wondered if maybe the Mannings would want to spare themselves another scene in public after what Anson just put them through. Give the town some time to forget.

"Very sure. I believe in a fair fight. True confession," Barb raised her hand like she was about to take an oath, "I find the whole process of political campaigns exciting, and this debate is just what you need to show the town your father isn't some cathouse hopping deviant. It's all arranged."

Of course, she had to slip that last part in. What just happened? It went from being a conciliatory gesture to pulling us into one of her events.

"Cathouse hopping deviant. I beg your pardon?" Mom said, nearly dropping her fork.

"Oh. I thought Dot here would have told you about our little conversation. Your husband's visit to Miss Daisy's was revealed to me. I, of course, will keep it to myself, but you know how people talk. Right, Dot?"

Gone was Dad's shyness. Just like the people he wanted to fight for, he recognized Barb's manipulation and tried to defend himself. "You do know that I was there to pick up someone else, right?"

"Of course you were, darling. And that's what I'll be sure to say when someone asks me about it. Too bad none of that was included in the official police report."

Mom spoke up. "It's true. His friend was in trouble. He saved a marriage that night if you want to put your nose into it."

Barb looked surprised at Mom's outburst. My mother may have been the quiet librarian type, but it was apparent Barb had never returned a book late. "And just another reason your husband's voice needs to be heard on Friday. I was delighted we could get the meeting room. So often it's booked months in advance. I'm already working on flyers to put up around town so everyone can attend. Isn't it wonderful? A real political debate right here in Camden."

"I don't know." My father rubbed his chin.

"There's nothing to think about, Mr. Morgan. We'll see you on Friday. So exciting," she said to herself. "I just love the political process."

After she walked away, Dad said, "Somehow, I think I'm going to be sorry for this in the end. I feel like a fly in a spider's web."

The next morning, I decided to start my journey investigating Anson Manning. I headed to where many people go to find answers, the public library. They might not have a book on my father's political opponent, but they did have my mother, a woman who knew where to find anything. She had always loved reading, and I could never remember her without a book. My attitude about work stemmed from her. I had grown up among old friends, both the books at the library and the ladies who worked there.

On my way to the library, I stopped by the diner and picked up some of Charlie Columbo's fresh bombolini, an Italian donut. Mother especially loved the chocolate-covered variety. As Charlie prepared my order, I couldn't help but notice his usual infectious mood was off today.

"Are you okay, Charlie? You don't look good," I said.

He held up a hand, "I'm still rattled—such a terrible sight. I can't get the memory of my newspaper boy's mama out of my head. She was right there by the side of the road. Left for dead." He shuddered and took another drink of coffee.

"What happened?"

"His mama had to go to the drugstore to get medicine for her little girl. She had to walk because their car is broken down, and they didn't have money to fix it. Mr. Draper opened the store early because she had a bad night. She's been sick a lot lately. Bertram and his mother almost never leave the house anymore. I found the poor woman by the side of the road this morning. She was struggling to stay alive. Her body was so crumpled up. I'm cursed with the vision of it." He folded over the top of the white bag.

"I can't believe this would happen, right here in Camden."

"Yes, and whoever it was didn't even stop. It's that corner. They ought to call it the Devil's death trap. Haven't I been saying all along we need a stoplight there? More people are driving around Camden every day. Now, this poor woman was hit and thrown to the side of the road like a piece of trash."

That corner was notorious for fender benders, but this was the first time I had ever heard of a hit and run. "Did Mrs. Benedict say what the car looked like? Maybe the police can track down the car by the make and model? There aren't that many people in Camden. Can Constance Benedict identify who hit her?"

"No. She kept worrying about her children. She left them home alone while she went out for the medicine. Were you aware her husband died in the war? That poor woman. First, her daughter is sick, and now she gets hit by someone who didn't even care enough to stop." He shook his head, his eyes cast upward. "Then, he passed out. No more talking. That was all."

I hadn't realized the Benedicts were a single-parent family. The way Arlene talked about them, they were the scourge of the earth because Bertram was vying for the same local entertainer slots Clara wanted. You never knew what kind of troubles the people around you might be carrying. If anything, I was beginning to feel Constance and her son were the bravest people I'd met.

"She kept saying to me, why is God so angry with us? First, my husband, then my daughter, and now me? It broke my heart as if God could ever be angry with a sweet lady like that." A tear slipped down his cheek. I patted his shoulder to comfort him.

"Is Constance...I mean, did she?" I couldn't bring myself to ask if Constance had died. It was too sad to think about.

"She was still alive when the ambulance came, but I don't know what is going to happen to her." The older man held him like a newborn baby, tears in his eyes. "I should have fought harder for that stoplight. Bad things happen when good people do nothing. If I had been stronger, that little mama wouldn't be fighting for her life at the hospital. I should have made them put one in."

"Did Mrs. Benedict ever get the medicine for her daughter Sylvia?" I asked.

"Yes. Mr. Draper delivered it himself after he heard about the accident. My missus is sitting with the children."

The sad news about Constance Benedict was still on my mind when I entered the library. It was quiet this morning, the long wooden tables were empty, and my mother was shelving books when I found her. The book towers cushioned our voices as we stood between the fiction rows.

She squirreled a book between two others, but her eyes widened when she saw the white bag from Columbo's I held in my left hand. "You brought me breakfast? How nice!"

Using my library voice, I whispered, "I had a long talk with Charlie. Did you know about Constance Benedict?"

She stopped placing a book on a shelf and then gave a "tsk." "The whole situation is tragic, and Charlie takes things to heart like no one else around here. I don't know why I didn't think of this sooner, but we should get the church ladies to deliver some casseroles to their house."

After she finished shelving the final book on the cart, we settled behind the spacious checkout desk, our sticky treats in hand.

"Charlie thought she was dead when he first found her. Can you imagine finding someone at the side of the road like that and then having to check to see if she's breathing? She's at the hospital, but from what I hear, it doesn't look good. I'm sure those kids are beside themselves with worry." I popped a donut in my mouth, savoring the powdered sugar on my tongue.

"I can't believe we have someone living in our community who would commit a hit and run on anybody, especially a widow trying to get medicine for her child. This is Camden. We have gossips and squabbles, but something like this? Do the police have any idea who hit her?"

"I don't know. I have to wonder if our local police department can handle more than traffic tickets. The whole thing is unbelievable."

My mother wiped her hand on a napkin. "I heard that Mr. Draper agreed to open early for her. She made a quick decision to step out while her children were sleeping. It was only a few blocks after all. She has to feel guilty about leaving them alone, but she was the only parent in the home and had to get that medicine. I still can't believe whoever hit her didn't even stop. What kind of person would do that?"

"Either they had to be drunk or really hated her." After I said that, my thoughts shifted to Arlene. Her desire to promote Clara's singing was important to her, but I couldn't believe she would be so motivated she would hit Constance with her car.

"Charlie blames the accident all on the need for a stoplight at the corner. He even blames himself for it."

Mother pulled her grey cardigan closer to herself. "I know. He's mentioned it once or twice. According to the city records, there have been four minor accidents at that corner in the last year. Of course, he's riled up. Each one of them played out right in front of his restaurant."

"I guess so. He was pretty shaken up when I spoke with him." With all this heartbreaking news, I had almost forgotten my real reason for visiting. As we finished the last of the donuts and she was pouring a cup of coffee, I changed the subject. "Mom, I wanted to ask you what you have heard about Anson Manning."

Her expression turned sour. "Plenty. He's the man everyone is talking about in here. He's a cad. He's a scoundrel. I'm not even sure how much of what I'm hearing is true. It's no wonder he went after you like he did. You know he's never quite added up to the Mannings' reputation of top citizenry. He went to several colleges, but I don't think he ever got a degree. He's had a few jobs here and there, but wherever he was, they didn't put up with him for long."

"It's amazing he's been unable to keep a job, and now he's running for city council."

"Yes. His hedonistic ways do not exactly jibe with the nine to five crowd. He's in his thirties, but he still acts like a college boy. You would think that would be all that we needed to win this campaign but…"

She walked over to the newspaper section and pulled out today's paper. "I debated showing this to you, but you're going to see it anyway. I guess someone tipped off that reporter. Pity. He seemed like such a nice man being there for you with Anson, but here it is. He found out the whole story about Miss Daisy's. If the *Camden Courier* wanted a story of debauchery, Anson could give him enough material to write a book. Why is it the press always goes after someone like your father?"

A library patron now stood at the checkout desk, a tall stack of books wobbling in front of her.

"Ready to check those out?" Mom asked.

I sipped my coffee as she pulled a card from the front of each book, stamped it, and filed it under the due date in a long wooden box.

When the woman left, I continued our conversation. "Maybe I should suggest to that reporter he check out Anson Manning's background. After all, fair is fair, right?"

"No. Just because somebody is mean to you does not mean you need to do the same. Anson Manning's habits are well known to the people in Camden. It won't surprise me if the Mannings control this reporter. The story here is not about your father but about the playboy trying to turn politician. Not easy for any reporter to resist, I would think."

I decided Mom's advice was worth taking. My father would never dish the dirt on a competitor, and I needed to do the same. That was why he was the better man for the city council seat. I had to hope other people could get past the Miss Daisy's article and see him for who he really was.

Chapter Three

Even though it had been sunny at the beginning of the week, storm clouds were gathering on the horizon. Constance Benedict was still in a coma, and the town was in a tizzy trying to figure out who among them would hit her and drive off to let her die. To Arlene's credit, she had visited her every day at the hospital. I couldn't help wondering if she was visiting her because she was a kind and caring person, or because she felt guilty about something. The more I considered the darker alternative, the more I had to be logical and ask myself, why would Arlene be out and about that early in the morning? There was no way she could have known Constance would be on an errand to the drugstore. For it to be anything premeditated was next to impossible.

Ellie continued to fret over Al's lack of attention to her. One night in our apartment, she paced the floor, the measuring tape she constantly wore swinging from side to side. "He's so comfortable and the place our relationship is in that he's stuck. He isn't thinking of getting married. He knows that if there is a party or any kind of function he has to go to, all he has to do is ask and good old Ellie will be there right next to him. I could be one of those big cardboard cutouts you see in front of the Rialto Theater. This is my girlfriend. She's a real doll."

"That's not true," I reassured her, although I wasn't convinced she was wrong.

"It is, and you know it. We've lost the spark. We kiss a little, but there's no passion. When we first started going out, I wasn't like anything like Maureen Johnson. I put the brakes on if you know what I mean. I gave him limits as far as what I was willing to do."

"Sounds like a good thing."

"Yes, but those were because we were still getting to know each other. Now we know each other very well, but Al doesn't even ask anymore."

Ellie threw herself on the couch and began to cry. "I'm in my thirties. When am I going to be the bride? I have enough bridesmaid dresses to outfit The Rockettes. Am I going to be an old maid? A spinster no one invites anywhere?"

"Of course not. Al's going to get around to asking you to marry him. You two are perfect together."

"Then why hasn't he? What's he waiting for? Tell me!"

I blew out a sigh. "I don't know…but I'm sure he has a reason."

"I need to do something drastic. Something to get the romance between us back." She turned, and her eyes took on a hard focus. "What do you know about birth control?"

"Excuse me?" Did she forget that I didn't even have a boyfriend at the moment? I had dated a few boys but had never had to consider something like preventing a pregnancy.

"You heard me." She stood up and began to pace again. "Does everybody just go to the drug store and pick up those prophylactic things or do they go to the doctor?"

"I don't know."

She turned and raised her hands in the air. "How do you not know? You're young and more beautiful than I ever hoped to be. Men have tried. I'm sure of that."

I gulped. "Yes, but like you, I made limits. I've never actually…you know."

She rolled her eyes. "I know. Sadly, I know." She went back to pacing. "I have a plan. Operation Land the Electrician has just begun. I am no longer waiting for him to make a move…no, the move. I'm taking destiny into my own hands. Maybe that's where it should have been all along, right?"

"What are you going to do?"

"What do you think? I'm going to the drugstore first thing in the morning, and then I'm going to make dinner for Al…at his place. Better yet, I'll write him a note and invite him to the debate and then for an intimate late dinner."

Her plans made me nervous. So much could go wrong. It would devastate her if it turned out Al was no longer interested in that kind of relationship. How did I support my cousin but still protect her from being hurt?

"And you think he'll go for that?"

"He's a red-blooded male, isn't he? Of course, he will." She seemed so convinced of it that I worried even more for her fragile heart.

"What if he doesn't?"

She stopped for a moment, and her face went slack. Then she switched back to Ellie the enthusiastic. "I can't think like that right now. I'm about to make a big change in my life. This could lead to passion, marriage, and then who knows? Little Als running around."

Somehow, I wished she hadn't gone that far as I imagined a set of children with red handkerchiefs in the back pockets of matching overalls. She cocked her head slightly forward and smiled. Bags under her eyes from crying, her long nose pointed downward, and yet at that moment, my simple cousin had just become a femme fatale.

On Friday, after a busy day at secretarial school, I promised my parents I would be at the debate. When Ellie and I left our apartment, the rain was pouring down with flashes of lightning and the earth-shaking booms of thunder all around them, causing even the bravest dog to hide under the coffee table. Ellie was her own source of a thunderstorm because after writing her version of a "come hither" letter to Al, he answered it with the same response he always gave. "Yeah. Sure." She whipped up something very slinky on her sewing machine and carefully compiled ingredients for their late-night supper. I couldn't help but think she was doomed to fail, but I never let on my true feelings on the matter. Whatever happened, I would be there for her.

My mother informed me that every day since the Founder's Day Banquet, Dad had dutifully practiced a set of questions and answers. I hoped the more he practiced, the more confident he would become. Now came the real test. He was trying out all those hours of rehearsal on real people. Even though he was exceedingly nervous at the Founder's Day Banquet, I decided to try to be positive. Maybe it was being exposed to Ellie all week, but I refused to let the negativity waiting around the corner get to me. Dad would overcome his paralyzing stage fright and show Manning and the community he was the worthiest candidate.

I had chosen to wear a red sleeveless dress with a string of pearls my mother gave me, hoping to look patriotic. Even though the dress was red, it wasn't as seductive as a dress Ellie had wanted me to try on at her store. The last thing I wanted was for Barb to make a judgment on my outfit as she did with the green shirtwaist.

When we got to the steps of the hall, Ellie said from under her umbrella, "Let me go in alone, so Al won't be shy about coming over."

"Sure," I touched her lightly on the sleeve. "Good luck."

She gave me a brief smile, and collapsing her umbrella, ran inside. Someone splashed through a puddle behind me.

"Wonderful night for a debate," the reporter from the Camden Courier muttered as he closed his umbrella upon entering the town hall. He shook it out and placed it next to another umbrella with fringe on the edges that rested in a brass bucket in the hallway. "I'm afraid we haven't been formally introduced. I am Ben Dalton."

"Nice to meet you."

I shook out my umbrella and placed it next to his. By the umbrella holder was an imposing highly polished bookcase displaying the town's time capsule dug up after a hundred years. There was a big ceremony when they unearthed it the year before, and our long-forgotten treasures were still on display. The capsule itself was a rugged-looking copper box discolored by patches of dirty green. Placed around it were the long-secured contents. There was a miniature Bible covered in black leather that over time had become ragged around the edges, a book of the town's laws, and an assortment of newspapers with articles from the then Southern Unionist governor Sam Houston. Amazingly, none of these items had suffered water damage and were still easy to read. A murmur of voices drifted toward us from a room down the hall.

41

"Sounds like a lot of people," I whispered.

"And if it's anything like the Founder's Day banquet I could end up with the Pulitzer out of this. Who knew small-town living could be so exciting?"

His words left a sting. "My family does not appreciate that article about Miss Daisy's. You printed it, and you don't even know the whole story."

He grinned and raised an eyebrow. "I realize sometimes the stories we tell make things difficult for the people we tell them about. For that, I apologize, but the story just sort of…showed up. In my business it's all about selling papers and a story about a brothel is money in the bank. You have more to add about the house of prostitution visit? I find that surprising. To me, it's pretty simple why a man would be caught there. Supply and demand, if you will."

I felt the heat rising to my cheeks. "It isn't as if I had ever visited there. I only know what I've been told."

"I guess you could say the same for me. In some ways, my education is lacking, not that I haven't been offered a quick study course." He offered me an arm. "Shall we go in?"

When we entered, the room was full of people milling about.

"Uh, huh." I took in a nervous breath, my anxiety mounting for my father.

"Your dad is going to do fine. I'm sure Anson Manning didn't spend too much time preparing for tonight. He strikes me as a seat of his pants type of guy. He doesn't want this job the way your father does."

I started to part ways from Ben, but he offered me his arm. "Would you mind if I tag along? I can't think of a better way to get to a story than through a lovely candidate's daughter. Besides, I believe you said you needed to give me some information on the Miss Daisy story."

"That part of the story is not for public consumption."

"Really?" He was very interested now. "I will be a gentleman. A journalistic gentleman."

We found my dad in the corner talking to some of the townspeople. He seemed fairly relaxed, but I knew better. I took in a short breath and then felt Ben Dalton take my hand.

"He's doing fine."

"Mike Morgan. He's our man," I said with the lilt of a singing cigarette commercial. He released his grip. It was the type of thing a friend would do, and I wasn't sure I wanted him to let go.

The large open room serving as the community meeting place was abuzz with chatter. I hadn't counted on so many people attending. According to the TV Guide, The Ed Sullivan Show was on tonight, and the Lettermen were supposed to be on it. If my father wasn't in the race, that was where I would be on this stormy evening. In one corner, Morton Manning and a group of men stood around a transistor radio listening to the static and crackles of a weather broadcast. I was surprised to see one of the teachers from my school, Miss Robinson, hanging off to the side of the group listening earnestly. Everyone else was focused on the radio, but she seemed to be fixed on Morton.

Barb stood with a gaggle of women engaged in conversation. As we walked by the topic was Constance Benedict's accident.

"Awful, just awful," Barb said. "Such a brave little mother. Someone like Constance is the heart and soul of this town."

The other ladies nodded in agreement. She turned to Jane. "Let's send the poor woman some flowers."

"Yes, Barb," she answered. I would think a financially comfortable group like these ladies would send his mother a cash donation instead of flowers. A widowed mother with an ill child would not have enough money to pay her medical expenses. Sending flowers seemed to be more the appropriate thing to do than the right thing.

Arlene waved at us from across the room as she sat among a group of older women. Ellie and my mother sat a row behind them, speaking with a third woman. From Ellie's hand gestures going from the woman's waist to hip, she was talking about designing a dress. Any occasion where the town's women turned out, Ellie almost always picked up a custom order. As Ellie listened to the woman's response, her gaze drifted to the doorway. I looked too. Al still wasn't in attendance. Was it getting so distant between them that he would not show up? I could feel the pieces of her heart splintering.

Anson Manning was seated up front looking surprisingly sober. A woman with short brown hair that curved around her jawline straightened his tie. Her look was simpler and less involved than Barb's, and she was beautiful, but more naturally. "Looks like Manning has found someone new to flirt with," Ben observed. "Sailors might have a girl in every port, but he seems to have a girl at every political function." He took in a breath. "Ooh, that's good. I need to write that down." He took out a piece of folded-up paper and pencil and recorded his brilliance.

I watched the proprietary way the woman tidied Barb Manning's brother-in-law. There was just something different about her. "I think that could be his wife."

"Oh my, take a look over there. I believe Maureen Johnson is also in attendance at tonight's function."

Maureen Johnson sat with her legs crossed, while her foot was swinging like a countdown to doomsday. She was not too happy with her favorite candidate, and a woman we were now assuming was his wife. Ben folded up the paper and put it back in his jacket pocket. "I think I smell a story."

"This could get interesting," I whispered. It made sense someone like Anson Manning would be married. He was quite a catch. Young, handsome, and rich. If an interested party could get enough of the first three, they might be able to overlook the fact he was an irresponsible cheating drunk.

"Anson looks like he could handle anything today which is good considering he's about to get caught between two women with issues," Ben Dalton whispered. "I guess your family couldn't count on him being drunk all the time."

"If we could start finding our seats," Barb announced.

"I know you wanted to follow me around, but I think you're on the trail of your story. I need to go check on my father."

"Sounds good," Ben said.

I walked over to my dad and patted him on the shoulder. His focus remained on the new sober version of Anson. "You can do this, and you know why?"

"Are you going to start talking about a little old ant who can move a rubber tree plant?" Dad asked, referencing my favorite song, "High Hopes" from the musical *Damn Yankees*.

"No. Because you are the best man for the job. The minute you open your mouth, the rest of the town will know that too."

As I was removing the sheer blue polka dot scarf, I had put on to protect my hair from rain and humidity, the pearl necklace my mother loaned me for the occasion suddenly broke. I caught the pearls in the scarf, saving myself from the embarrassment of chasing after the little white balls. My mother's eyes flashed.

"Oh dear, now we'll have to take it to the jeweler to be restrung."

"Sorry, Mom." I crammed the whole mess into my purse, which now refused to close because it was designed to hold a single lipstick and a comb, nothing more. As I attempted to snap my bag shut, Barb Manning approached us. "So nice to see the two of you, but what are you doing back here? You Morgans love to hide out in the crowd, don't you? Your place is at the front of the room." She swept her hand in the direction of the front table. "Anson has been waiting for you." She particularly reveled in this. Her brother-in-law was now ready and living up to her expectations. "I think you'll find him quite the adversary today."

"Of course, thank you," Dad said, his low voice a mixture of politeness and caution.

"Thank you," Barb beamed. "We are so excited for this debate today. You always learn so much about people in these settings. It's just like watching Nixon and Kennedy all over again, but of course this time we have two handsome men, not one."

Mom smiled at Dad. "You sure do."

Barb drew in a breath and raised a finger. "I completely forgot. You haven't met Anson's wife, have you? Let me introduce you. Maybe the two of you can sit together while your men duke it out?"

We followed Barb to the front as the lights above us flickered. "Quite a storm. I'm just so happy all these kind people made their way out in this weather. Aren't you?" Barb turned, "Linda, I'd like you to meet Mike Morgan, your husband's opponent, and his lovely wife, Opal. Oh, and this is his daughter, Dot."

Linda Manning wore a green suit with a blue-collar that scooped at the neck. It was very stylish, if not a little warm for the stuffy hall. She extended her hand. "It is nice to meet you. I know we are in a competition of sorts, but I do hope we can all become friends."

"Nice to meet you..." I started to answer but was interrupted by Maureen Johnson, who was now standing behind me. The scent of perfume rose up around us, the hypnotic fragrance causing us all to look around.

She reached a hand around to Linda, causing me to step back on my mother's foot to let her into the circle. It was as if I wasn't even there. "Nice to meet you, Linda. I'm a friend of your husband's. A very good friend." There was no denying what she was hinting.

Linda's eyebrows rose, and a spot of red came to her cheeks. She glanced at Anson whose eyes were cast downward and then turned squarely to face Maureen. "How lovely to meet you. How long have you known Anson?"

"Long enough." She gave Anson an inviting grin.

"Yes," Anson said, standing to shake her hand. "We've just met. Maureen... I'm sorry. What was your last name?" I couldn't believe he was going to pretend the two of them hadn't been all over each other at the Founder's Day banquet. The way he went into action denying her existence, I had to wonder if he had done this more than once?

"Johnson," Maureen said, still smiling.

"Johnson," he reached out and shook her hand. "Well, I certainly hope I can count on your vote."

"You certainly counted on it last time we met," she licked her lips seductively. An awkward pause fell between us.

Linda reached for a white woven handbag behind the chair and slung it over her shoulder. "I'm sorry. I feel a terrible headache coming on." She turned back to us, "Nice to meet you." She pushed her chair under the table and headed for the door.

This was better than watching soap operas.

Maureen's seductive tone turned cold. "Funny, you forgot to tell me about a wife, Mr. Manning."

Barb looped her arm through Maureen's and physically turned her from

Anson. "Maureen, have you met my husband, Morton? He's right over there listening for reports on this terrible storm." Taken by surprise, Maureen put her hand over Barb's.

"Why would I ever want to meet your husband?" She released herself from Barb's grip and slunk back to her seat.

We were about to join Anson at the table when a bolt of lightning hit right outside the window. The lights flickered off, plunging us in the twilight of the day. The sound of the radio announcer cut back in through the grey pall of the room.

"A tornado is expected in the Camden area. Please find shelter immediately. This is not a drill. We repeat. This is not a drill."

Morton Manning turned around, cigar in hand. A siren could be heard winding up to its high note through the closed windows. "That's it, folks. Let's all head to the basement. Gather your belongings."

People scattered, grabbing purses and rain jackets. Anson walked around the table. "I'll be right with you, Morton. Need to visit the men's room." Instead of taking the unencumbered path to the door, he walked over to Maureen, who rose and followed him. I presumed they wouldn't end up in the men's room. It was kind of funny to think just a few minutes ago he barely knew her.

"Come on," my mother slung her purse over her shoulder. My father stood with his hand on her elbow.

I wanted to see where Anson was going. Was he going to meet Maureen while everyone else found shelter in the basement? Ellie joined my parents. "Let's go, Dot."

"You go on ahead. I'll be right there. Need to use the restroom."

"Now? Can't you hold it?"

"No. If I'm not there in ten minutes, come back up and get me."

"Ten minutes," Dad said.

The room quickly emptied, and when I started to find Anson, Ben Dalton stood in the doorway, his eyes on the weather. "I'm up here to get a picture of the storm. What's your excuse?"

Before I could answer, a window on the far side of the room shattered into pieces as a tree fell through it. I dropped my purse, and because the latch was never securely closed, the pearls bounced out onto the floor.

"Oh, no. I hope those weren't valuable. This is going to be a whopper of a storm. I don't think I brought enough film." He began to dig through his suit pockets. Another bolt of lightning hit. Branches, debris, and rain poured in through the broken window. "We need to go," Ben said.

"I have to get those pearls. My mother gave me these. I'll catch up with you."

Ben came to me from his spot at the door. "No, you won't. I wouldn't dream of leaving you here. The pearls aren't going anywhere. You can ask your mother's forgiveness when we get downstairs. I'm sure she'll understand."

Ignoring him, I began scrambling around the floor, retrieving the pearls.

"Dot please, just leave them," Ben said.

"I can't. It will only take me a second. I think there were thirty, and I have," I counted, "11 in my hand." Giving up, Ben joined me in grabbing pearls while we both said the number out loud as we retrieved them." When there was a thud in the hallway, followed by brisk footsteps, we had just hit thirty.

"Someone must have fallen trying to get to the basement. We have to go now." Ben slipped an arm around my waist, guiding me to the door, and we made our way out of the room. The lights had left us for good, but the light through a broken window on the double doors of the town hall dimly illuminated the item that had caused the loud noise. A branch from the massive oak tree that stood proudly in front of the town hall had pierced through the window and lay next to the bookcase on the hall floor. Even with the wind and rain blowing around us, I smelled a familiar perfume. The oversized bookshelf that held the precious time capsule was now face down.

"Oh no," I gasped.

"Yes, it's awful, and I would love to stand here and get the whole story," Ben said, still tugging on my arm, "but we need to get downstairs."

"No…"

"Reporter's code. A story is only good if you're alive to tell it. Staying up here isn't safe."

"No…we can't," I pulled away from Ben and ran to the bookcase. "There's someone underneath it. Look." I pointed to a man's leg, sticking out on the other side.

Ben rushed over and pitting all his strength, tried to move the bookcase. He stood up and let out a breath. "Yell down the stairs and get some of the other men up here." He returned to the bookcase and kept trying to move it. I screamed down the stairs, and several of the men ran up to help.

A few minutes later, they lifted the bookcase off its victim.

"Oh, God," Morton Manning said as he viewed the dead man. Pulling a handkerchief from his pocket, he placed it over his mouth and turned away. On the floor, his chest crushed in, and a piece of display glass protruding from it, lay city council candidate Anson Manning.

"And you say, you walked out, and the bookcase was already on the ground?" Officer Sprague asked a half-hour later, his forehead, bereft of hair, still glistening with rain. He wrote everything I was saying into a small black notebook he had pulled from his front pocket. The stub of the pencil he was using was near extinction, but he wrote in a gruff, sloppy hand on the lined pages. He was surprisingly small for an officer of the law, and it looked strange he was in command of much larger men.

"Yes," I answered, suddenly feeling tired. Exhaustion was setting in after the shock of seeing a person so brutally impaled.

"And was anyone else in the hallway when you entered?" He asked.

"No."

"I was with her," Ben said.

"And you are her…" Sprague searched for the correct word.

"I'm not her anything. We were leaving the room at the same time," Dalton answered.

"So, it was only the two of you when you found the body?" Sprague's eyes intensified as he tried to get his answer. Finally, he began to write again.

"Although…" I stuttered.

He looked up from the notebook. "Yes? Although what?"

"I smelled perfume in the air." Officer Sprague returned to the notebook but then stopped.

"Perfume?"

"I know. It sounds silly, but that was the first thing I noticed after seeing Mr. Manning."

Another uniformed officer joined us in the corner of the hallway. He was much younger than Sprague and bent down to hand a card to him. "Sir, we found this in the deceased pocket."

It was one of my dad's promotional postcards. My father's image had scribbling around the face resembling a goatee and devil's horns.

Sprague took it and began to read aloud, "Mike Morgan. He's your man." He smiled. "If solving a crime was only that easy. Where is Mike Morgan?" His voice echoed down the hallway. "Is he still here?"

Dad, who had been hanging back, stepped forward. "Right here."

"And what connection did you have with the victim?" Sprague questioned.

"Not much of one. We were running against each other in the race for the empty city council seat, sir."

Sprague nodded knowingly as if an "ah-ha" just went off in his brain. "Oh yes, poor Phil." Was the death of the last city councilman a cautionary tale for everyone? It seemed even the police knew about the chicken bone incident. "Did you and Mr. Manning get along?"

"I barely knew the man, although I did not care for the way he was looking at my daughter at the Founder's Day banquet." Sprague pursed his lips together and began to look around.

I spoke up. "I'm his daughter."

Morton Manning stepped forward from the crowd of onlookers and placed himself between my father and Ben Dalton. "These men engaged in fisticuffs with my brother at the Founder's Day Banquet."

"In all fairness, he deserved everything he got," Ben Dalton said.

Officer Sprague straightened at the district attorney's words. "Mr. Manning, nice to see you again. I am sorry for your loss." He turned to Ben. "Is that true? You and the victim got into a fight?"

"Not a fight," he assured him.

Morton took out the white hankie and dabbed at his mouth as he spoke. "Not true. He had my brother pinned up against the wall. Morgan's daughter made the mistake of flirting with my brother, and these two went after him."

"So, it was a fight. Did you have words with our victim this evening?" Sprague asked Dad.

"Not really. We were just about to sit down, and the tornado siren went off."

Morton jumped in. "But possibly they have been planning this since the banquet to get back at him."

"And that is not true. He had been drinking that day," Ben Dalton tried to explain, "and this young lady did not flirt with him. He was making lewd suggestions toward her. Tonight, he was sober and a much different man."

"More than likely," Sprague said, "what happened here is an accident, but I like to be thorough. How long were either of you and the victim together tonight?"

My father stepped up. "As I said, we had just arrived when the storm siren went off. We met his wife, and then everybody broke up to seek shelter downstairs."

Sprague's attention shifted to Ben Dalton. "And you?"

"I didn't say a word to him. I was watching him though hoping to get a story. Little did I know I would get one this big."

"And about what time did you first come into the town hall?"

"Um, I came in with Dot," Ben said.

"Let's see," I interjected. "We got here sometime before 6:30 and I would have to say the siren went off at around 6:40. That was when Morton instructed us to go to the basement."

Sprague nodded and recorded the times. "And what time did you and Ben Dalton discover the deceased?"

"We didn't go right away. It was probably about 6:45 to 6:50."

Sprague tapped his pencil on the notebook. "Why didn't you go to the basement when everyone else did?"

Ben stepped forward slightly, "Dot's purse spilled out. We were picking it up."

"*Spilled-out-contents-of-purse*," Sprague said as he scribbled each word. "So that means Mr. Anson Manning was out in the hallway alone from 6:40 until around 6:50 and that would be the approximate time when the bookcase fell on him. Are you telling me it took you ten minutes to pick up your personal items?"

"Okay. Maybe five," I said. "Less than five. My necklace broke, and we were picking up the pearls. We heard the thud when the tree went through the window, and then we heard footsteps."

"Footsteps? Whose footsteps?" Sprague repeated.

Why was Sprague's questioning so painstakingly slow and methodical? The policemen on television were much quicker than this. "Why, the murderer of course," I said. "Isn't it obvious?"

Officer Sprague scowled, blinked rapidly, and then said, "Miss Morgan. This is not some lady's detective novel. Just because you heard footsteps does not mean they are a part of some nefarious plot to kill the deceased. As I said earlier, at this point in our investigation, it appears to be an accident."

Before I could disagree with him more, Ben interrupted. "I heard the footsteps, too. Dot is not imagining this. You wouldn't be trying to cover up the crime, would you?"

Sprague's eyebrows rose. "When was this?"

"Right after the thud. Whoever was in the hallway, they had just exited when we came in."

Sprague turned to the young officer. "Who was the last person in the basement?"

Morton Manning butted in even though Sprague's question wasn't directed at him. "Miss Morgan yelled down the stairs for us to help her. Technically, that would make her the last person in the basement."

"That is not what I asked," Sprague said.

"Well, then I really couldn't say." Morton backed up.

Sprague nodded. "So, you can't recall who entered the basement before Miss Morgan yelled down for help?"

Morton Manning splayed his large hands across his middle. "No. There was quite a crowd down there, and I wasn't keeping track of the comings and goings. We were trying to listen to the radio."

Putting the hand with the pencil up to his chin, Sprague looked to the outside door. "That means the killer…I mean, the person you heard, had to have exited out that door before the bookcase fell killing Mr. Manning."

I couldn't hide my smile. Although he hadn't admitted it, Sprague was starting to adopt my theory. The officer walked over to the bookcase, his eyes drifting to the back of the rough-hewn wood. He turned to the uniformed officer. "Let's check this for prints," he looked to me, "Miss Morgan, here thinks this was no accident. I think a simple fingerprint test will put her histrionic theory to bed. Television cop shows will be the death of us all."

With a wide smile, I folded my arms. My gaze drifted to Ben Dalton, who was listening intently. Had he heard that? The police were going with my idea. Morton Manning was also looking my way. This was not the public persona I normally saw. His menacing glance sent a chill through me. Not everyone in the room appreciated my theory.

"I think you're missing the point here, Sprague." Morton eyed my father. "It would be prudent to know this man's whereabouts when the bookcase fell over and crushed my brother. I don't know if you are aware of Morgan's background, but he was recently caught in a raid at a brothel. My brother Anson, trying to do good by his future constituents, was going to be addressing this very matter tonight. Mr. Morgan, here, had to have known it would come up as a topic at the debate. If this awful thing wasn't an accident and you're looking for a motive, go no further."

Sprague's right eyebrow shot up with this new information. "Mr. Morgan, is it true your unseemly behavior and eventual arrest was exposed by the victim of this accident?"

With the tables turned, Dad stepped back slightly. "I'm not sure who leaked that information to the paper, but I wouldn't put it past him, or anyone from the Manning family for that matter. For the record, I wouldn't have been comfortable discussing the newspaper article, but it would not be reason enough for me to kill this man. It was only a city council race, after all."

"But you were caught in a raid at a house of prostitution?" He licked the tip of his pencil and began to scribble.

"I was… helping out a friend, and before you ask me the next question, we didn't engage in any of the services provided."

Sprague shook his head. "I see." Again he started writing *helping – out – a – friend.*

Dad turned to me and then back to the officer. "If that's all…"

"All for now, but don't leave town," Sprague answered.

"Are you sure about releasing this man, Officer? He obviously has motive to kill my…" Morton started to choke up as his wife gently took him by the arm.

"Come on, Morton. We need to see about arrangements for Anson."

As the Mannings left, I whispered, "How did the focus shift to you so quickly?"

"I have no idea. Anson Manning was a real son of a gun, but I wouldn't wish this on him." Dad shuddered as he looked back at the body of Manning.

Ben pulled out his camera. A policeman held up his hand. "No pictures."

"Had to try." He winked at me.

Arlene and Ellie came up from the basement, out of breath from the stairs. I couldn't help but notice Al was not with them. Had he stood Ellie up? From the red spots on her angled cheekbones, the answer was probably yes. "Officer, may we leave now? The people downstairs are getting restless."

Sprague looked up from his notebook. "As soon as I get everyone's name and number, you're free to go."

Arlene held her pocketbook over her arm. "Then start with me, young man. Such a sad thing to have happened."

"And then me," Ellie mumbled after her.

"Did either of you know the deceased well?" Sprague asked.

"Not really," Arlene answered. "Although it doesn't matter to me. He wasn't a very nice man."

"Why do you say that?" Sprague's notebook flipped open.

"He insulted her niece," Ellie said. "Just another careless man."

Sprague looked confused. Arlene said, "She was singing for the Founder's Day Banquet, and he called her a cow."

"A cow?" Sprague's eyebrow went up again. "That is interesting. Let me get your information, ladies, and then you can be on your way."

As my parents and I crunched through the glass at the shattered door,

Sprague lifted his head from his copious notetaking. "We'll need you to be available if we have more questions."

"Anything you need," my father said. "Glad to help."

Chapter Four

Even after such an eventful Friday night, life went on in Camden. Ellie sulked all weekend, and when I asked her about Al, she told me she didn't care.

"Al who?" She answered as she hemmed one of the many bridesmaids' dresses she was making for a local wedding.

"Did he tell you why he didn't show up?"

"He tried. I'm not talking to him right now."

We went around like that all weekend when I finally got out of her that Al had a last-minute emergency with the storm coming in and had to help the city with the electric poles. It sounded like a valid reason to me, but I didn't have as much at stake as my cousin did.

"Are you going to try again next weekend?"

She set her needle on the light blue satin. "I don't know. I'm just not sure if I can get my courage up one more time."

"Sure, you can."

"Easy for you to say. You have men fawning all of over you."

"I do not."

"I saw how the reporter was looking at you."

Interesting, but was Ben Dalton looking at me romantically or as a story for the newspaper? I had to admit when he drew close, he made my heart speed up.

"No, he wasn't."

"Oh, and now I can see you're interested too." She sighed. "Oh well, at least one of us will find love this summer."

The next Monday I was sitting front and center at the Hudson Secretarial School. Seeing the dead body of Anson Manning had unnerved me and even though I tried to study, I spent more time looking out the window. I felt guilty for not getting to the hallway sooner. If I hadn't dropped the pearls, we might've been able to save him before the bookcase fell, especially if it was a freak accident caused by the tree coming through the window. I turned in my test to my teacher Miss Robinson, a woman in her forties with cat-eye glasses and a sorry plaid knockoff of a Dior suit.

"You certainly took your time, Miss Morgan." Because of my poor job of studying, I needed all the assigned time given to decipher the shorthand scribbles on the page. Nothing boosts your self-esteem less than being the last person to finish a test. Looking into Miss Robinson's face, it almost felt as if she was enjoying my shame. What I chose not to share with her was that while she left the test unattended to go on one of her many smoke breaks, another student noticed the key to the test laying on her desk.

"Hey, everyone. Robinson left the key," she had announced. When she let the rest of the class know, several students went forward to copy the shorthand symbols on the paper. I did not. I wasn't in this school to get a perfect grade, but to learn something, especially if someone was going to expect me to use shorthand in a future job. Cheating on the test would not only be shortchanging the class but shortchanging the future abilities I was there to receive.

When it was clear I would be the only student not to use the key, one of my classmates came up to my desk. "Why are you still doing the test? This is a free pass, sweetie. Go on up there," she urged.

"No. I think I'll take my chances," I said.

"Fine, Saint Dot, but don't you dare tell on the rest of us." An edge had crept into her voice.

Now I stood in front of Miss Robinson's desk, remembering that threat. "I wanted to get it right," I told her. Did she have any idea the other students cheated?

Miss Robinson peered at the paper through her pointed lenses and drew her lips into a line. "I guess we shall see about that." Again, she gave off the feeling she was getting her kicks from my potential failure.

Trying to put the unfortunate experience of the test behind me, I drove home. It was a beautiful summer day, and the park was full of the yellows and golds of coreopsis and more shades of gold in the coneflowers lining the walks. The trees were in full bloom, providing much-needed shade, and the air smelled like freshly mown grass. With so much rain in the forecast, I tried to take a moment to treasure the here and now. So, what if I might have just blown a test? I comforted myself by looking at the glorious blue sky. When I walked in Arlene, Clark rushed out of the kitchen and made a beeline for me. Letting out a sigh, I gave a wave. I wasn't sure if I was in the mood for landlady gossip. "Hello, Arlene. How are you today?"

"Not good. Not good at all. My poor little niece is devastated and told her mother she refuses to sing ever again." Out went my joy of the moment and in came Arlene, beside herself with worry.

"Well, she is sixteen," I reminded her.

Arlene shook her head no. "That's not it. I'm telling you, this is traumatic for the dear girl, and I'm hotter than a wet hen over this." She put her fingers to her temples as if she was getting a headache.

"I'm so sorry to hear that. I thought her voice was beautiful. Of course, I've heard her sing before, so I know what she can do. After all that had happened with Anson, she was a little nervous at the banquet. Barb should have never thrust her up there like that."

"I'll tell her you said that and thank you. I'm just hoping your father beats that scoundrel in the race for city council. Why did Phil have to choke on a chicken bone? What happened to Anson Manning was a terrible thing. What a way to go. As shameful as this sounds, I'm glad he's gone. His words to my Clara were cruel. When someone hurts your family, you want to draw blood."

I was a little shocked to hear these graphic words coming from such a nice churchgoing lady. I had always thought of her as a sweet person who would catch a fly and shoo it out the back door rather than smash it with a fly swatter. She was kind. She gave away baked goods, for goodness sake.

Arlene changed the subject, her frustration expressed. "I'm sorry. I guess I let this get under my skin. How was your test?"

I shrugged. "Who knows? I hope I passed, but it couldn't have been by much." Miss Robinson, happily making red marks all over my paper and humming a merry tune, flashed in my mind.

"I think it is very admirable of you to learn a vocation, just in case Mr. Right doesn't come along. Ellie has proved it doesn't always work out. You never know what the future will bring. I wish I'd learned a trade. I don't need the money, because Wilfred provided for me, but you know, some days it's hard to get excited about gardening."

"It's never too late to learn something new. I think you would make a good secretary," I said.

"That's true, but I don't think I want to be a secretary. Although I have thought about being a talent agent. With my perseverance, I could get Clara all kinds of singing jobs. That would be worth getting up for every morning. Who am I kidding? I'm not getting any younger. You, my dear, are an inspiration."

"Thank you for saying that. When I look around at all of the happy families in Camden going the traditional route, I sometimes feel not everyone supports the idea of me getting a job one day."

"What do your parents think? I know they support you, but how do they feel about your independent streak?" she asked.

"They think I have a mind of my own, and respect that. At least that's what they say. My father told me I'm too smart not to do something with it." I could still remember the night I told them I was enrolling in the Hudson Secretarial School.

"Well then," my mother had said. "I guess we've raised a smart, beautiful, independent woman. Right now, I think I'm surprised but proud of you for having this kind of goal."

She couldn't have said anything better to make me feel like I was making a good decision. I was on my way, and my parents were willing to support it.

Arlene gave a nod. "Times are changing, and it's time to get the traditional role of women out of the 1950s, right? Things like the Camden Ladies' club are going by the wayside. No matter what you might hear, you don't have to land a successful marriage to have a fulfilling life."

"Yes, well I'm sure there's one successful marriage in this town suffering today. Anson put that family through hell. First, he showed up drunk to the Founder's Day Banquet, and then, when Barb tries to make it right with a debate, we find him crushed beneath a bookcase."

Arlene drew closer. "You're telling me." She gave a low chuckle. "I know, I know it isn't polite to laugh, but everything always seems to go so right for those people. Now, all of a sudden, bam bam. Speaking from the ranks of the little people, I find a guilty pleasure seeing someone else suffer for once. God forgive me."

"I just wonder if Barb is so distraught it will mean the end of the ladies' club."

"Are you kidding? Oh, it will come back. That ladies' club is like cockroaches in the dark. You couldn't get rid of it even if you tried. One thing about the Mannings, though, is whatever they set out to do, they always succeed."

That evening as I tried to reapply myself to my studies hoping to make up for the low test grade, I heard the phone ring downstairs.

"Dot, Barb Manning for you." I laid my transcription pad aside and ran down the stairs where Arlene stood with the phone extended and a smile on her face. "Cockroaches."

Barb didn't waste any time getting to the point. Her voice sounded rough. "Could you do me a little favor?"

"Sure. What can I do?"

"I need you to call the members of the ladies' club and tell them there will not be a meeting this week. We have so much going on with the funeral, and I'm just not up for it. You can understand that, can't you?"

"I guess so," I answered, although curious why she would pick me for something like this and not her best buddy, Jane. "I think I have the phone list around here somewhere."

"Good. I don't feel like talking to anyone right now, and I thought you would be the best choice for this job. I've known some of these ladies since high school, and with you being an outsider, they probably won't want to gossip with you about this terrible event."

"Of course. I'll be glad to help. How is Anson's wife doing?"

Barb harrumphed. "Surprisingly well. I do think it's pretty peculiar she left early and then our beloved Anson met with an untimely death."

"I hadn't thought of it that way." Was she pointing the finger at Linda for Anson's death? That would mean that she thought he was murdered and it wasn't an accident. What about Maureen? Would Barb bring up all the trouble she caused that night or was this the kind of thing the upper crust would try to dismiss as if it never happened? Linda Manning might have left early, but it was because Maureen Johnson was making it very clear she was on intimate terms with her husband.

"Then again," she said. "I think I would have left the debate early if someone was flirting with my husband like Maureen Johnson." And there it was. She wasn't going to sweep Maureen's behavior under the rug. "That woman is like a bee to honey, and that awful perfume she wears is atrocious."

"It was pretty strong," I said as Ellie came in the door from work. Pointing to the phone, I mouthed "Barb". Ellie rolled her eyes and walked to the kitchen, and then I could hear the tap running. She stepped out again with a glass.

"Subtlety is not that woman's forte, shall we say," Barb said.

"Do you have any idea where Linda went when she left?" I asked.

"No. We found her later that evening at home. We called right after it happened, but she never answered. She wasn't at home when the police went to tell her about Anson either. She rolled in about an hour after they took Anson's body away. I have no idea where she was when Anson died." There was a pause on the other line. "I'm sorry. This is all getting to be a little much. If you could make those phone calls for me, I'd appreciate it."

When I hung up, Ellie was scowling at me. "What could Barb Manning be calling here for?"

"She wants me to call the members of the club to tell them there will not be a meeting this week."

"You're still in the Camden Ladies' Club? I thought, after all that's happened…"

"Just for a little while longer," I assured her. "We need to be charitable, Ellie. She's just lost a family member. It wouldn't be right to say no to her."

Ellie scrunched up her shoulders and then stretched her neck, something she often did after long hours over a sewing machine. "If you say so."

An hour later, as I finished my last phone call alerting the members of the Camden Ladies' Club, there would be no meeting, I looked up to see Arlene waiting patiently in the hall.

"I hope I'm not interrupting?" Arlene asked.

"Not at all. I just finished."

"One of the things I like about your boarding here is that you don't spend a lot of time on the phone. At least until tonight. I can't believe she had you call the entire group. Nothing stops that woman." Arlene said wistfully.

"I'm sorry. I should have asked. Were you expecting a call?"

"No. At least I don't think so. Are you finished?"

"I spoke to everyone but Linda Manning, and under the circumstances, I don't think she planned on attending, anyway."

Arlene's lips pursed. "Well, that was very nice of you. Unexpected, that you would make calls for her, but nice."

"I know what you're thinking, but Barb wanted me to do it to keep the gossip down. I guess she thinks no one wants to talk with me, and from the shortness of the responses I got, she was right. I think she's having a hard time trying to deal with Anson's accident."

Arlene's eyes flashed. "You mean Anson's murder. Don't you?"

"That's not how the police see it. Do you know something I don't know?"

"Did you know I was one of the last people to go downstairs? One of the things they don't tell you about getting older is your bladder has to be constantly attended to. If I was going to be locked up in the basement with half the town, I needed to be sure and make a trip to the little girl's room first. On the way there I ran into Anson, and he was with none other than Maureen Johnson. They were going at it in every which way right up against the wall. It was quite a shock."

"Did you tell the police about what you saw?" I asked.

"I thought about it," she answered.

Arlene was an eyewitness and for some reason had chosen to keep it to herself. Maureen's presence also explained the smell of perfume in the hallway. The town's hottest divorcee might have been the last person to have seen Anson alive. "So why didn't you?"

Arlene shook her head. "I know Maureen has quite a reputation with her history of husbands and all, but I thought maybe she wouldn't want a description of her amorous activities in a police report. I mean against the wall, for goodness sake. Who does that?"

"Now you're the one who is being nice, but this information is what the police might need."

"I suppose you're right."

"Of course, I am. The police can't do anything without information. Don't you see? She had to be the one wearing the perfume I smelled when we found him? Maybe Maureen killed him?"

"She was pretty angry with him before the debate, but they were kissing and making up when I walked in...unless she's the Mati Hari type. Seduce them and then kill them..." She stopped and then after a second, "Nope...I just don't see her killing him after...you know."

"I know. Still, I think you need to tell the police. Do you want me to go with you?"

"I know this sounds strange, but I feel like it wouldn't be right unless I tell her first. Is that crazy?"

"Considering she might have pushed the bookcase over on him, and she could be a killer...maybe a little."

"But why would she do that? From what I could tell, she wanted him alive. Real alive, if you know what I mean." She drew out the last word, making her meaning quite clear.

"Did you see anything else? Did they see you?"

"I'm not sure, but when I came out of the ladies' room, I made it a point not to look back. I marched myself straight down the hall, minding my own business. Some people would spread that kind of thing all over town, but not me. I live by a moral code."

I leaned back in my chair. "So, you won't tell the police until you talk to Maureen?"

"It is such a delicate matter. I'm a little embarrassed. What if she thinks I'm a peeping Tom?" Arlene asked.

I checked my watch. "Tomorrow morning I have a little time before class and," I pulled up the piece of paper I had been using to make Barb's phone calls. "I have Maureen's address here on this list. Why don't we go over there together?"

"Miss Maureen isn't home, ma'am. She's getting her hair done at the beauty parlor," the housekeeper said when she opened the door at Maureen's home the next morning. Maureen was also a resident in the King's Hill subdivision and lived in a two-story white frame home with an entryway light resembling the outdoor version of a chandelier. Most of the houses in my neighborhood had one bulb, but her porch light had twenty.

I started to step back on the large front porch that in this neighborhood would be called a veranda when I nearly stepped on Arlene's toe.

"Sorry," I said.

Arlene stepped to my side, still addressing the housekeeper. "Would that be Mr. Armand's or Betty's Beauty salon?"

"Oh, Mr. Armand's Ma'am. Miss Maureen is not the kind of customer you would expect to see at Betty's."

Mr. Armand's had been around for several years catering to the ladies of King's Hill. He charged double what Betty charged and offered services like facials and hair coloring. Betty's was good for a cut and a roll-up, no extras. She featured good coffee, Hollywood tattletale magazines, and the freshest gossip in town.

"Then I guess we'll have to talk to her at Mr. Armand's," Arlene said, giving a curt nod to me.

"Are you sure that's a good idea?" I asked when we returned to my car. "I wouldn't think she would want her activities broadcasted across Mr. Armand's." I was pretty sure even high-dollar hair care came with a healthy smattering of gossip.

Arlene settled into the passenger seat, her hands resting on her tan leather pocketbook. "Even though I don't want it in the police report without her permission, Maureen Johnson doesn't seem like the kind of person who would be shy about anything. She certainly didn't seem to care when she knocked heads with Linda Manning or attached herself to Anson when he was drunk. If anything, she was gloating about her latest romantic tryst with Linda's husband. She may want us to speak up so the whole crowd will hear."

Mr. Armand's was in a cluster of Camden's busiest downtown shops. As I locked the car, I expressed my doubts about our upcoming mission. "Let's just hope we're not going to a lot of trouble for nothing."

"Exactly how I feel about teaching most days," Miss Robinson from the Hudson Secretarial School said. I hadn't realized she was behind me, but she was close enough to join our conversation. How had I not seen her before?

"Miss Robinson, what a pleasant surprise," I said even though I didn't think I sounded remotely believable. "Were you in Mr. Armand's?" Mr. Armand's exterior was drowning in pink and ornamented with great white daisies cut out of metal. There was an awkward pause after I said it. I judged Mrs. Robinson hadn't changed her hairstyle since sometime in the 40s.

"No, unfortunately, that place is out of bounds on the salary they pay me to educate people like you." I didn't miss her slight as she emphasized *people like you.* "I was over at the dry cleaners, but it is fortuitous I ran into you. It saves me a phone call about your test."

I swallowed hard. From the indulgent smile on her face, I could tell it was going to be bad news. "I already know. I didn't do well. You see, I, I didn't have time to study what with..."

Miss Robinson's back straightened, "Not my concern, young lady. I am well aware of your meddling with the lives of others in this town. I don't know if you are savvy to this information, but Hudson Secretarial School graduates are a part of the hiring pool for the courthouse and Mr. Morton Manning. Our esteemed D.A. did not shy away from how displeased he is with you. It's bad enough he is suffering the trauma of his brother's accident, but to have you tell the police it might be murder is beyond the pale."

I folded my arms and said, "I certainly didn't mean to upset Mr. Manning."

"That's the problem with your generation. You tromp through life with no self-awareness. If you plan to succeed in business, then it's best to know who your superiors are and never, I mean, never cross that line. Common sense is vital, young lady, and something you don't seem to have in abundance."

Was that meant to be helpful advice or a threat? I held my tongue before I said something that would get me kicked out of secretarial school. It wasn't out of respect for Miss Robinson, but more for the time and money I had put into my education.

"As far as the test goes, I will raise your failing grade to a C when you turn in the first 100 pages of the textbook written in shorthand." She gazed down at me, her eyes magnified by her thick lenses. "Have I made myself clear?"

"Abundantly."

"Good day to you, then." Miss Robinson walked past us in her sensible crêpe heels, making no sound on the sidewalk. No wonder she was able to sneak up on me.

"She's worse than a mother-in-law who finds an inch of dust on your furniture," Arlene whispered. I felt my shoulders slump as Miss Robinson turned the corner.

"One hundred pages. Do you realize how long that will take?"

"However long, you can do it. I believe in you." Arlene squeezed my arm in a motherly fashion. "Don't let her get to you, sweetie. Let's find Maureen the homewrecker. Are you ready?"

I nodded, trying to slough off Miss Robinson's negative effect on my mood.

We opened the door of Mr. Armand's and found ourselves in a galaxy of sparkling white counters, pink floral wallpaper, and the overwhelming fruity smell of shampoos and lotions. There was a counter on one wall, and the young woman behind it was the gatekeeper.

"Good morning, ladies. Do you have an appointment?" She asked, her skin glowing, and her lips perfectly shaded a deep red.

Not only did we not have an appointment, but I doubted either one of us could ever afford one. Arlene spoke before I could answer the cover girl beauty.

66

"So sweet of you to ask, dear. We need to chat with one of your clients."

The receptionist batted her doe-like eyes. "I'm not supposed to let you into the salon area without an appointment."

Not only was she a walking advertisement for Mr. Armand's talents, but she took her job as a door sentry to the beauty salon seriously. I had to think of what would change her mind. Should I tell her she might be protecting a potential murderess or was that too much reality for someone in this oasis of spectacular glamour? I needed a different approach.

"We're from the Camden Ladies' Club and were running an errand for Barb Manning. Did you hear about the unfortunate incident that ended her brother-in-law's life?"

Her posture slackened, and she looked a little more open to us now that I had brought up what had to be the most sensational thing that had happened in Camden in a while. "Terrible. Just terrible," she whispered. I had her.

"Yes, well Barb wanted us to talk to Maureen Johnson. She needs to cancel some of the business of the ladies' club. It will just take a minute, and then we'll be out of your hair."

She pursed her lips. Had my story worked? Then, she relented. "I suppose it wouldn't hurt. Just this once."

"Wouldn't hurt a bit," Arlene echoed sweetly. Coming around her desk, she led us through the door. It was like landing on another planet full of luxuriously robed aliens who possessed enormous brains hidden by white fluffy turban towels. Those towels also meant Maureen Johnson's signature red hair was now covered up, so spotting her from across the room was going to be difficult.

"Mrs. Johnson is in Miss Hazel's chair." Our guide motioned to a woman who was fully leaned back in a pink tufted vinyl chair. Miss Hazel was filing the nails on Maureen's left hand while it looked like she was sleeping under round slices of cucumber placed on her eyes.

"Excuse me, Maureen?" I asked as we moved next to her chair. "We were wondering if we could speak to you for a moment?" Using her free hand, Maureen removed a cucumber, and a single blue eye darted to me and then Arlene.

"Do I know you?" She asked.

"I'm Dot Morgan. We were at the Founder's Day banquet and then the debate."

She looked irritated. "If you say so." Arlene stepped forward her shoulder rubbing mine.

"You probably don't remember us. You mostly paid attention to..." Arlene was going to say Anson Manning loud enough for everyone to hear.

I interrupted her in a softer voice before she could continue. "We won't waste your time, Mrs. Johnson. We wanted to talk to you about the night Anson Manning was killed." Maureen yanked her hand away from the attentive Miss Hazel and barked, "take a break, honey."

Sitting up in the chair, she removed the other cucumber completely revealing her eyes without makeup. They looked smaller and set further back into her skull.

She scowled. "What would I possibly know? I barely knew the man."

"That's not what you said before Anson's wife left in a huff at the debate," Arlene reminded her, not too tactfully.

"I don't know what you're talking about," she clipped.

The more Arlene directly confronted her, the further away she went from any type of cooperation. I shifted gears. "That's a lovely perfume you're wearing. What is it?"

Her eyes riveted to me, and then she smiled and shrugged. "April in Paris."

"Oh, it's unforgettable. You know, I smelled it when we found poor Mr. Manning's body."

Her eyes hardened. "So what? I think we're finished here." She snapped her fingers to signal Hazel's return.

Arlene spoke before the white-uniformed worker could resume her seat next to Maureen. This time she lowered her voice. "Not to be too crude, my dear, but when I was on my way to the basement, I saw you and Mr. Manning in the middle of well, you know, right there up against the wall."

"You must be mistaken. It wasn't me," Maureen said.

"We think it was," I said.

"Fine," she admitted, anger in her voice. "But when I left Anson, he was alive, and for your information, it was only a kiss. Nothing more. There wasn't enough time for anything else. Our little attraction was harmless."

"Not if that's what got him killed," I said.

"What are you talking about? It was an accident. The tree came through the window and knocked over the bookcase on top of him."

"That's partly true, but what if the bookcase went over first? Or should I say, someone, pushed it over first?" I asked.

Maureen shook her head. "Are you serious? That bookcase was solid. It had to weigh a ton."

I leaned closer, and almost whispering said, "you'd be amazed what adrenaline fueled by anger can do. Were you upset Anson didn't seem interested in you once his wife showed up? He couldn't even remember your name."

"We are only mentioning this because I feel like what I witnessed with the two of you in the hall…well, I won't go into it, might be important to the investigation. I was planning on telling the police about it, but wanted to talk to you first," Arlene said.

"Do whatever you like," Maureen answered, returning the cucumber to her eyes. "I had nothing to do with his death, and I don't care what you think." She adjusted her white towel turban and returned to the alien world of unnatural beauty.

Chapter Five

"And you say you saw the victim and this Mrs. Johnson embracing before the incident?" Sprague asked at the police station. He didn't look as if he had changed his clothes in days indicating he might have been working nonstop trying to solve the murder he was calling an accident.

"Yes, sir, but they were doing more than embracing," Arlene said.

Sprague cleared his throat. "I'm well aware of what you're implying, Mrs. Clark. Well aware."

"Just so you know," Arlene said.

"I do. Thank you for bringing this information to my attention today. We are gathering all the facts in this case right now, and every little bit helps."

And that was it. I expected Officer Sprague to wax on about motives and homicide theories, perhaps make us a cup of tea and then enlist our help to solve Camden's latest tragedy, but we were ushered out the door with great efficiency.

"Do you think this was even worth the effort? I don't think he cared at all," Arlene said as we pulled back into the driveway at our shared home.

"Who knows. I don't think Joe Friday would have let a tip about a last-minute rendezvous slip by him." On the television program Dragnet, where Joe Friday solved crimes every week, the police had it all wrapped up in half an hour.

"I agree," she said.

I attended class, and then after returning home, I settled into writing my assigned pages in shorthand. Not too long into the secretarial school torture, the phone rang downstairs. Thank God. Upon hearing my name, I took the stairs two at a time.

"The Ladies' Club calls again," Arlene said, handing me the phone.

"It's Barb. Just checking in to make sure you got everyone called. Did you have any trouble?"

"Except for your sister-in-law, Linda, I believe I spoke to everyone. They all send their condolences, by the way."

"Thank you so much. As you can imagine, it's been a trying time for our family."

"How is Linda doing?" Even though I had just met Linda the night her husband was killed, I was sympathetic to her loss. Not only that, but I felt bad she was dealing with that nasty scene involving Maureen.

"Fine, I guess. As a couple, they were never really close. I don't know what he saw in the woman."

Barb was unusually candid. I would never have expected her to reveal this kind of thing. It seemed out of character for her to say anything disparaging about a member of her own family. "They were married to each other. How could they not be close?" I asked. All you had to do was go to the movies to see pairings like Doris Day and Rock Hudson. The perfect couple. Now I knew not everybody was like that, but I hoped that my marriage would be just as wonderful.

"Oh, you know how it goes. Then again, you're still living in the Sandra Dee days of life. After so many years together, you begin to grow apart. Don't get me wrong, the love is still there, just not as urgent. You get comfortable."

Listening to her description of a long-term commitment, I wasn't so sure I'd be looking forward to the future. If I ever got married, would my union lose its steam? Would we get comfortable as she said? Anson and Linda were not that old. Surely, they couldn't be so loveless already? Could they have been high school sweethearts whose passion was gone even before they married?

"How long had Anson and Linda been married?" I asked.

"It would have been their fourth anniversary this Christmas. Can you believe they chose Christmas Eve for their wedding? What a beastly idea.

Of course, there was no accounting for taste when it came to those two. She was a daddy's girl, and if she wanted a Christmas wedding, that was what she got."

I thought a Christmas wedding sounded romantic. Red velvet dresses, twinkling lights, snow. I returned my thoughts to Linda and Anson.

"Four years doesn't seem like that long."

"I suppose not, but it is when you're stuck in a bad marriage. Anson was not what I would call the marrying type if you can understand that. Oh my, I've talked too much. I hope you'll forgive me. It's been a trying few days."

This was the first time I had heard Barb be so vulnerable. "Don't worry about it. I'm just glad I could help," I answered.

"And please keep the status of their marriage to yourself. I'd hate for that to get around town. Especially now," she added quickly, her guard going back up. It was as if I could hear the doors of King's Hill slamming shut.

That was what she was concerned about? Had she already forgotten Anson's last fling with Maureen Johnson? You could bet the rest of the town hadn't.

"To be perfectly honest, I think most people around here already know after what happened with Maureen Johnson at the Founder's Day Banquet."

No one wants to hear negative things about a family member, especially Barb Manning. Think first and then speak, I reminded myself silently.

"Maureen Johnson." She said the divorcee's name as if it left a bad taste in her mouth. "I should have known she would set her sights on Anson eventually."

"Is it true she's had four husbands?" I asked.

"Quite true and you would think after a record like that, she would have had enough of men," Barb said, "or at least they would be wary of her. It always amazes me what red hair and a large bustline can get a girl in this world."

"Does that mean she collects four alimony checks?"

"Hmmph. Something a lot of people don't know is she isn't getting that much. Husbands three and four wised up and insisted on what they call a prenuptial agreement. You know, one of those legal documents to keep the assets with the husband if things don't work out. Maureen Johnson isn't all she seems. If you had closely observed her, you would have noticed her shoes were nice, but last year's style, her umbrella, and raincoat were cheap, and that perfume she wears all over herself is only French if there's a Paris in New Jersey."

Listening to Barb describe Maureen, I surmised two things. I hadn't looked closely enough at Maureen, and Barb despised her, or should I say her type. I also had to figure she had checked up on Maureen's marriages the same way she found out about my dad's trip to Miss Daisy's. Was she allowed to dig through the courthouse files with complete freedom?

"Anson was such easy prey for a woman like that, but then again, Anson was easily drawn into anything he thought would upset us.

Morton was at the end of his rope trying to deal with him. Well, I've said enough. Thank you again."

As I hung up the phone, Barb's words echoed in my brain. Could it be even families who lived on King's Hill had their share of troubles? Maybe they were just better at hiding it.

Chapter Six

"To our next city council candidate!" Art Duran lifted his coffee cup toward my father.

"We are just so glad you could come tonight, Art," my mother said. She had broken free of wool skirts and sensible shoes and wore a floral dress and heels. Her hand strayed to the gold chain that held her bifocals.

Even though I had heard the story about Miss Daisy's, I had never met the man he rescued. Now that it was out in the paper, he suggested this dinner so that I could meet Mr. Duran and his wife.

Art looked at me. "I suppose you're wondering just why your father had to come and pull me out of a place like Miss Daisy's?"

"You don't have to say anything," my father advised his friend.

"No. It's time I came clean about all of this." He pointed to his wife, who fidgeted in her chair. "You see this woman? She's the love of my life and the reason I've come along as far as I have, but one stupid night I almost lost it all." He took her hand gently in his. "You know I love you, Eloise."

"I do, although sometimes you have a funny way of showing it."

"So true. I was having a bad day. I was at the same job for over thirty years when management in all their wisdom decided to replace me with someone new. Better looking. More efficient. They didn't want the old man anymore."

"That's terrible," Mom said. "It seems society doesn't value the older worker anymore. Years of experience amounts to nothing when someone newer and flashier comes along."

"You're telling me," Art said. "So I started drinking, and the more I drank,

74

the more desperate I became. That was when I decided to go to Miss Daisy's. Rumors around the office were the boss liked to spend some of his evenings over there, so I thought I would try to talk to him. I didn't even think about how it would look when it came to my own marriage. Somewhere in my drunk-addled brain, I was sure I could change his mind. I was so drunk, though Miss Daisy told me to call someone and get a ride home. She wasn't having me harassing one of her best clients. I was ashamed to call Eloise, so the first person I thought to call was your father, and thank God I did."

"And how did you know my dad?" I asked. Surely Art Duran had not been a plaintiff at court.

Dad took a scoop of salad from a large bowl. "Bowling league. We were the county champs last year. Surprised you don't know that."

I bit my bottom lip. "Sorry, Dad. I don't always keep up on that."

"That's okay. You're young. Only old fuddy-duddies like us think of bowling as entertainment," said Eloise.

"After everything happened, I told Eloise everything. Losing the job, getting drunk, and going to Miss Daisy's," Art said.

Eloise smiled at her husband. "It was the most honest talk we'd had in a decade. Sometimes you get so comfortable with each other, you forget to enjoy life."

There was that word again. Barb had said comfortable when she described marriage. Eloise continued, "I'll admit it. We needed something like this. Oh, sure I was mad at first because instead of turning to me when he lost his job, he got drunk. Then I was mad because of his hair-brained scheme to track his boss down at Miss Daisy's. It was like I didn't know this man anymore."

"Yes, and there was still the little matter of my not having a job," Art added.

"Yes, so we took a little vacation and found ourselves again. Then we came back, and Art got a new job." Eloise reached out and lovingly pinched her husband's cheek.

"Doing what?"

"Well, he'd always been a camera nut, so now he takes portraits of children at school. We're preparing picture packages for each child. It keeps us busy."

"And I'm doing what I've always wanted to do and getting paid for it."

"Plus, you get to work with your wife."

"Of course," he answered dutifully.

"The kids are all grown, and I'm having the time of my life helping Art run the business," Eloise said, giving a little clap.

"I think that's wonderful how the two of you worked through it," I said.

Eloise smiled at the compliment. "So, tell us, are there any young men in your life right now? I just love a good love story."

Ben Dalton's face flashed into my mind. "Um, not at the moment."

"Too bad, but you are a beautiful young woman, and I'm sure the right fellow will come along someday," Art said.

"Yes. Someday."

"You know I expect to hear wedding bells for her Cousin Ellie any time now. She and her boyfriend have been together for several years," my mother nodded.

If they only knew what Ellie had planned with Al. Would mother think it was scandalous to plan to sleep with Al or would she say it's about time? I was crossing over into an area with which I was unfamiliar. Just what were the ground rules, and was it okay for Ellie to sleep with Al if they were going to get married anyway?

"I will always feel incredibly lucky to have this lady right here," Art reached over and took Eloise's hand, "and to have a friend I can call in an emergency. Thank you, Mike, for being there when I needed you."

"What have we here? Our next city council candidate eating dinner with one of his constituents?" I turned around to see the last person I expected, Ben Dalton from the Camden Courier.

"Mr. Dalton? What are you doing here?"

"Call me Ben, and even a reporter has to eat."

"Art Duran." Art extended his hand.

Ben's right eyebrow rose, and a grin played at the corner of his lips. "The same Art Duran, who was the other person at Miss Daisy's that night? Even though I didn't put it in the paper, your name was in the police report. It's nice to meet you."

Opal sneered. "Wait a minute. Are you the person responsible for putting that story in the paper?"

"I am."

"How could you do such a thing? Don't you realize that article ruined people's reputations?" Duran said.

"I do, but I also know that there is a reasonable explanation for the whole incident and that Mr. Morgan here, can give me an interview and clear the whole thing up. I mean, how noble is it to help out a friend before he plunges himself into the depths of depravity. It's a regular Peyton Place plotline." He reached into his jacket pocket to pull out a pen. "If you like, I can take some notes right here and now."

There was something about Ben that made me happy to see him, but this conversation was getting me angry. He wanted to do an interview in the middle of our dinner? "I think you should go. What you did was inexcusable."

"I know freedom of the press can be painful sometimes, but honestly, folks, it's just my job. I'm serious about giving you a chance to straighten it out. Trust me. People will like you even more when they see you're a human being, not a cardboard cutout like the Mannings seem to be."

My father patted the empty chair between the two of us. "Have a seat. I'll give you something to print." My father's knee started to bob under the table. On the outside, he seemed calm, but inside, he had to be a bundle of nerves. "Here's the story. I was there to help a friend."

Ben started furiously writing on a paper napkin at the table.

"But that friend is to remain unnamed."

Ben opened his mouth to protest but then nodded and continued to write. "He had just lost his job, drank too much, and was trying to find someone."

Ben's eyes widened, but my father stopped him before he could speak. "Not one of Miss Daisy's girls, but the person who fired him. I came to get him and we were raided before I could help him to the car."

Finally, Art broke his silence. "One more thing. For the record, we never… enlisted any of the services of the young ladies present. We love our wives. The police came in and raided the place, and we got caught up in it."

Ben put the eraser end of his pencil in his mouth and grinned. "So, tell me, Mike. When the rooms started emptying, did you see any other high-ranking officials coming out with their drawers down?"

"And that is something I choose not to tell you."

"You sure are a friend of your fellow man. Well done, but if you ever have a change of heart, you can call me at the Courier."

"Yes, well that's all I have to say in the matter, and I expect you to correct it in the paper immediately."

Ben stood up and saluted. "Yes, sir. Glad to know there are a few good men out there. The press can't side with one candidate or another, but in light of recent events, I'd say you're a shoo-in."

As Ben stashed his napkin in his jacket, he said softly in my direction, "Well now, it seems as if we're thrown together again. Hopefully this time we won't be taking down any drunks or picking up pearls in a storm."

"Here you go." Charlie Columbo delivered our order himself which was unusual. Our waiter had disappeared. "I'm you're fill-in waiter now. Giuseppe's mama just called, and he had to rush to the hospital. He has a bambino on the way."

"That's wonderful," Eloise said. "Babies do have a way of making a family whole."

"Babies are a wonderful thing," Charlie said. "They can take even the worst situation and make it better. Lately, I've been so worried about what happened with Mrs. Benedict right outside my restaurant that having a new baby in the family is a blessing for all of us."

"Have you heard anything new?" Art asked.

"No. It is like the invisible man hit the woman. I guess we wait," Charlie told him as he set down the last plate. "I better be going. More orders for my wonderful customers. Enjoy!"

Charlie's talk of Constance put a damper on the celebratory mood. Luckily, my mother broke the moment. "And how is your schooling going? I haven't seen you at the library as much."

"I've been busy," I answered.

"She's been running Barb Manning's errands for her," Dad said to Art and Eloise. "Dot figured if she was Girl Friday to the Empress of the Camden Ladies' Club, it might help my campaign."

"Oh, yes, the Mannings. What a terrible business," Eloise said. "And now I hear it might not be an accident?"

Ben sat up slightly. "Where did you hear that?"

Eloise shrugged, "I'm not sure, but you can bet people are talking."

Art patted Eloise's hand. "Now dear, let's not gossip."

"I heard it too," mother checked in, ignoring Art's paternal if not slightly condescending warning. "I listen to what people say." Her gaze met Art's, "and then I shush them."

Ben buttered a piece of bread. "You never know what is true and what is gossip. Sometimes even I have trouble telling it apart." There was a humbleness about Ben Dalton that I liked.

"I know. It was awful to be one of the first persons on the scene. I spent a little time looking at everything involved in Anson Manning's death. For now, the police are saying it was an accident, but I'm almost sure it was murder. Just look at all the run-ins the man had before he was killed." I stopped myself and reworded my statement. "...died. He had a quick affair with Maureen Johnson and then dumped her. Then his wife Linda found out about it and got so angry she left the debate."

"If I had to bet money, it wasn't the first time Anson strayed," Mother added.

Ben nodded. "I agree, and don't forget he insulted Arlene Clark's niece at the banquet and made her cry."

Eloise tucked her napkin in her lap. "Boy, that's a line you don't want to cross. Arlene thinks the sun sets and rises by that little girl."

Ben shrugged. "You can't mean you think of Arlene as a killer or that sweet little girl?"

"Of course not, but then there was also the scuffle at the banquet. I don't know what I would have done if you and my father hadn't tried to put a stop to it," I added.

Ben's gaze met mine, "I'm just glad I could help out."

My mind drifted to Anson's behavior toward the women in the room that night. If anyone ever cheated on me, I would be angry and heartbroken and then angry again. Who knew what I might do? Had Linda Manning been upset enough to come back to the debate and kill her husband with the bookcase somehow? Perhaps she planned to have it out with him, but then her anger got the better of her. Or maybe she came back planning to kill him all along?

"Deep in thought, Dot?" Ben whispered.

"Maybe."

If there was something to this theory, maybe I could get her to talk about it. I had lowered Barb's defenses, why not Linda's? Even though he would have loved to hear my theory, splashing a widow's business across the front page was not my idea of being kind.

The next day, armed with one of Arlene's casseroles, I made a bereavement call at the Manning house. According to the newspaper, the funeral was that morning and most of the funeral reception would be at the elder brother's home. Somehow, using the simple word "house" wasn't quite right. The word palace or estate would have been a more apt description. Towering elms were shading the front porch. On either side of the massive door were vases filled with a liberal spray of pink and white geraniums. The neat white trim reflected a well-kept stately older home. I could have attended the funeral earlier in the day, but I didn't feel right attending such a solemn occasion for a man I barely knew. There was also the thing at the Founder's Day Banquet, where I had to defend myself from his lecherous glances, making the whole speaking ill of the dead thing challenging to achieve. There was a tasteful black wreath on the door and the rumble of voices inside.

I rang the doorbell, and after only a few seconds it swung open, revealing Morton Manning, his face partially turned to me. He spoke to someone further in the house. With a glass of amber liquid in hand, he turned and gave me his full attention.

"Hello, Mr. Manning," I said, trying to look as if my actions were entirely innocent. I was just a friendly neighbor there in a time of need. "I brought over a casserole. I'm sorry for your loss."

"Thank you," he took the casserole and began to shut the door between us.

"I was hoping I could have a few words with Linda," I asked before he could get it closed.

He scowled and his profuse eyebrows knitted together, making me feel as if I had just asked to go through the contents of his safe. "This is not a good time, Miss Morgan. I appreciate your condolences, but this reception is private." He put his hand on the doorknob, intending to close the door and end our conversation. I raised my voice and threw the words out to him.

"I wanted to ask her a few questions. Nothing too intrusive."

Morton Manning in a well-fitted dark grey suit, but with the tie loosened at the neck, looked tired. Very tired. His steel-grey eyes bore into mine, and his thick neck started to redden.

"Not too intrusive? I don't think you quite understand what that means, sweetheart." I cringed at the way he made me feel like a child when he called me sweetheart. Before I could protest, he continued, the ice clinking in his glass.

"Let me make it simple enough for you to understand. You need to mind your own business. I see and know everything that goes on in this town. I know you were determined to get into the middle of Officer Sprague's investigation of my brother's death. You're not a cop. Hell, you're not even a secretary, yet. You make this whole thing sound like a cheap paperback from the bargain rack at the drugstore. You were trying to turn an accident into some sort of scandal, and the Manning family has an unblemished record when it comes to that kind of thing. I am heartbroken at my brother's accident, but that is all it was. An accident."

He was really wound up now, and as he took a gulp of his drink, he continued. "I hear you have aspirations to work in an office one day. Maybe in the very building where your father is currently employed. If this is true, you should know I have a lot of influence where I work, and if I refuse to hire you, no one else in the courthouse will either. Hell, no one else in the city will hire you. You'll be waiting tables for the rest of your life, sweetheart." He shrugged his shoulders, one hand holding the drink and the other hanging loose at his side. "People listen to me. Why not? I'm the District Attorney for God's sake. I can make an innocent man look guilty without batting an eye. You'd be smart to remember that." His arrogance, so skillfully hidden before, was leaking out everywhere. He was a self-appointed king and was happy to put me in place as a peon.

He closed the door in my face, this time succeeding at ending our conversation. Morton Manning had not only proved he was a powerful man but how he had achieved that power. He wasn't afraid to mess with someone else's life or reputation if it benefitted him. If I wanted to continue to ask questions, I would need to do it without it getting back to him. Better yet, maybe I should heed his advice and leave the whole matter of his brother's death alone? It could be bad for my father or Ben if like he said, he decided to make them look guilty.

Chapter Seven

"We must always honor our brave veterans...." Barb's words floated through the fog, barely surfacing in my brain. I sat near the back at the Camden Ladies' Club a week later having serious doubts about the need to be here. After my encounter with Morton, I decided I would stick it out for at least one more meeting. I needed to keep my eye on the Mannings, but I couldn't stop asking myself if belonging to this organization was worth it. I reasoned politics was all about making connections with people in power. I was attempting to play the game and become one of them. Unfortunately, that was where I couldn't make it work. I would never be one of them. My father would never try to make an innocent man look guilty to further his career, and I would never treat another woman the way Barb had treated me.

Maureen sat in the corner, staring down at her fingernails. Her behavior was subdued and quiet. Could it be she was sad over Anson's death or was it because there were no men in the room to flirt with? It was hard to believe she was upset by his death because of her short exposure to him, but still, there was something on her mind. I would bet it had nothing to do with honoring veterans.

"So, can we count on you for the grave markers?"

It took me a moment to realize Barb was still talking and now directly to me. A smug look settled into her face causing her foundation to crack a little around her mouth.

"Excuse me? What?" There was so much going on in my brain at the moment, that the president of the Camden Ladies' Club had caught me daydreaming. A few of the members exchanged smiles.

She made eye contact with a couple of the ladies and then zeroed back in on me. "Miss Morgan, a few weeks ago, you elbowed your way into our little group promising great things. Now we can't even expect you to pay attention?"

"I'm sorry."

"I was asking if we could count on you to help with placing the grave flowers to celebrate the boys who fought and died in other countries for the American way. Of course, you seem to be in another country altogether." More titters of laughter. They were enjoying her calling me out. I felt the heat rise on the back of my neck. Was she so like her husband that she would make fun of me to further her agenda?

Rising in my chair, I returned my pen and notebook to my purse. The more I watched Barb's lips move, enjoying a laugh with the other ladies over my lack of response, the less I wanted to be a part of her world even if it was to keep an eye on her. I didn't want my father to ever be like Morton Manning. Dad was an honest guy who just wanted to help others and make the world a better place except without the cape and tights. I realized that had been the problem all along. Our family was different. This group belonged to the 1950s country club set, but for our campaign maybe we didn't need to be. With Anson dead, we didn't need to campaign it all. I was wasting my time with this group.

"No, Barb, you cannot count on me. You'll have to find somebody else to make your grave flowers, but that's okay because I know you already have the cards printed to take the credit." I turned my back on Barb and addressed the assembled group. "Even though I am choosing not to be a part of it, I do hope you continue with this project. It's a wonderful idea. We should always honor our veterans. When I joined this club, I had hoped I would make some friends, as well as helping my father's campaign. Neither of these things has happened." I walked to the front and now stood next to Barb, the imperious leader of the ladies' club. "What did occur was ridicule and a sneaking feeling I was being taken advantage of by you, Barb."

Barb raised her finely manicured hand to stop me. She was beginning to look nervous, and I had to wonder if there weren't women sitting there who shared my feelings but had been too afraid to speak up. Jane shifted uncomfortably in her chair.

Before Barb could utter a word, I continued. "The most amazing thing I've learned from all this, and my mother always told me that even in your worst moments there is something to learn, is I don't need you or the ladies' club."

One of the members clutched her pearls in shock, and I was smart enough to step back my words a bit. "Of course, we need your votes for the city council race, but my father envisions a world where everyone's voice is heard. Not just the people with the fattest wallets."

I snapped my purse closed. "I resign from the Camden Ladies' Club, but then again, was I ever really a member?"

Feeling the eyes of the club members burning a hole in my back, I made a quick exit, closing the door behind me. Had I just told off Barb Manning and her lackeys?

The door opened behind me just slightly, and Maureen Johnson slipped out. She wore a form-fitting pink suit that highlighted her abundant magenta hair with the obligatory set of pearls around her neck.

"That was amazing," she whispered as she gently closed the door. "I can't believe you did that. You look so sweet, and well, with a name like Dot, I figured you were trying to be the next Donna Reed. Boy was I wrong. You're nothing like the rest of those women."

Her words were complimentary, but seeing myself as Donna Reed, the kitschy TV housewife whose most significant problem was dishpan hands, was a new one for me. "I can't believe I did it either. I'm shaking."

She put an arm around me. "When I saw you at Mr. Armand's, I misjudged you, honey. I want to buy you a cup of coffee down at Columbo's."

We scooted into a red vinyl booth a few moments later and settled around two steaming mugs of coffee. Dean Martin was singing in the background about a kick in the head, and I was beginning to feel like I had just done that very thing, but to the Camden Ladies' Club. Maureen held her mug up and took a sip. "What you did today was amazing. I've never seen anyone actually quit. I've seen people get kicked out, sure, but you quit them. That's a first for Barb, the queen of mean."

I ran a finger along the rim of my cup. "I joined the ladies' club because I thought it would help my father in his city council attempt, but after a while, I think I realized we didn't need it. A person should run on what they believe in, not who they know. Don't you think so?"

"If you say so. What a kick! You just took down Barb Manning. Do you realize how big that is?"

"Is it?" I had quit a club where I never belonged, so Maureen's excitement over the whole matter was almost a little too much to me. Still, with this victory under my belt, I felt like Cassius Clay taking down Sonny Banks in the boxing ring.

"I just wish I had enough courage to tell Barb off," Maureen said into her coffee.

Had I started something? Once again, as in our conversation at Mr. Armand's, she seemed way too concerned about a man she barely knew. Maybe she was one of those women who fell in love instantly, but with as much romantic experience as she had, I had a hard time thinking that was the case. "Is this all because of the time you spent with her brother-in-law? Because of Anson?"

Maureen took a sip from the white stoneware mug. She nibbled on her lip and then said, "because of Morton."

"Morton?" She had been flirting with Anson Manning, not his brother.

"I only flirted with Anson to make Morton jealous. You see," she looked around the diner, "we've been having an affair."

I never expected that. I had totally missed Maureen's real motivation for flirting with Anson. "So, you didn't have an attraction to Anson?"

Maureen waited for a moment as a couple of locals passed by us on their way to the register to check out. Once satisfied, we had some privacy, she revealed, "Anson was a screwup. I should know. Morton spent a lot of time talking about him. He only helped him with this campaign thing because he was blood. Anson failed at everything he tried. I guess politics was the perfect fit for a lifelong loser. At least, that's what Morton said right before he put his name in for Phil Bogg's seat. Anson didn't even know about it until after the fact."

"And he was quite the embarrassment for the perfect Manning façade, I guess."

"Oh, yes. Every time Morton and I...you know, got together, we'd have to spend the first half an hour talking about what a pain in the ass Anson was. Nothing like complaining to enhance the mood, if you know what I mean."

"So, why would you throw yourself at Anson?" After I blurted this out, I worried she would think I was being judgmental, but she didn't seem phased.

"Morton and I have been together for over a year. At first, it was glorious. He was so romantic. So caring and generous, but then this thing with Anson started taking more and more of his time. He told me he felt guilty for all of the embarrassing problems Anson was creating, and it wasn't the right time to tell her about us. No matter how in love I thought we were, I could see that he never intended to leave Barb. What I saw as a future with him wasn't happening. We're stuck. He's not dumping his wife anytime soon, and well, I'm not getting any younger. This will probably surprise you, but having been married several times already, I'm no longer as desirable as I once was. I don't feel complete without a man in my life." She gazed down into her cup. "I just want my happily ever after. Does that seem unreasonable to you?"

It did not seem in the least unreasonable, but just how many times did she have to race to the altar to find it? I thought of Ellie and her desperate plans to land Al. Was it because women like Maureen had oversampled the population of eligible men? It hardly seemed fair.

"You flirted with Anson to get Morton's attention?"

Water piled up around her light blue eyes. "Yes, and because I threw myself at him now, I'm afraid..."

"What are you afraid of?" Did she know who Anson's killer was? Was she afraid Linda killed Anson and now planned to come after her?

"I'm afraid Morton killed his brother out of jealousy." She stifled a sob into a napkin.

I hadn't thought of Morton as the killer. He seemed aggressive enough, but his brother? That didn't seem possible.

"Morton was downstairs with everyone else. He was the person who directed the crowd to go to the basement. It couldn't have been him," I reassured her.

"I heard people were going up and down those stairs. Who's to say he didn't slip back up? Hell, I wanted him to come up and see Anson and me together in the hall. Maybe he did, and I didn't know it? Maybe he was skulking around the corner just like Arlene. When I didn't see him, I left. Maybe I was wrong? Maybe he was waiting for me to leave?"

Listening to her talk about the trap she had tried to set for Morton, I supposed he could have murdered his brother. But then again, it could have been Maureen herself who had turned over the bookcase. Even the prettiest face can tell a lie.

"I guess it's plausible," I said. "But do you think he could kill his brother?"

Maureen set the napkin down, her tears subsiding now that she had voiced her fear about her lover. "As I was leaving Anson, I heard footsteps. There was someone else there."

Why didn't she stay to see if it was Morton? That was her plan, after all. "As you said, people were in and out. Maybe it was Ben or me?"

"Maybe. Oh, I'm not sure. I'm not sure about anything anymore."

"So, what is going on between you and Morton now?" I asked.

"That's just it. Morton seems even more distant."

Maureen was a beautiful woman used to getting whatever she wanted. I would guess this was the hardest she had ever had to work to get and keep a man. Maureen was a gifted seductress who had just struck out. It sounded like now she had lost him and didn't have the first clue as to how to get him back. It was like watching a straight "A" student struggle with her first failing grade. I was sure Cousin Ellie could have told her a thing or two about getting over failing to get a man.

Chapter Eight

I told Ellie the whole story that night as she measured me for one of her experimental designs.

"I don't know who I feel sorry for more, Morton's wife or his mistress."

Thinking of this dilemma, I realized I was siding with Maureen.

Ellie looked wistful. "If the situation had been different, and a man I was in love with had been the recipient of Maureen's attention, I don't know how I'd feel. What if she went after Al?"

I hardly saw that happening. Maureen wouldn't look twice at a guy like Al. His looks were passable, and he didn't have the bankroll she had with her other husbands.

"I don't think he's her type."

"Yeah, well electricians make a lot more money than people think. And if she did go after him, I would be yesterday's news. He's not committed to me."

"That's not true. Al's your boyfriend of five years. I would say that's commitment."

"That's not what I mean. Al is there for me as a friend, but we don't have that physical bond. We've never had it. Maybe we don't have the sparks true lovers have. Maybe we haven't…you know…because we don't have enough dynamite to blow up the mine…figuratively."

I had to stop her before she pressed me with more metaphors to hide what she was really saying. "I'll admit, things like dynamite are easy for Maureen, but I think you and Al have gotten comfortable. Friendship is important in a relationship, but the two of you need more."

"So, you are saying I should sleep with him?"

"I don't know. Your mother and mine would say no."

"Sure, they would. They have their men."

"So does Barb, or at least she thinks so. You know, she was bossy and condescending to me, but it must have been difficult for her. Looking at it differently, she was the victim in all of this. Why can't I feel bad for her? What kind of person blames the victim?" I began to feel guilty for my lack of compassion.

Ellie barely heard me. "I think I'm going to call Al. Put it all out on the table. Fish or cut bait."

I blurted out, "I should tell Barb about the affair. She should know. I would want to know."

"And if he says yes well, then….What? You have to be kidding me. A married couple's troubles are not the kind of thing you want to get in the middle of, Dot."

"I know, but this is the kind of thing people love to talk about."

Ellie tried to return to inserting pins in the material but stopped.

"Now you're confusing me. Who else knows?"

"I don't know. Probably anyone who saw the way she was acting at the banquet."

"But her attention was directed at Anson, not Morton."

"You have a point there…ouch" Ellie missed the hem of the dress, and I felt the stab of the pin.

"Dot, I know you think you mean well, but if you go marching up King's Hill and tell Barb Manning about Maureen, it could break up their marriage. Do you really want to be responsible for that?"

"And who's fault would that be?" I asked. "I'm not the one who's been secretly meeting a notorious redhead in a hotel for the last year."

Ellie put a finger on her chin her gaze drifting upward. "Hmm, if it works for Maureen, maybe I should try that route."

"Ellie! What would your mother think?"

"That it's about time? Listen, Dot, just promise me you will keep this business about Maureen to yourself. I agree that what they are doing needs to be revealed to Barb, but it's not your job to do it. Let them work it out on their own." Ellie put down her pins. "I'm going to call Al." Ellie got up and went downstairs. I could hear Arlene's TV going in the living room, so whatever Ellie said it would have to be quiet. What would Arlene do if she found out one of her single ladies was setting up a rendezvous?

A minute later, she returned and began pinning my hem, as if nothing had happened.

"Well?"

"I'm not sure. He was kind of quiet."

"So, what did he say."

"He'd think about it."

I thought all men wanted to jump into sex. Could Al be more interested in someone else? "When will you know?"

"I don't know, but you can bet I'm not going to let it lie. I want an answer. I feel all jittery inside, and I almost wish I hadn't messed with what we have."

"You aren't happy, and you haven't been for a while. You want more. You want to get married and have children with Al."

"Yes, but the man makes the schedule. Not the woman."

And why was that? Sometimes asking difficult questions and bringing up subjects that people shy away from is healthy, which brought me back to Barb.

The next day as I drove down Barb's street, she was out in her yard trimming roses. Ellie's advice was dancing around in the back of my head, but the problem was, I felt so bad for her that my resolve to keep this information quiet blocked it out. Sorry, Ellie.

"Hello, Barb," I said as I climbed out of the car. After quitting and telling her off at the ladies' club meeting, she looked surprised and a little wary of me.

"I know I have people to do this, but if I want my roses to bloom all summer, they need to be pruned correctly." She took her gardening gloves off and peered at me from under the brim of a large white floppy hat made of straw.

"What can I do for you?"

I suddenly felt awkward as I searched for what to say. Should I say it or work it into the conversation with subtlety?

"Well? I don't have all day," she said impatiently.

"It's about Maureen Johnson."

She pursed her lips together tightly. "What about her? Is she quitting the ladies' club too?"

"No. It's not that." What was I doing? Ellie was right. Finding out her husband was cheating could crush her. My heart was pounding, and I wished I had listened to my cousin and kept driving.

"Then what?"

My words ran together as if I was about to run out of time on a television game show. "Maureen Johnson is sleeping with your husband."

She slapped her hand with her glove. "I see," she said quietly. I expected Barb to have a stronger reaction. Tears, fainting, anger. She seemed slightly perturbed but overall calm upon hearing the news. "Thank you for letting me know." Before I could force any more bad news on her, Linda Manning pulled into the driveway in the same lime green Camaro I had seen so badly parked at the Founder's Day Banquet. It must have been Anson's car. Now that I was closer to it, I could see a few nicks and dents that were probably due to driving while drunk on occasion. Today she wore a simple black sleeveless top and tight-fitting pants making me think of Audrey Hepburn. On her well-shaped bicep, a purplish-brown bruise showed on her fair skin. She walked toward us, lowering her sunglasses. Her eyes were surprisingly well made up for a woman who had just lost her husband.

"About time you got here. Morton has it ready for you. I'll be right back." Barb turned to me. "Thanks for stopping by."

She was dismissing me as if learning her husband was cheating with a buxom redhead was the equivalent of finding out the local butcher had his finger on the scale.

Linda, curiosity in her eyes at Barb's dismissal, smiled and said, "I didn't realize the amount of paperwork involved when one's husband dies."

As a secretarial student, that was precisely the kind of thing I loved working through. We had been given a few "story problems" in my legal assisting class, and it was fascinating. Hopefully, someday I might be working with an attorney helping people with their legal matters, just not Morton.

Barb returned with a bulging black leather pouch.

"Thanks, Barb," Linda said. "I need to see what Anson was doing with our finances."

"Oh, my dear." Barb gave her a withering look. "You had no idea what was going on, did you? Anson gave everything requiring an ounce of figuring to Morton. Surely you didn't think he could pay attention long enough to fill out a form?"

Barb turned to me, realizing I was still standing there. She went from surprise to annoyance. "You'll have to excuse us now, Miss Morgan. As you can see, we have family matters to discuss."

"Of course," I said. Before I reached my car, I turned back on a whim. "If you would like, I could help you fill out the paperwork for probate. That is what you're dealing with, isn't it? We had a class about it and other legal matters in secretarial school. I know a little bit about it and what I don't know will be a great experience to figure out."

"Don't be silly, Morton takes care of that sort of thing," Barb said, rejecting my offer. "I am simply handing over these details to begin the process of his working with Anson's widow. Once she gets a handle on Anson's obligations, we will take over the executorship of the will."

"Aren't I the executor, Barb?" Linda asked.

"Well yes, dear, but we can't ask you to bother with the nitty-gritty of the finances at this point. We've been handling this all along and will continue. Really, it's no bother. Morton does this kind of thing all the time," Barb assured her.

"Mrs. Manning, you don't want to bother Morton at a time like this. Besides, I'll help out for free. I welcome the opportunity to try out my skills in the real world."

Her eyes widened slightly. "Dot, there is no need…"

Linda Manning cut into Barb's words before she could dismiss me again. "I'll take your help."

"Linda, you're distraught," Barb comforted, putting a hand on her arm. "Good Lord, what have you done to yourself?"

Linda covered the bruise with her hand. "It's nothing. Clumsy." She veiled her eyes with her lids. I had two ideas on that bruise. Either someone had done that to her, quite possibly Anson, or she did it herself pushing over a large piece of furniture. Something like a bookcase at the town hall.

"How clumsy could you be to drop something that big on yourself?" Barb asked.

"It's nothing. It happened a couple of weeks ago," Linda said. Barb waited for more, and she finally answered, "Anson was drunk, and he ran into me. He didn't see me, that's all. Sometimes when he drank, he could get a kind of tunnel vision and not see things around him. He opened a door not knowing I was on the other side."

"I see. Poor Anson, a victim to the devil drink."

Poor Anson? Once again, Barb had taken the side of the Mannings, even if the actual victim was standing before her.

Chapter Nine

"If you're willing to help, it would be a lifesaver to me." Linda turned to Barb. "I don't want to bother Morton."

"You're not. I don't see how this woman…"

"Then it's settled," Linda said before Barb could say anything else.

Barb's mouth still hung open, and then she closed her lips with a little popping sound. It was wonderful to see someone not bulldozed by Barb Manning.

"Would you happen to have some time today?" Linda asked.

I checked my Timex watch. "Yes, but only about an hour," I answered. "I still haven't finished a hundred pages of extra work assigned by my teacher at secretarial school." I glanced at Barb. "It was a sort of punishment."

"That's interesting. You'll have to tell me all about it. How about if we run by the burger joint on the way?" Linda suggested.

She was referring to a new place on the edge of town, but I was unsure of what the quality might be like, I dined out mostly at Columbo's. The "burger joint" as she put it, was a small square building with windows and two ridiculous looking arches on either side of the building. Every time I saw it, I kept thinking of Dorothy telling me to follow the yellow brick road.

"I'll buy you a hamburger," Linda said. "You're going to love it. They call it fast food."

"I always thought if you fast, you don't eat food." Had the people who had come up with this new invention thought of that? Maybe instead of being a secretary, I should go into advertising? I could certainly do better than what this revolutionary new food movement was doing.

"I can get you a hot fresh meal in just a few minutes."

"And how much do you have to pay for all of this speediness?"

"Did I mention the prices? Listen, this place is ingenious. Instead of offering a big menu, they only sell hamburgers, French fries, and drinks. Because all they make is one dish, the time to prepare a new order is much shorter. One of these places started serving burgers near the highway a couple of weeks ago, and luckily, not many people have discovered it, yet. I've been there twice."

"Sounds interesting." I looked in my purse and held up a dollar bill. "Do you think this is enough?"

"Hamburgers are $.35. How can you beat that?"

What amazing things this decade was beginning to offer. Someone out there finally figured out people want cheap food fast.

I was cautiously optimistic but had never seen a restaurant that looked like this place. The smell of the cooking food drifted over when we pulled up, but instead of sitting down inside at a booth or table, we ordered food from a window, like getting a corndog at the fair. A few minutes later, I held a small white bag in my hands and had to admit it smelled heavenly.

"Try it," Linda suggested as she started pulling her sandwich from the wax paper.

I unwrapped my burger and took a bite. "Hey, this is good."

"See? I told you so. It's because it's all they do."

"And it was so fast." I took another bite, and this time, my teeth sunk into a pickle.

Linda took a napkin and dabbed at some mustard on my face. "What a great idea, don't you think?"

"Mmmm," I answered. "Sometimes, change is good. Even if it does go against the grain of tradition."

We sat quietly and ate our burgers. I was lost in thought considering what we were about to do with her husband's affairs, both legal and otherwise.

After a short lunch, we made our way to Linda and Anson's home, a much smaller house than what Barb and Morton owned. She pointed me to Anson's makeshift office, a former bedroom in the Victorian home. Once inside, I remembered I had been in this house once for a party when I was still in high school. A different family lived here then, and I tried to remember the name of the girl who hosted the party, but like the family itself, her name had vanished from my memory. Some of the cabbage rose wallpaper had been removed and replaced with modern prints of striped earth tones. The home seemed brighter all around as I noted, the former red drapes that hung on the windows were now a summery white linen.

"I'm afraid Anson's office is a little messy," she confessed. There were papers everywhere, and a picture of Anson in a rowing uniform lay broken on the floor. "One of Anson's drunken tirades. He missed his college days when he was the captain of the rowing team. I married Peter Pan, who never wanted to grow up."

"Do you have the probate forms?" I asked.

"Yes." She pulled a couple of sheets of paper off the center of his desk. "Here they are. Maybe you can make sense of them."

As I read through the legal terminology, I began to think maybe she would've been better off with Morton. After all, he was a lawyer. They were more complicated than the forms we had in class. I slowed my brain down and attempted to dissect word by word and then phrase by phrase of the legal terminology. Finally, it started to make sense, and I gave Linda a grin.

"Well?" There was a mix of anticipation and desperateness in her voice.

"You're right. It is gobbledygook, but I think we can start a to-do list. Anything I'm unsure of we can ask my dad. He handles court documents all the time." Even though Miss Robinson had been my teacher in legal assistance, there was no way I would bring this to her not after she had already accused me of meddling in the Manning's affairs. What would she think when she found out about this? I'd be copying the entire textbook in shorthand.

Linda smiled, flashing straight white teeth. "Wonderful." She grabbed the black leather bag Barb had given her.

"Barb said Morton helped Anson keep his finances straight, but of course, Anson never shared that with me. I was ignorant of a lot of things, I guess."

She handed me the bag. "He showed up with this bag at the beginning of every month, although Anson barely acknowledged his help. I thought they were investments or something. Anson acted like Morton's visits were a nuisance."

I unzipped the bag and pulled a few of the papers out. At the bottom were a couple of smaller pieces of paper with rough edges looking as if they were torn out by someone in a hurry. After closer inspection, I realized they were I.O.U.'s from Anson to Morton. I counted the amounts and realized he had borrowed a couple of thousand dollars from him.

"Did you know about these?" I asked.

Linda examined the I.O.U.s and frowned. "No. I was wondering why we were always flush with cash since coming to Camden. Then again, I guess after four years I should have known. He loved those get-rich-quick schemes. At first, he told me about them when he started on some new venture. Then I would have to drag it out of him after he lost money. I guess he was borrowing money from Morton to cover himself. I told him no more so-called easy money businesses."

"How did you two meet, if I may ask?" The more I came to know Linda, the more she didn't seem a good match for Anson. She had been beautiful at the debate wearing the latest style, but the outfit looked like something a different kind of woman would wear—someone like Barb.

"You won't believe this, but when we met, I lived on a ranch with three older brothers. I spent most of my days outside working with the horses, so I didn't get to meet too many men. I thought I would die of loneliness, and even if I did meet a man, they had to get past my brothers. Anson and I met purely by chance at a hotel in Dallas. I was there for a wedding for an old friend I knew from school. The groom invited him. I don't know what it is about weddings that give the unmarried the desire to chase the happily ever after, but that's what happened with us. He was the most handsome man I had ever met, and for some strange reason, he was interested in me."

"That's very romantic."

"Sounds that way doesn't it? We got carried away and married in Las Vegas a month later. My brothers were livid. It was the craziest thing I had ever done. When you make your living from ranching, you plan out everything and then still proceed with caution. I have no idea what got into me."

"It still sounds romantic. Spontaneity can be pretty intoxicating," I reminded her.

"Yes, except with any form of intoxication, you always wake up with a hangover, and I had a whopper of one once I found out what Anson was really like. He spent money we didn't have and flirted with other women. It's like he never stopped being single."

"So why do you think he proposed?"

"At first, I thought he was in love with me, but then I figured it might have a little something to do with the ranch. We own over 1000 acres and have seven oil wells. Someday, I will be a wealthy woman, but that's the irony of it all. Our family has money, but we don't spend any more than other families. We're too busy working, you know?"

At this point, I didn't know what to say. A family like that in Texas was like royalty. You could be a hayseed with a third-grade education, but with seven oil wells people tended to overlook your faults. Anson had married her for her money, plain and simple.

"After we were married, Anson showed his true self. He wasn't too happy. My father expected him to support me, not the other way around. I finally started talking to them all after the funeral. I should have called them years ago, but I was so afraid they would try to talk me out of my marriage. Pride is a terrible thing, and I didn't want to be the one coming home with my tail between my legs."

"I don't know. It sounds like you come from a strong family and they'd be glad to have you back."

"I know. Family is everything, and that was one thing I realized early in the marriage. If Anson was such a lousy husband, I couldn't imagine him as a father. Even though some people don't approve, I went on birth control. Actually," she laughed, "it was the only thing I was in control of in our four years. I hope you won't judge me for that."

Judge her? It sounded like growing up in an environment that flourished by planning had had a good effect on her. Besides, women were going on birth control everywhere now. "No judging."

Then she smiled again, and I realized she had never been this way until Anson died. Even though she belonged to the Manning clan, she was more like my family than Barb and Morton. My comfort in finding her real personality didn't last too long when my thoughts drifted to the bruise and how strong she must have been from growing up on a ranch. I believed her about Anson being a terror when he was drunk, but it was her word against his, and he wasn't here to tell me his side. Was that a victim or a murderer, smiling back at me?

"Well, I think that's all the bills, but according to this form, you still need another document. Are you up for a short trip to the courthouse?"

Linda ran a hand through her hair and sighed. "I suppose so. The quicker we get this done, the quicker I can disconnect myself from the Mannings." The name Manning was a very prestigious handle around here, but Linda wanted out. Even though the rest of the town might not understand, I couldn't blame her for wanting to be rid of it.

"That bad, huh?"

"You could say that." She took in my surprise. "Let me put it this way, at least when I was on the ranch all I had to deal with was horses. Horses are honest, stubborn, smelly animals, and after dealing with the upper crust of Camden, I will happily return to them."

I checked my watch. I had a class in twenty minutes. "We need to hurry. I'm in the final part of my secretarial course, and I don't want to be late."

"Okay. We'll run in and out. Thanks again for doing this."

"Well, you did educate me about fast food."

"My refrigerator is crammed with casseroles right now, and as thoughtful as our community is with gifts of food, I would love another milkshake. Yes, I know Barb would say I'll get fat, but I'm in mourning."

"You know, I've always felt ice cream is healing, especially chocolate," I reassured her.

Once we had retrieved the paperwork from the probate office, I poked my head into the court clerk's office where my dad was slaving over a typewriter.

"What a delightful surprise," Dad said, kissing me on the cheek. Behind me, Linda Manning came into the office. Dad cleared his throat.

"Mrs. Manning, how nice to see you. How are you doing?" It was the polite thing to say, but I could tell he was a little flummoxed by her sudden appearance.

"Better now, thanks to your daughter. She's helping me organize myself to file probate for Anson."

"Really?" His eyes widened, and then they connected with mine. "I would think Morton would be handling that."

"No. I wanted to do it, but then I realized I had no idea where to start. Dot volunteered to help me, and with her secretarial schooling she's been a godsend."

"Linda, is that you?" A woman stepped in from the hallway. I vaguely recognized one of my father's coworkers from my comings and goings at the courthouse. She probably knew Linda through her connection to Morton.

Linda's lips pressed into a smile. "Excuse me for a minute." She exited into the hall as the courthouse employee began to offer her condolences.

Dad put a hand on my arm. "Do you think working with my dead political opponent's wife is a good idea? I know you mean well, honey, but the Mannings can be more trouble than what they're worth."

I fidgeted a little, not entirely understanding his frustration with me. To me, it had been simple. Linda needed help, and it gave me the chance to use some of the lessons I had been learning under the guidance of Miss Robinson.

"She needed a secretary. I'm training to be one." I was trying to express the logic of it, but from the look in his eye, I could tell he wasn't buying it.

"Hmmm, and what else?"

He knew me too well. I love a challenge whether it was breaking into the business world or solving a puzzle like the suspicious death of Anson Manning. I kept asking myself, who dies like that? What are the insurance statistics of a person being crushed by a bookcase?

His scrutiny seemed to go through me like Flash Gordon's death ray. "Okay, maybe I'm trying to get more information on Anson Manning."

He shook his head, "I knew it!"

"I'm weak. I couldn't help myself."

"Maybe that's why I love you so much. Always expect the unexpected with my daughter. I'm not completely comfortable with you doing anything with the Manning family, so promise me you'll be careful okay?"

"You worry too much. I'm just helping a woman who has sadly lost her husband. Besides that, she's harmless. I've started to get to know her. She's a country girl who found herself in the middle of our town's most conniving family."

"That may be true, but with this probate assistance, now you're in the middle of it too." Dad might have been progressive in his attitude toward women's equal footing in this world, but there was a side of him that was fiercely protective. It always made me feel safe, and I knew he'd be there for me, no matter how much of a mess I might be getting myself into with my unofficial investigation.

After Linda returned, I bid Dad farewell, and we made our way out of the courthouse. We were almost to the door when Morton Manning came rushing out of the elevator. His eyes were focused straight ahead, and there were patches of color on his cheekbones. The telltale veins of a longtime drinker spidered down his nose, further augmenting his flushed appearance.

"Morton, are you okay? You don't look well," Linda said as her voice echoed off the marble tiles of the courthouse lobby.

"Huh?" He turned toward her. "Linda. What are you doing at the courthouse? I thought you'd be home with Barb."

"No, I've hired Dot here to help me with the probate of Anson's estate. Did you know she is studying to be a secretary?"

Morton stiffened. "I've heard. Regardless of whatever qualities this woman has told you she has, I'm a little insulted you didn't choose

to leave it up to me. When I agreed to share that packet of bills with you, I was willing to let you become informed. It was never my plan to have you attempt to close out Anson's affairs on your own."

After he said affairs, he cleared his throat as if the double meaning of that word dawned on him.

Linda came back at the speed of a discount divorce attorney. "And if it turns out someone pushed the bookcase over on him, it will be Anson's affairs that led him to premature death."

Morton looked at his watch. "I have another appointment, but mark my words, this isn't over." He turned and gave me a curious look. "And once again, Miss Morgan, I find you have inserted yourself into my business. I suggest you take heed of this advice and don't place yourself where you don't belong. It could be detrimental to your well-being."

As he rushed out the door, his large hand splayed the glass as he shoved it open. I turned to Linda. "Does he always act like that?"

"He's always been pretty overbearing, but today he seems to be even worse than normal. Who knows? Maybe it's his way of grieving for his brother?"

I should have considered that. He had been so abrupt with me. I hadn't attributed some of his behavior to mourning—people process grief in different ways. When my grandmother died, I spent days crying but then felt a weird kind of release during the funeral. I was still sad but found I could better control my emotions and move on. My mother had been the opposite. She remained stoic through the funeral, but when she went to her home and began sorting through drawers and boxing up her mother's possessions, she began to cry and then sob. My grandmother's things were all around her, but she wasn't and would never be there again. That was when it became real to her.

Was Morton Manning feeling anger through his grief? Even a troublesome family member can leave a hole in your heart when they die. It would make sense a man might turn to anger and then rage. Or could he be feeling guilty? Killing one's brother could make a man feel very guilty.

Even though Morton attempted to make his dramatic exit, it seemed the business of the courthouse would not be letting him go anytime soon.

"Mr. Manning!" Beatrix Crabtree, Manning's long-suffering secretary, trailed after him. She was a good friend of my mother's and her square heeled shoes clumped across the floor, creating an echo as she tried to catch her boss. She pushed through the outer door, leaving it open as she spoke.

From my vantage point, I could see Morton turn around to face his secretary, a look of irritation displayed by the furrowing of his brow. His annoyance was evident. "What is it, Mrs. Crabtree?"

"Your appointment. The location has been changed. You are now to meet at Dr. Henley's office."

Dr. Henley? There was only one Dr. Henley, and every woman of childbearing age in Camden knew him. He was the town's obstetrician. I glanced at Linda, and her interest seemed to have been peaked as well. After her admission about birth control, she had to know what kind of doctor he was, too.

Morton snatched the note out of Beatrix's hand glaring at her. I didn't think I'd be happy with someone who had just announced to the world a clandestine meeting at the local baby doctor. He glanced at the note, grumbled something to her, and then continued his way to the sidewalk.

Beatrix Crabtree returned to the lobby holding a hand on her chest as she caught her breath. "That could've been a disaster. Mr. Manning does not like to be stood up."

"Yes," Linda said. "Even if it's his wife."

A smile played on Beatrix's lips. "I never said it was his wife, now did I? I'm not sure who it was. It has to be something quite important for him to leave the courthouse and postpone a trial. Very unusual for Mr. In-at-9-out-for-lunch-out-at-5." She smiled and patted me on the shoulder. "Tell your mother hello for me," and then hurried off to her post. God forbid she misses one of Morton's calls.

Linda and I exchanged a look. "If it wasn't his wife, then who is waiting for him at Dr. Henley's office?" I asked.

"I have no idea," Linda said. "No wonder he got angry. My brother-in-law has a secret, and now I'm beginning to believe he wasn't all that different from Anson."

"I read somewhere blaming the other guy is a classic political move. Take your worst fault and project it on someone else," I said. Now that my family was involved in politics, I was finding out it wasn't a very nice place.

"Except, this time it had nothing to do with politics," Linda said as her shoulders began to slump. "I still have a lot to do today. I'll get started on the forms, but then do you think you could check them over to make sure they're correct?"

"Sure, but you still need to see a lawyer. I may have been a little presumptuous volunteering my services." I glanced at my watch. "And now I'm officially late for class."

She linked her arm in mine. "Thank you for your help with this. I think you're the first real person I've met since I've come to Camden. Keep this up, and you might be the only one I'll miss when I leave."

Chapter Ten

After everything that had happened, I had to sneak into the back of the class. Miss Robinson was out on another smoke break, and I was lucky I didn't run into her in the hallway. She barely noticed me when she returned to find the students hammering away at a shorthand transcription assignment. Today's lesson was easy, but finishing the endless pages of shorthand transcription she had assigned outside of class was another matter. The next morning with an aching arm and a lack of sleep, I slapped the first hundred pages of the textbook gloriously recorded in neat little strokes on Miss Robinson's desk. She was tearing through another student's work, merrily marking it with a cruel red pen. When she finally looked up, her eyes were cold.

"Thank you for finally getting your work to me." She leaned back in her chair, and taking off her glasses, rubbed the back of her neck. "However, it is unfortunate these pages cannot outweigh your latest blunder."

"I beg your pardon?" How could I have made a blunder so soon after the last one?

"They say a little knowledge is a dangerous thing. You are a prime example of this. It has come to my attention you've been calling yourself a secretary in our community. A noble thing for sure, but a position you are not yet trained for."

Did Miss Robinson have me under surveillance? Everything I did was making its way back to her. Had it been a coincidence she was walking down the street when we happened upon each other in front of Mr. Armand's or had she been following me? "Are you...referring to..."

"Linda Manning. How dare you offer her secretarial services you are highly unqualified to perform." Miss Robinson made me feel like a doctor operating on someone's appendix while still reading the instructions out of the medical book. Don't worry about a thing—it says here it's just a simple cut.

"I only offered to help her with probate for her husband. I made an A in my legal assistance class. I hardly think helping another person with business affairs is out of line. Besides, it gives me experience outside of the school."

Miss Robinson shook her head in disgust. "Do you realize the problems an untrained individual can cause in proceedings of the court? Are you even thinking of the legal fees you could end up causing this woman?"

Legal fees? I hadn't thought of it that way. Feeling a little less sure of myself, I said, "Linda...Mrs. Manning needed help, and I offered. Besides that, you were the person who trained me. Don't you have any confidence in your curriculum? Yes, some of the items were confusing, but I think I did fine with it. What I did wasn't wrong."

"The simple financial affairs you encountered in the legal assistance class are not the same as the family of Morton...Anson Manning."

They say sometimes you can tell more about a person in their blunders than their words. Miss Robinson had just made a significant one. Morton Manning had put her up to this, of that I was sure. Just like Bertram and putting the words into the mechanical wooden mouth of Mr. Sammy, Morton was putting words in Miss Robinson's mouth.

My frustration rose as I felt Miss Robinson's scolding of me for using something she, herself, taught me was getting ridiculous. If I wanted to help Linda Manning, then I would. "Honestly, it's just filing a few forms."

"This is a glaring misuse of your education and why I am demoting you back to first semester. It is obvious you haven't learned anything." She picked up my pages of shorthand transcription and threw them in the trashcan by her desk.

I had worked hard to get to the final semester of secretarial school. First semester? Could she even do that? The secretarial school course lasted two years, with each class taking half a year. Miss Robinson's decision left me with a choice. I could try to get a job without my certificate of completion, or I could delay my entrance into the workforce for another two years. Either way, it wasn't right. "I don't think that's fair and I'm not even sure you can get away with it. You don't own this school. You only teach here."

Other students began to filter in behind me laughing and talking, unaware of the showdown going on between us. "You are correct. The Hudson family owns this school, and Mr. Hudson trusts me completely. That includes a student's placement in our coursework. It is my opinion this course of action is indeed fair and ultimately for your own good." She wagged an unvarnished fingernail at me and grinned. "The hardest lessons are the ones from which you gain the most knowledge."

"You want to know what I think?" My voice was becoming a little louder than I would have liked it, but it was either that or let the tears that were threatening take over. "I think Morton Manning put you up to this."

Miss Robinson bristled at the mention of his name. "I don't know what you're talking about, but you can be assured your amateur attempts at secretarial assistance have not gone unnoticed in our community. Seeing as you are starting all over again, you can go home today."

I was still seething that night when Ellie came home from work. I was ready to unload on her, but she seemed to be in a sour mood already.

"What's wrong?" I asked.

"Nothing." She threw down her purse and a bag of hand sewing she brought home every night.

"Doesn't look like nothing to me."

"It's just…this thing with Maureen Johnson getting to have any man she wants has been on my mind, and it's starting to tear me up."

Maureen's ability to seduce a man and Ellie's inability to do the same was killing her. "I should probably admit this to you now. I know you told me not to, but I told Barb about Maureen and Morton."

"You did?"

"Yes, and here's the kicker. She didn't care. She went right on with her business as if I had just told her slip was showing."

"That means she already knew. The woman who looks like she has everything has a man who chooses to sleep with someone else. I guess that's life on a cracker."

"So that is what has you upset?"

"No, and yes." To my surprise, she began to cry.

I rushed over and put an arm around her, and we both sat on the bed. "Ellie, what is it?"

"Al still hasn't answered my...proposition," she said through tears.

"He said he wanted time to think about it."

"How much time does the man need?" She threw her hands up in the air and wailed. "I'm not getting any younger, you know."

"Do you think you should call him again?"

Ellie gave me a sideways look. "Now, that's just desperate." She took on a small voice. "It's me, Ellie. Have you decided to sleep with me, you big electric man?"

I laughed at her voice, and she smiled. "If it weren't so sad it would be funny. I don't know what to do."

"Maybe he's frightened? I've never seen Al with anyone but you. Maybe he's ...inexperienced."

"Good grief, the man is in his thirties. He isn't inexperienced."

"And you don't know that for sure."

"I guess all I can do is try to be patient."

"You want me to blow a fuse? I bet we could get him over here."

"Maureen Johnson has had four husbands, and I can't land Al the electrician. What's wrong with me?"

"There's nothing wrong with you," I reassured her.

She began to cry again, and my hugs and kind words were not even making a dent in it.

"I think..." She stopped for a moment.

"What?"

"I think I need to...get more serious with him."

I wasn't entirely sure what she was talking about, but I had an idea. "You've said that."

She rose and went to her room. When she came out, she was holding a piece of black silk lingerie. "Sex. Tonight's the night."

"Sex? You mean you're going to go to his house tonight, without an invitation? He opens the door, and there you stand?" I began to worry about how much a rejection could hurt my cousin. "Are you sure that's a good idea?"

"Sure. I'll put on the nighty and then wear my raincoat over it. Just like Marilyn Monroe." She ran back into her room, and I could hear her changing. "When I come back," she said through the door. "I'll be a changed woman."

"I thought you were waiting to get married."

"Well, that's not happening anytime soon. If Maureen Johnson can have that many husbands, then so can I."

"Do you want four husbands?"

She came back out, securing the belt of her raincoat. "Of course not. I'd be happy with one. It's just a comparison, that's all."

"I don't know Ellie. What if he says no?"

"He won't."

"You can't be sure of that."

"If he doesn't want to sleep with me, I've been barking up the wrong tree, and maybe I should introduce him to some of my male friends."

We both laughed at that, and it felt good after what Miss Robinson had just put me through.

"Just so you know, you're not the only one who had a terrible day. Because of what Miss Robinson calls my interfering with the Mannings she's demoted me back to first semester at Hudson Secretarial."

I explained about my helping Linda with probate and how quickly it got back to her through Morton.

She was quiet a moment and sat with her arms crossed against her thin body. "This was just because you helped Anson Manning's wife? Unbelievable. I told you it wasn't a good idea. Any time you mix with those people, bad things happen."

"I don't see why everyone is so upset about it. Is there some unwritten law? Can't I help somebody out? Am I only qualified to bring a grieving widow a casserole and judged inept at doing anything that requires a brain?

Honestly, Ellie, I thought you'd be on my side in this."

"I'm always on your side. You know that. It's just sometimes when you get a notion about something, you act first and think about the consequences later."

"Yes, well, newsflash. You're about to do the same thing."

"This is different."

"Is it?"

"It's just that I would expect Linda's own family to handle that sort of thing."

"…And maybe I deserve to be put in the beginning classes at the secretarial school? Those are my consequences?"

"Now, I didn't say that," she quickly answered. "I'm sorry. I guess I have a lot on my mind. You do what you think is right, Dot."

"The same goes for you."

"Well, then. I'm off." She hugged me and went out the door.

Chapter Eleven

The next day, the anger gnawed at me from Miss Robinson's unfair decision. I heard Ellie come in during the night, but she was gone before I got out of bed. Whatever happened between her and Al, I had to hope for the best. I couldn't let my demotion to first semester go. Morton Manning had caused this setback, and I had the right to confront him about it. I pulled my hair back into a ponytail, threw on a pair of slacks, and debated whether or not I should wear a top with a Peter Pan collar. It was the perfect match, but it wasn't intimidating enough to go up against Morton Manning, D.A., it wasn't intimidating enough. Only Doris Day could pull off righteous indignation and a Peter Pan collar. It was still early, and according to Mrs. Crabtree, Morton never graced the courthouse until 9 in the morning. I decided to drive directly to his home and confront him there. A housekeeper answered the door with a dust cloth in her hand.

"Mr. Manning left about an hour ago, did you want to see Mrs. Manning?"

The last person I wanted to talk to this morning was Barb Manning. She had caused me a great deal of calamity, bossing me around in the ladies' club, but this morning's complaint was solely with her husband.

"No. Did he go into the courthouse early?" Maybe I could catch him there, and in my thinking, it might be better. He could call the secretarial school and get the decision reversed.

"I don't believe so, but wherever he was going, he was in a hurry. I thought he was going to choke on his eggs and bacon." The Manning's housekeeper looked to be about my mother's age, and if she was anything like her, wolfing down carefully prepared food did not sit well with the cook.

112

"Can I tell him who stopped by?" She drew out her words at the end, and she waited with a knowing smile on her face. Maybe I wasn't the first young woman trying to get her hands on Morton.

"Nope. I'll catch up with him at the courthouse," I stammered, making a quick exit. What was I going to tell her?

How do you do? I'm Dot Morgan, and I'm here to tell your boss he's an interfering idiot.

As I was driving out of the King's Hill subdivision, I went by Maureen Johnson's house. Was there a chance Morton could be there? A quickie before work? I didn't see his car, but I doubted if he would park it in the driveway this time of day. On impulse, I pulled over. Maybe his car was safely hidden further down the street.

When Maureen answered the door instead of a housekeeper, her hair was no longer held in place by a dome of hairspray. Instead, it reminded me of a lion's mane with auburn tendrils sticking out in all directions. There were dark patches under her eyes, and it was apparent I had gotten her out of bed.

I didn't bother to say hello, which I was sure was a clear violation of Emily Post's manners book. "Is Morton here?" I still had anger fueling my social skills, not politeness.

Her upper lip curled. "No. Why are you looking for him here?" She seemed to have parted with the niceties as well. Could I blame her? I had just roosted her out of bed and demanded information.

"Because I need to talk to Morton. He got me demoted at secretarial school. Do you know how many classes I'll have to retake? I don't even think that's legal."

"Sounds like something Morton would..." Before she could finish her sentence, her cheeks paled. She looked like she was going to be sick. She put her hand over her mouth and sprinted away. If we were friends, I would have followed her, but I didn't think we were even close to being throw-up buddies. I was unsure as to what to do.

I stepped inside. "Are you all right? Should I call the doctor?" I yelled after her, my voice echoing down the front hallway.

After a moment, she answered, "No. I'm fine."

I heard water running and occupied myself studying the pictures in her foyer. If you have had four husbands, which husband's picture do you hang up? The last one? The dead ones? I was still pondering this when Maureen returned.

The color was coming back into her cheeks, and she had taken a moment to tame her wild tresses.

"I'm sorry." Her voice was gravelly. "That's been happening a lot lately."

"I'm sorry for knocking on your door this early. I didn't know you had the stomach flu."

"I don't." Her words were flat and yet telling. I don't know why I hadn't figured it out before. I just assumed it was Barb seeing the baby doctor. She was a little older than most new moms, and now that I thought of it, why didn't Barb and Morton have children? They were way past the average child-bearing age. They should have a couple of teenagers running around. Was their relationship that bad? Was she unable to have children? Maybe I was as naïve as Barb said.

"Are you…" I had a hard time finishing my sentence, so Maureen finished it for me.

"Pregnant? According to Dr. Henley, I killed Bugs Bunny."

So, she had taken a pregnancy test, also known as the rabbit test, at the local obstetrician's office. It had been her waiting at the baby doctor. She was pregnant with Morton Manning's child.

"You went after Anson to get Morton's attention. It was more than just trying to revive your relationship. You needed help with the baby."

"And now you know. I can't believe after all I've been through, I've found myself in this position. I told you, I would never be interested in an unambitious loser like Anson Manning. Please, I have better taste in men than that. Why would I want a leech I would end up having to support? I've become accustomed to living here on King's Hill. A selfish confession, I know, but it's the truth."

"How long have you known?"

"About a month or so. Of course, it was a shock to realize I was pregnant, and quite another when I noticed my child's father suddenly cooling and

114

trying to end the relationship. I had to do something. If I told him outright about the baby, I was afraid he'd come back to me only because I was pregnant. I stupidly thought he would come back to me because he loved me."

Now I understood even more why she was flirting with Anson. If she was waiting for the results of the pregnancy test and hadn't told Morton, any signals of him trying to end the affair could have been catastrophic. She wouldn't be the first woman who tried flirting with one man to catch the attention of another.

"I'm sorry, but maybe this is a good thing? A child?"

"At first I wasn't sure, but now...I think it is," she whispered. Then she sank into a chair giving out a wail as she hit the cushion. "But Morton doesn't. He wants me to go to some shady doctor and have an abortion. I could get arrested or worse, I've heard some of those doctors are butchers." She began to sob, making my heart break. I pulled a chair up next to her and put my arms around her. We sat there for several minutes, her crying and me saying things like it will be all right. I had no idea if it would, but it seemed to comfort her some.

"He's going to kill the baby," she said, her voice now quiet.

"Don't say that. Besides, this is your baby, too. He can't make you do anything you don't want to do."

"You don't know him." She wiped her nose with her sleeve. "He has a way of making things happen."

On the subject of his ability to mess up other people's lives, I was becoming very familiar, but I let her go on.

"I've always had men around me. They arrive, and everything's great, and then they're gone. They cheat, they get tired of me, they die. It never changes. This baby will be mine. I'll finally have someone I can love and will always love me back. I need this."

I thought of my reason for tracking Morton down this morning. He and Miss Robinson had thrown away all my hard work at the Hudson Secretarial School. I knew all too well about the manipulation of Morton Manning. If he didn't want this child, she would have a challenging time keeping it.

She continued to speak. "He probably killed his brother because of my charade, and now he's going to kill my baby." That sent her off into another bout of sobs, and while I rubbed her back, I couldn't get her last statement out of my mind. Her words were hammering at my skull.

"You think he pulled the bookcase over on his brother?"

She shook her head. "He couldn't move that bookcase an inch. Not with his bad arm. A mortar shell hit him in the war. He can't lift above his chest, but that doesn't mean he couldn't get someone else to do it."

His infirmity was something I had been unaware of, but now when I thought back, it explained several things. The stiff hugs, handing others drinks with an awkward hand, and backing off from shaking hands. That meant he couldn't have killed his brother, and with it being in the middle of an unpredictable storm, he couldn't have had time to hire anyone else to do it. It was a crime of passion, not planning.

Morton Manning, as big of a puppet master that he was, had to be innocent and off my suspect list. Of course, he only needed to mention it to Miss Robinson, and she would do it for him. She'd move mountains for Morton Manning. She had undoubtedly wielded her power to put a stop to me.

Chapter Twelve

I glanced at my watch. Morton would be in court by now. If he hadn't come to see Maureen, where had he gone so early in the morning? Could he be seeing another woman? It would explain his cooling down their affair. After my conversation with Maureen, I decided I needed a little time to think about confronting Morton. My ambition squelched, I returned home. When I pulled up to the house, Arlene was walking to her car, holding a small white gift box with a red bow on top. My landlady had continued her daily pilgrimage to the hospital to visit Constance Benedict. I wasn't sure if it was because of the outrage we all felt at Constance being run down or if she felt guilty for being so vocal about wanting to eliminate her son from Clara's competitions.

On the sly, I checked out the hood of her car. No dents, although there was some mud around the headlight on the right side.

"Good morning, Dot. I thought you'd be at school right now. Playing hooky?"

"Not exactly. I'm having a disagreement with the Hudson Secretarial School." I didn't want to go any further with the details because it would involve telling on the girls who cheated, girls, Arlene might know.

"A disagreement? I'm sure there's more to the story," Arlene said, giving me a leading look.

Attempting to change the subject, I pointed to the gift she was carrying. "Is that for Constance?"

She gazed down at the package as if she had forgotten she held it in her hands. "Oh, yes. Actually, it's for Bertram. Mrs. Columbo is dropping him off at the hospital today to visit his mother. Doctors are not sure when or even if she'll recover from the accident. When I think about all the mean things I said about him and his mother, I feel just awful." Her bottom lip began to tremble, causing an extra set of lines around her chin.

I reached out to comfort her. "Oh, Arlene. Don't do that to yourself. You were trying to help Clara. I knew you never really meant all those things you said. You were wrapped up in competing for places for her to perform."

Arlene began nodding her head, her jawline now set. She was taking in all I had to say, but I wasn't sure if she was buying it. She was what they called a "stage mother" even though she was an aunt.

"I know. I know."

"Listen, why don't I go with you to the hospital? If I'm going to play hooky, I might as well do some good in the world."

"I would love that," she agreed.

When we arrived at Constance's hospital room, she was hooked up to an IV, and dark circles showed under her eyes. Bertram sat quietly in a chair next to her, holding on tightly to his ventriloquist dummy, Mr. Sammy. Arlene walked to Bertram's side.

"How is she?" she asked.

"She hasn't woken up yet," Bertram said, his eyes never leaving his mother. "The doctor says he has no idea when she'll wake up."

"And how is your sister doing?" I asked, coming up behind Arlene.

He gave me a weak smile. "She's better. Thank you for coming to visit my mother, Miss Morgan." He was so polite, even though he must have felt like his world was crashing around him. The hospital smell of disinfectant and rubbing alcohol haunted the room, the Venetian blinds blocked out the sunlight, and the stillness of the little boy's mother in the bed was heartbreaking.

"Arlene brought a little gift," I said, trying to lighten the mood. Arlene extended the box to Bertram.

He grinned and untying the red bow, lifted the lid on the box. Inside was a tiny green argyle sweater. Bertram pulled it out and cast a confused glance at Arlene. "Seems a little small."

Arlene gently took the homemade sweater from Bertram. "That's because it's not for you. It's for Mr. Sammy. When all this is over and your mother is well again, I'm expecting to see you out there delighting us with your performances."

Bertram clapped his hands in delight as he touched the little sweater. "It's swell. Thanks, Mrs. Arlene."

Arlene took off Mr. Sammy's coat and slipped the little sweater over his head. Once she had it on and adjusted the doll back in the chair, he looked quite stylish.

"It's amazing how good the fit is," I remarked. "What do you think, Mr. Sammy?"

Bertram responded with his high-pitched dummy voice. Constance jumped at her son's performance and then grabbed his hand.

"Mommy? Wake up, Mommy," he pleaded.

Constance's eyes flickered open for a minute as she licked her lips. "Look, Mommy, Mrs. Arlene made Mr. Sammy a sweater."

Constance's eyes opened as Bertram held up the doll for her to see.

"Green," Constance said in a whisper.

Arlene stepped forward, her smile bright. "Yes, the sweater is green. That's wonderful. Sammy has a new green sweater. Won't he look spiffy on St. Patrick's Day?"

Constance repeated, "Green," this time more emphatically.

Bertram nodded. "Yes, green, Mommy. Isn't it pretty?"

Constance spoke again. "Green." I had almost decided Constance Benedict's mind had been affected by the accident when she attempted to speak again. "Car. Green car."

"A green car hit you?" I asked.

Her eyes began to close. "Constance. Was the car that hit you green?" Arlene asked, but she didn't answer. She was back asleep.

Bertram began to cry, squeezing Mr. Sammy tightly against his little chest. "She came back. She can come back again. She's going to be alright."

Arlene hugged him. "You bet she will."

"It was that lucky green sweater you knitted," he said. "You helped her

119

wake up, Mrs. Arlene."

Arlene stammered. "It was my pleasure. Knitting has always been a kind of therapy for me. Busy hands help my brain to slow down a bit."

"And just what is it your brain is speeding away about, Mrs. Clark?" Officer Sprague stood in the doorway.

I had been focused on the little sweater and Bertram and hadn't heard him approach. "Do you have any new information on Mrs. Benedict's accident? Have you identified the hit and run driver?"

Holding his hat against his jacket, he shrugged and then gave a sad smile to Bertram. "Sorry, no. We are trying to locate any possible witnesses, but that early in the day no one was out and about. Even if they were, it would have been hard to see everything clearly with the sun just coming up."

Bertram glanced back at his mother and then turned to Sprague. "Mommy spoke."

"She did? That's good news."

Bertram, now full of excitement gulped and nodded, his eyes big. "She said a green car."

"Green car?" Sprague looked intrigued. "You mom woke up, and that was the first thing she had to tell you? I wonder if she saw who was driving it? This is something I can work with. Sometimes when a witness wakes up, it is nearly impossible for that person to remember what happened. You are a brave boy and should be commended for your police work."

Bertram beamed and Arlene stepped forward. "It was because I made Mr. Sammy a green sweater." Sprague glanced over at the doll.

"And that made her say, green car? I see." He chewed his bottom lip, "How do you know she wasn't talking about the doll? Was her speech clear?"

"Mostly," I said. "She was coming in and out of the coma. We are almost sure she was talking about the hit and run driver."

"Whoever did this needs to be brought to justice," Arlene said. She gestured to Bertram. "This boy and his sister need their mama back."

"I agree with you, wholeheartedly, Mrs. Clark. Too bad she didn't give you a name as well as the color of the car. That would certainly speed along the investigation."

"Do you think we'll get lucky twice and she'll be able to tell us who it was when she wakes up again?" I asked.

Officer Sprague walked over to Constance's bed and rested a hand on the side rail and shrugged. "It's hard to tell. Sometimes in traumatic experiences like this involving a head injury, people don't remember what happened to them. I've never been sure if it is the impact on the brain or if they don't want to remember. I guess we'll all continue to watch and wait."

"So much has happened in our little town this summer," Arlene said.

"That it has." Sprague's gaze shifted to me. "Speaking of unfortunate incidents, you'll be glad to know I now support your theory about Anson Manning. When I closely examined the crime scene photos, I noted there were branches under the bookcase where Mr. Manning was killed. I am now leaning on the theory Mr. Manning was killed by the bookcase falling on him, and it was not caused by the tree branches crashing through the window. I believe the tree crashed through the outer doors and Mr. Manning turned toward it. He then twisted back as someone pushed the bookcase over on him. With the storm going on, no one would have been able to distinguish the difference between the sound of thunder and the sound of the bookcase hitting the floor. As heavy as that piece of furniture was, we are looking for a strong man with a grievance against him."

He could be talking about my father or perhaps Ben Dalton, the reporter. I thought of Morton Manning telling me he could make an innocent man look guilty. I had to find out who pushed over that bookcase.

Chapter Thirteen

That evening I stopped over at my parents' home for dinner and told them what I had learned from Officer Sprague at the hospital. "So, he seriously has murder on the table? I hate to tell you, Nancy Drew, but I think this one is headed for the cold case file," Dad said with a touch of sarcasm.

"Why would you say that? Officer Sprague may be slow to see the obvious, but I think he's a competent detective."

Dad leaned on his elbows with his hands extended. "Look at the list of people who wanted to do him in. His wife hated him because he has a penchant for cheating, and Maureen Johnson hated him because he has a wife he forgot to mention. Then you have Arlene who hates him because he humiliated her niece. Oh, and don't forget his brother, who keeps having to clean up his messes."

I held up a finger shaking my head. "No, it couldn't have been him. He can't raise his arms above his head. There was no way he could've pushed over the bookcase. He has very little upper body strength from an injury left over from the war. So, Morton is out. He didn't have the strength or mobility to kill his brother."

"I never knew that about him," Mom said as she spooned up a piece of meatloaf. It was a little dry, so I added extra catchup to mine, and now it was bloody enough to resemble a grisly crime scene. "And after all this pondering, you still forget there's a chance it was an accident."

Anson Manning had been so unlikable and offensive to me personally, could I be wishing an accident into murder? If that was the case, I needed to explore this idea. I learned from my bookkeeping course, that if you have a column that won't balance, you have to dig in, find the error, and fix it.

"So, what do you think? Was it all just an accident?"

Mom tapped the table and gave me that withering librarian stare. "Seems to me Camden is having more than its share of accidents lately, don't you think? Even though you probably don't want to hear this, if there is a murder to solve out there, I don't want you mixed up in it. It's too dangerous."

I hated to admit she was right about my amateur sleuthing. I didn't have the training or the knowledge the police had, but how many people in this world were killed by falling bookcases or crushed by copper time capsules? I found it to be a fascinating oddity. It was an error in the books that stuck out like a red flag.

Mom continued, "I did want to bring up another subject, and I'm a little nervous about it." I braced myself. Was this the "when are you going to meet a nice young man" speech?

Her eyes were solemn, and I held my breath as she began to speak. "Are you actually going back to the first semester in secretarial school?"

I blew out a sigh of relief and felt an overwhelming rush of love for my mother. I wouldn't have to explain why I hadn't found Mr. Right tonight. Mom looked surprised.

Miss Robinson's manipulation of my future had been unfair and nothing more than retribution for going around Morton. I knew now what I had to do. "No matter what Miss Robinson thinks she's justified in doing, I refuse to let it happen." I pounded my fist on the table, causing a bowl of green Jell-O to shimmy. "I will not be bullied by a woman who is nothing but Morton Manning's puppet."

"And that's our little girl," Dad said with an element of pride in his voice.

"We were afraid you'd be too upset and let this woman get away with it," Mom added.

"I am upset, but I am also at the end of my coursework, and what she is trying to do to me is unethical. I plan to lodge a complaint with the owner, and if that doesn't work, I'll go to the press." What would Ben Dalton do with a story like this? I was more than willing to find out.

Dad looked at me sideways and raised an eyebrow. "Are you sure the right one of us is running for office?"

"Absolutely. I'm qualified to help Linda Manning. I'm doing a good job, and it's what I've been trained to do." After I said it, I realized the death of Anson Manning had just crept back into the conversation.

"I commend your giving spirit, but I have to ask myself if you aren't really helping her to get more information on Anson's death?" I hated that my father knew me so well.

"A little of both." I gave a weak smile. "Besides, I think I want to ask Officer Sprague a few more questions."

Mom gave a knowing nod. "And that's our girl."

When I left my parent's house and pulled into the driveway at my own home, I was surprised to see Al sitting in his truck watching the house.

"Al? Are you going inside?" I asked through the open window. He took a drag from a cigarette and nodded no.

"No. I'm not going in right now."

"So, what are you doing here?"

"I'm not sure. It's just that...something has changed with Ellie, and I don't know what to do about it."

"Uh, would you mind if I sat in your truck with you for a minute?"

He opened the passenger door. "It's a free country."

I piled in and turned to the electrician. "How has she changed?"

"She's ...more forward."

I realized she had been so busy in the last day, that she had made it impossible for me to find out what had happened the night she went over to his house in the sheer negligee. "I don't want to embarrass you, but I saw her right before she came to you last night. I know what she was wearing and what she intended to do."

He stubbed out his cigarette and ran a hand through his hair. "Wonderful. Now the whole world knows about it."

"Not the whole world, just me, and I won't tell anyone. What happened?"

"Didn't she tell you?"

"No. Ellie's been avoiding me."

He took a deep sigh causing his chest to float upward. "Nothing happened. I turned her away."

I would be the first to admit that maybe I wasn't always in tune with the way men think, but I thought men always wanted sex. They stopped thinking with their brains and let other vital organs take over. "Why did you turn her away? You two have been dating for five years."

He glared at me. "Yes, and I liked it that way. What we had was perfect. Why did she have to go and mess it up by asking for more?"

"You didn't want to…you know?"

He looked down at his fingernails. "I don't know. Yes, I guess, but …it's a big deal, you know? I guess I wanted to be the one who started it up."

"But it's been five years…"

He held up a hand. "Yes, I'm aware of that."

"What happened when you told her no?"

He returned his glance to our second-story apartment. "I'll never forget the look on her face. She was so hurt. I did that to her. I hurt her bad." He sniffed.

I put a hand on his arm. "It will be okay. Why don't you go in and tell Ellie that you're sorry and that you didn't mean to hurt her? Tell her that it was just too sudden for you."

"I can't. If I do, I have to answer for what happened last night. I don't want to do that."

"You're going to have to talk to her sometime."

"I know. Just not tonight. It's still too painful. A man wants to be ready when he has to confront something."

After listening to Al, I figured I had just learned a little something about the opposite sex. They didn't like surprises.

For instance, unplanned pregnancies and brothers who show up drunk to banquets.

Chapter Fourteen

As much as I wanted to speak with Ellie the night before, she was already in bed when I came in from speaking with Al. I decided to try to talk to her in the morning. She left before dawn. How much longer could she keep this up? After hearing how Al reacted to her seduction, I needed to know she was alright. I quickly dressed and headed down to Bluebonnet Fashions, Ellie's dress store. Her car was parked on the street, so I knew she was in there.

The closed sign was still showing through the glass. Because I knew it was hard for her to hear when she was sewing in the back, I pounded on the glass door.

"Ellie! It's me, Dot. Let me in. What happened the other night? Ellie?"

"Something happened the other night?" A shadow fell over me, and Ben Dalton stood on the sidewalk curiously peering into the glass window. "Is this a story for the *Camden Courier?*"

I looked behind me. "Where did you come from?"

"I was born in Texas, but I don't think I'm comfortable discussing the birds and the bees with you," he said with a grin. Was he flirting or just making me look silly?

"You know what I mean. I didn't see you walk up."

"Nope. I was on my way to work when I observed you trying to break the glass of the dress shop. Is there something going on in there we need to contact the police about?"

"No. It's nothing." I waited for him to walk away, but his size eleven feet seemed to be glued to the sidewalk.

"You didn't sound like it was nothing." He leaned closer in full reporter mode. How did I get this man to drop it?

"It's my cousin. She made a…hasty decision about something, and I want to make sure she's alright."

The door to the dress shop opened, and Ellie, bags under her eyes, and slightly disheveled stood there. "I'm fine. Now go away."

Completely forgetting about Ben's presence, I walked into the dress shop. He followed me like a puppy.

"If you don't mind, this is a private conversation," I snapped.

"Who cares if he hears?" Ellie threw her hands up in the air. "Here's a story for you. I went after a man last night in next to nothing, and that was exactly what I got. Next to nothing."

Ben blushed and cleared his throat. "You know, maybe I should leave you two ladies alone."

"Don't leave. Let me pick your brain," Ellie said, her tone so sarcastic she almost sounded drunk. "Just what is it that attracts a man? I thought I had all the necessary equipment, but it seems I must be missing something."

Ben looked very uncomfortable, but she continued spilling information about her failed attempt to seduce Al. I had to stop her. "Ellie, you're upset… "

She crossed her arms and wobbled a bit. "You bet I'm upset."

"I'll be going," Ben said, backing out of the store.

"Chicken," she called after him.

He stopped at that word and turned around, "This is a bad time for you. I don't know why you would ask me of all people for advice, but for what it's worth, I think you aren't missing anything, and the man you speak of is a fool."

Ben got out of the store before she could say another word. Ellie began to cry. "He didn't want me. I can't believe it."

"I know. Maybe, it was just too sudden for him."

"And maybe he's been lying to me all along."

I stayed with Ellie until she could pull herself together. When she seemed to throw her mood into sewing up a bridesmaid dress, I left her alone. Stitching could be therapy for her, and now all she needed was a few hours of the hum of the machine, and the feeling that sewing a straight seam could straighten out the rest of her world.

Deciding to concentrate on finding out more about who killed Anson Manning, I made a stop at the Camden Police Station. Even though I had lived here all my life, this was the first time I had set foot in this building. The initial thing I was hit with was the smell I always associated with government buildings. It was a mixture of paper, ink, filing cabinets, and cigarettes. There was a faded Formica counter that had once been white with elements of silver that formed star shapes. The counter divided the room and prevented any unauthorized entrances by the general public. There were two uniformed officers behind the counter, one man and one woman. The man was standing with his back to a giant emblem painted on the wall behind him, TO PROTECT AND SERVE. He shuffled papers next to a black boxy looking phone similar to the one my parents owned in the 50s. Since then they had replaced it with a newer model, but the Camden PD still had one. There was a nameplate in front of the man that read Officer Jerry Roland. Further, into the room, the woman with warm brown skin sat behind a typewriter with a ten-inch stack of files next to her. Her straight black hair was pulled severely into a military-style bun.

When I drew closer to the counter, she looked up and acknowledged me with deep brown eyes but did not rise to wait on me. If I had to guess a pecking order, he spoke to the public, and she was the one who handled the paperwork. How predictable that even at the police department, women were expected to do the grunt work of filing and typing.

When he didn't immediately acknowledge me, I asked, "excuse me?" The man ran his finger along a typewritten line of a piece of paper as if he were searching for spelling errors.

"One minute," he answered crisply. I waited, not too patiently, as he finished and then snapped the file shut. "What can I do for you, Miss?"

"I wanted to talk to Officer Sprague about the death of Anson Manning."

"I see, and did you have an appointment?"

"No. Do I need one?" I thought the police department was always open to the public, and appointments were not required. Does a good detective turn away help on a case? I think not. The next thing they would be asking us to schedule our emergencies at more convenient times.

"Of course, you do. Officer Sprague is a very busy man. Do you have new evidence to add to the case?"

"Well, no," I stammered. I didn't have information to give, but it was information that I wanted.

"Then what is the purpose of your visit?" He crinkled his eyes at me, making them look beady.

"I wanted to ask him something."

"I see." He looked at a form taped to the counter while once again running his finger down the page. "He's out in the field right now. I can't tell you when he'll be back, but you can have a seat over there if you wish to wait." He pointed to one of the long benches lining the institutional grey walls.

"Thank you." As I sat, I noticed an inscription carved on the bench. "Bootsy loves Ricardo. From the intricacy of the work and the number of letters involved, whoever wrote this, and I assume it was Bootsy, had a lot of time to carve away. A wave of discouragement passed through me. Why did my life always seem to be one step forward and two steps back, lately? After about an hour, my bones were beginning to ache, and I was seriously considering making an appointment. Officer Jerry announced he was going to lunch. As the door to the office shut, the woman at the desk pulled a brown paper bag out of her drawer and began unwrapping a sandwich. Was she supposed to work both desks over lunch? That hardly seemed fair. I was starting to dislike Officer Jerry quite a lot. I must have been glaring at her because she smiled.

Like a good police observer, she picked up on my mood. "Oh, don't worry. Officer Jerry and I have a deal. I work through lunch so I can get my kids from school on time. I go home an hour earlier."

"I thought he left you all alone."

"I prefer it this way. It's quiet here over lunch, at least most days." She broke her sandwich in half and walked past the counter and over to my bench.

"Would you like some of my lunch?" She offered a ham and cheese sandwich on white bread.

I held up a hand. "Oh, no. I couldn't."

She smiled and cocked her head to one side. "Come on. It won't bite you. Besides, you look hungry." She was right. I had been in such a hurry to get to the police station, and I hadn't eaten breakfast.

I gave in and took the sandwich. "Thank you."

"My name is Mary Oliva, by the way."

"I'm Dot Morgan," I said between bites.

"You were checking on the Manning investigation?" She asked as she sat down next to me.

"I wanted to ask Officer Sprague if he had any new theories. As hard as I try, I can't seem to get rid of this feeling I'm missing something." She seemed intrigued as her eyes brightened at my suggestion. Suddenly I realized I was talking to a police insider who might have access to the information I wanted. "Do they have you working on the case, too?"

"Hardly. I'm a records clerk. The only way they will let me get involved with any case is to file the paperwork."

"Is that because you're a rookie?" She didn't look any older than I was. I had never known anyone who worked for the police but assumed you had to work your way up to more desirable positions, just like anywhere else.

"It's because I'm a woman. Have you ever seen a woman detective?"

"No."

"And you won't."

"And yet you stay."

"I started with some pretty crazy ideas. When you check out those Sherlock Holmes books in the library, nobody stops you because you're female. I loved those books, and I had a good reason for searching them out. When I was six years old, my father delivered the milk. He had to work early in the morning, you know. It was the same time the drunks were driving home from the bars. My mother always worried about him, and he told her he was fine. He could take care of himself. They found him dead by someone's front porch. They think he delivered milk to a house on Oak Street and somebody held him up. He never carried more than ten dollars around, but they killed him for it. The police never solved his case. Somebody has been walking around free all these years not even caring he killed a father who was a loving son and a husband."

"That's awful."

"And the entire reason I wanted to work in law enforcement. It sounds silly to me now, but I had dreams of solving his murder. What I didn't expect was to become a glorified file clerk."

I took another bite of my sandwich. It was delicious, and I hadn't realized how hungry I was. "Did you look up your dad's case?"

"Just as soon as I got a moment alone. Another reason I like it when Jerry goes to lunch."

"And did you come up with any answers?"

She crumpled up the wax paper that had been around our shared sandwich and threw it into a nearby trashcan, bouncing it off the rim. "I'm afraid not. There weren't any witnesses. Even though his milk route customer heard the gunshot, she says she never looked out the window. Now I realize it was silly of me to have even tried. If there is no evidence or an eyewitness, you are out of luck."

"Don't say that. I admire you for becoming a policeman... policewoman and trying to solve your father's case. I would probably do the same thing."

"You don't think it's terrible that I'm a mother working outside the home? My mother and her sisters all think it is." She glanced at my outfit. "I'll bet you're a housewife. I mean, not only am I here because of my dad, but we needed the money."

"Not at all." I held up my left hand, showing the absence of a ring. "I'm not married. I'm studying, or should I say I was studying to be a secretary. I hope to do more with it someday."

"I would never have seen that, and I'm a pretty good judge of people. A secretary, huh?" Mary asked.

"I'm trying, but like you and your dream to become a detective, I'm running into some obstacles."

"After watching you sit on this bench, I think you must be pretty stubborn.

I'll bet you figure it out."

"Could I ask, do you have access to the files on Anson Manning's death?"

"Honey, I have access to all the files." She rose from the bench. "And while Camden's finest are all out to lunch getting their blue plate specials, you do too." She flashed a gloriously wicked grin, and instantly, I decided I liked Mary Oliva.

A few minutes later she splayed out several photos from the Manning police report. "Here are the photos they took." The upturned bookcase was centered in the gritty black and white photo.

I ran my finger along the ragged scratch on the back of the bookcase. "Did the police ever figure out what caused this?"

Mary pointed to a line in the police report. "It says here it could have been there, even before the bookcase fell." She pointed to a scribbled line. "And Sprague changed the classification from accident to possible murder after noting the branches under it."

I pushed the large grainy black and white photos around on Mary's desk. The bookcase falling as it did scattered the umbrellas we had seen stored neatly in the brass canister across the marble floor. They looked like the childhood game of pickup sticks crisscrossing each other as they encircled the bookcase that had fallen on poor Anson Manning. I spotted the umbrella with the fringe on it near the wall, but now it was bent almost to the point of breaking. I could not understand how the bookcase could have done that.

"Do you see that?" I pointed to the fringed umbrella.

"The broken one?" Mary asked. "It must've happened when it fell."

"Do you think that umbrella could be sturdy enough to use as a lever to bring down the bookcase?"

Mary looked closely, "I don't know. Maybe?"

There were footsteps in the hall, and the doorknob started to turn. The outline of Officer Jerry shown in the mottled glass. He was saying his goodbyes to his lunch companions. Mary and I quickly reassembled the folder, and I dashed to the bench, nearly spraining my ankle on the way.

Officer Jerry walked in, and upon seeing me, a guilty grin crossed his face. "You still here? I probably should've told you this earlier, but Sprague called, and he'll be out the rest of the day."

I rose and grabbed my purse. "That would've been thoughtful."

Jerry laughed. "I never thought you'd actually stay, Little Missy."

"That's okay. I got to spend time with a real police professional, Officer Oliva over there." He looked puzzled as Mary, and I exchanged knowing glances, then we were the ones laughing.

Officer Jerry scowled. "Whatever you say, ma'am. Now be a good girl and scurry on home."

Chapter Fifteen

After being stalled by Officer Jerry but still getting the information I wanted, I felt empowered. I didn't have to follow a set of arbitrary rules set by someone else. Okay, maybe I wanted to be a good person and follow the rules, but I didn't have to allow someone to use them against me. I picked up the phone and dialed the Hudson Secretarial School. It was time for them to hear my side of the story. Better yet, I would demand it. Miss Robinson didn't have a monopoly on the decisions there. An hour later, I found myself sitting across from Miss Robinson and the owner, Mr. Leonard Hudson. He was a petite man with a delicate bone structure and a pencil-thin mustache outlining his top lip. He wore standard-issue, regulation Army glasses, which told me he'd once been in the service and was too frugal to buy more stylish civilian frames. His voice was higher than most men's but still lower than mine. He wore a brown suit jacket with a white shirt and a tan paisley tie placed precisely between his collar points.

"Now, Miss Morgan," he started, "let me see if I can take in all of the details here. Miss Robinson feels you would achieve more success repeating our program, correct?"

I started to reply, eager to explain, but before I could, Miss Robinson interrupted. "Miss Morgan lacks in some of the most basic skills needed to succeed in the world of business, namely professionalism. She has said some things among our business colleagues I consider highly inappropriate. Frankly, with all this meddling going on, I became concerned about how this would affect the school's reputation." She placed a hand over her heart. "You know I'm always loyal to Hudson Secretarial."

She was making it sound like I had been telling dirty jokes in the executive lounge. I could not let this go on. I started to speak again, but this time, Mr. Hudson jumped in first.

"Oh my. We can't have that—not one bit. Professionalism is the key to the services we provide. We can't have one of our Hudson girls acting in any way untoward."

I tried to tell him I would never be untoward, whatever that meant, but Miss Robinson cut me off again.

"Exactly. So, you agree it would only benefit Miss Morgan to repeat her courses," she said, her hands clenched tightly in a prayerlike pose.

"At a ten percent discount, of course," he answered with a little smile directed at me. Was this meager offering supposed to cheer me up?

"Of course," Miss Robinson smugly agreed and rose to go without ever listening to a single word I had to say. Before Mr. Hudson could get his petite behind out of his chair, I stood and put both hands in front of me like a traffic cop at rush hour.

"Wait! Don't you want to hear my side?" I blurted out. Miss Robinson's eyes narrowed and gave me what my grandmother would've called the stink eye.

"Certainly," Mr. Hudson said uncomfortably clearing his throat, "if you feel you have been inaccurately represented in this procedure, then we will be glad to listen to what you have to say. Isn't that right, Miss Robinson?" Who was he kidding? My side hadn't been represented at all. Miss Robinson still stood at the door, unwilling to give up her hold in these proceedings. Maybe she thought she could leave because she and Mr. Hudson has settled the matter to her liking?

"Miss Robinson, please return to your seat," Mr. Hudson said. She turned and yanked the chair out from the black lacquered table.

"Thank you," I said as Miss Robinson settled herself.

Once she finished sitting down, Mr. Hudson waved his hand for me to begin. I tried to clear my mind and focus, hoping the speech I rehearsed would come out smoothly. "Miss Robinson felt I had been unprofessional because I voiced my opinion about Anson Manning's death."

Mr. Hudson tapped his fingers together. "Oh, yes. Awful what happened to that poor man. My heart goes out to the widow."

"I feel the same way, Mr. Hudson, which is why I volunteered to use some of the excellent skills I've learned here to help her with the probate process."

Leonard Hudson beamed and nodded like the proud father of a successful child. "That is very good of you, and just what I would expect of a Hudson girl."

I nodded. "Thank you. Miss Robinson, though, felt my actions were not out of compassion but interference. That's why she said I was meddling. I felt sorry for Mr. Manning's widow and felt confident in what I had learned in my legal assistance class, where I got an A by the way. I offered to help. That was it. Miss Robinson didn't see it that way, so she demoted me to first semester."

A look of confusion came over Mr. Hudson's face. "Miss Robinson, is this true? Was that the reason you felt she should redo the coursework? I have always wanted our students to be well-rounded enough to enter the business world with an attitude of service. It seems to me, Miss Morgan, here was doing something that would make our school shine."

I had her. There was no way she was going to wiggle out of this one.

"Of course, Mr. Hudson, but it was also the last test she turned in," she said, adding a tongue cluck on the end. "The rest of the class made nearly perfect scores, but Miss Morgan failed miserably. It was quite enough evidence to me she was not only unprofessional but was failing at comprehending the material. Some of these girls are just not bright enough to be Hudson girl material no matter how good their hearts are. You can understand I was looking out for the school's reputation, can't you?"

"Is that true?" Mr. Hudson asked. His gaze turned to me. "You were unable to pass a test every other student found easy?"

Miss Robinson's eyes were like daggers, and now they were dripping with my blood. The difference between the two of us, though, was I did have a heart and a secret weapon I hadn't wanted to use. "There was a reason for that, and I would prefer not to discuss it," I said.

"Come, come now. If we have failed you, we need to know why. Right,

136

Miss Robinson?" She issued a grunt and pumped her shoulders. She could care less whether I passed, and she had no idea what I was about to say.

"If I tell you, I would also be telling on my classmates."

"If there is something wrong, then it is your duty..."

I interrupted Mr. Hudson this time. "I would also be telling on Miss Robinson."

Miss Robinson pushed her chair back. "This is ridiculous. I will not sit here and listen to this woman, making up stories about me to save herself. I have given you the clear facts of the situation, and that is all I have to say on the matter."

"Sit down," Mr. Hudson ordered, his squeaky voice filling out a little.

Miss Robinson sat.

"Before I tell you this, you need to know Miss Robinson and I don't always get along, but she is a good teacher. I've learned a lot in her class."

Mr. Hudson sighed and put his hands across his middle. "That is a comfort, but if she is such a good teacher, why did you fail?"

"I failed because I didn't have time to study."

Miss Robinson spoke up with the speed of lightning, slapping her knee. "And there you have it."

"I appreciate your honesty, Miss Morgan. If you don't study, you don't pass. I still don't see what Miss Robinson has to do with your lack of preparation, young lady," Mr. Hudson said.

"There's more. Most of the other students received A's because Miss Robinson stepped out of the room to smoke a cigarette. This is something she does quite often when she gives us work to be completed in class."

"Is that so?" His glance shifted to Miss Robinson, who now squirmed as if she was sitting on a bed of coals. Leaving a class unattended to smoke a cigarette had to be against the rules, even if the students were adults. "Go on."

"After Miss Robinson left, one of the girls was sharpening her pencil and noticed the key to the test left on Miss Robinson's desk. She told the rest of the class and everyone, except me, answered their questions using the key. I didn't. Whatever I learn at your school, I plan to take with me when I enter the work world. Cheating on the test would have solved my problem of not getting time to study, but it wouldn't help me in the real world."

"So, you failed, and they all achieved high scores." He adjusted his glasses. "I have to say this does change things."

Miss Robinson, who had been so vocal about my failure, was now quiet about hers.

"In light of this added information, I am granting you a second testing date, and you will continue your coursework, where you presently are." He turned to Miss Robinson. "You should be thanking Miss Morgan here for sharing her favorable opinion of your abilities as a teacher. Otherwise, I would've fired you on the spot. I believe she has a great deal of the professionalism you desire, but you, madam, may need a refresher course of your own."

Miss Robinson sulked.

"As for the other students, I will require them to retake the test as well. Because we were told this in confidence, you can say, I revised the test and wanted it given again. Do you understand, Miss Robinson?"

"Yes, sir."

"And there will be no more smoke breaks while I'm paying you to teach," he said with an edge in his voice.

"Yes, sir."

He turned to me. "Thank you for bringing this to our attention, Miss Morgan. I also applaud you for volunteering to help another in need. Our community needs more people like you, and I'm quite honored you chose our school to further your education."

I glanced at Miss Robinson. Her complexion was somewhere between dusty rose and fire engine red. I only had to hope I wouldn't be paying for this in the future.

Chapter Sixteen

I was bursting to tell somebody my news. I decided I would surprise my parents with takeout from Columbo's Diner.

"Congratulations, Dot," Charlie had said when I regaled some of my victory at the secretarial school to him while I waited for the kitchen to bag up our dinner. He stroked his mustache, looking out on the street in front of his restaurant. "Sometimes standing up to authority can be a good thing. It is a brave man...or woman who can recognize that."

"My parents had to help me pay for those classes the first time. I couldn't see having to ask them to foot the bill twice," I said.

"And you are a thoughtful daughter. You are going to be a big success at whatever you do. Not forgetting other people's feelings and sacrifices is one of the best parts of humankind. Mr. Hudson was right. The world should have more people like you in it." Guiseppe brought my order from the kitchen, and Charlie placed it in a paper bag. Bringing his hand to his mouth, he blew a kiss. "Enjoy!"

When I carried the delicious-smelling food into their home that night, I felt a little guilty about the cost, but I was about to be finished with school. Once I completed my final semester, I could get a job and stop depending on my parent's support.

"What's this?" Dad asked when Mom directed him to the kitchen that evening. He sniffed the air as he took in the aroma of my surprise. "Something smells wonderful."

I pulled the tinfoil off a plate of lasagna. "We're celebrating. I went into the Hudson Secretarial School and argued my case. Miss Robinson thought she had it in the bag, but I wouldn't let her take over, and Mr. Hudson listened to me. They are keeping me in my last semester."

"That's terrific," he said softly. There was something about his tone that bothered me. He didn't seem happy about my news. I expected a pat on the back, a hug, or at least an attta girl.

"What's wrong? I don't have to repeat my classes, and we don't have to pay for it. Do you know they offered me a measly ten percent discount as if that would make it all better, but your daughter convinced them to reverse their decision? Isn't that wonderful?"

His eyes avoided me, and instead, he continued to look at the takeout lasagna. "You shouldn't have. How much did this cost you?"

"A little, but not too much. You have always been there to support me. I know, I shouldn't have, but I…"

He threw his jacket on the chair and then plopped down on top of it.

"Mike, don't do that." My mother ran after him and quickly picked it up. "You'll wrinkle it." Dad only had three suit jackets. He was usually so careful with his clothes.

"I got fired."

"Fired?"

Dad was a model employee at the courthouse. It would be tough for them to have a reason to fire him. He always showed up to work on time and did whatever they asked of him, and then some. "What happened?"

"We had a police report go missing, and I was blamed." He blew out a breath. I had been so excited to give him my news that I hadn't noticed his mood.

"That's impossible." Throwing the coat back down, Mom placed her hands on her hips. "Are they sure it was your fault? I'm sure a lot of other people handle paperwork like that."

"Morton Manning spearheaded the whole thing," he said. "The judge called me to his office, and Manning was standing there, gloating. In all my years I've never been called into the judge's office like that. Judge Carpenter kept saying how disappointed he was in me, and a criminal could go free because of my negligence."

My dad had worked in the same building as Manning for years, but he rarely talked about him. Now all of a sudden, this man was becoming a regular part of our conversation. My cheerful, sweet father was devastated, and I knew I had Morton Manning to thank for it. I also knew who might have called him after my victory at the secretarial school.

"You say it was in the late afternoon?" I asked.

"Yes, and he even mentioned you."

"Me?" My sense of accomplishment at facing down Miss Robinson faded.

"Yes. The whole thing was just weird. Manning kept saying something about how both of us were trying to be more than we were meant to be. He called us attention-seeking irritants. What did he mean by that? All I've ever tried to do is my job to the best of my ability. I don't get it."

Even though he didn't spell it out for me, I was getting a clear idea about what was going on. Upset, Miss Robinson called Morton Manning. He, in turn, got Dad fired on bogus charges. He had come through on his threat making an innocent man look guilty. Dad was now out of a job, and it was all my fault. I had shown the audacity of questioning the system and then winning. Getting my dad fired was about power, and Manning had just exercised his power on us.

"This is my fault. I never should've crossed Miss Robinson and then she wouldn't have gone running to Morton."

He looked over with sad eyes. "Don't say that. Although," he was silent for a moment, "do you think that could have been what happened? It seems incredibly petty."

"Yes," my mother said, "but the more I think about it, have you ever asked yourself why Miss Robinson has this weird friendship with the D.A.?"

It did seem to go further than her being a resource for the steno pool. What was their history? Did she know about his romantic liaisons and was using that knowledge to her advantage? With such a sudden retaliation, if these events were connected, it was an odd sort of loyalty.

"Is there any possibility you could have lost this report?" I asked, not believing it myself. Dad's garage looked like an ad for the Sears and Roebuck tool display the way he carefully lined up his drills and saws on the pegboard that graced the walls.

"No. I don't go home until my desk is completely clear. I always file before I leave. There was nothing on my desk after court."

"I know they're wrong, and you've been falsely accused. If it makes you feel any better, this is exactly how I felt when Miss Robinson demoted me."

"I don't know what we're going to do. It's not so easy for an old guy like me to land a new job. Even with your mother working, we need my salary."

I suddenly felt guilty they had paid for my secretarial school. Dad didn't say it, but that had to be the reason they were still scrimping on luxuries and unable to make it without two salaries.

"I suppose I could try for that job at the gas station. They've had a sign in the window for a while now, so they're desperate to hire someone. I'll have to withdraw my name from the City council race tomorrow. Nobody wants an unemployed city clerk or worse, a gas station guy for city council."

As Dad made plans on how to survive his sudden unemployment, I made a few of my own. I was not going to let Miss Robinson and Morton Manning win. I would find more jobs like the one I was doing for Linda Manning. I could also make a call to my mother's friend, Beatrix Crabtree. If anybody had the inside scoop on Morton, it was her.

"Dot?" Beatrix Crabtree looked up from her typewriter the next morning, her rhythmic tapping stopped. "Is your mother okay?"

"Yes, everything is fine, well, not really, but my mother is fine. I need to talk to you about my father."

A look of recognition came to her eyes, and she pulled her hands from the keys. "Oh, yes, I heard about that. What happened?"

"Your boss, Mr. Manning, says he lost evidence."

She pursed her lips together in confusion. "Mike lost evidence? That man files his paperwork better than me. I guess we can thank his military training for that. If I had to choose who would lose paperwork around here, it sure wouldn't be him. What was the paperwork exactly?"

"A police report on a case," I said. "Now Manning and the judge are saying someone who committed a crime could go free."

"Well, sadly, that does happen, you know. Mike wouldn't be the first one to make a clerical error that changed a judgment. That's the unpredictable side of the judicial process. We make mistakes sometimes. All of us do, even me."

"I don't think it had anything to do with him. I made Miss Robinson from the secretarial school look bad with her boss, and now she's angry with me, and you know how close she is with…"

She grinned. "You're telling me you think Mr. Manning isn't telling the truth? Aren't you?"

I was so relieved she understood even though I was stumbling around with my words. I didn't want to accuse Morton Manning in front of her outright. He was her boss, and she had to have some sort of loyalty to him. "Yes. I think he took that report from Dad's desk. Would you have any idea where he might hide it?"

Beatrix slipped off a pair of tortoiseshell glasses she kept on a gold chain around her neck. Her white blouse and skirt were a little old-fashioned, but they fit her well. She stood with a finger on her chin, her gaze upward.

"He has a few locations around his office he doesn't think I know about. It's where he keeps his receipts for all those long lunches he takes with Maureen Johnson. Poor girl, is she going to have the baby?"

"You know about that?"

"Honey, if it has to do with the great and majestic Morton Manning, I know all about it. I figured it out."

"I'm finding his affair with Maureen might be the world's worst kept secret. I'm sure his wife knew."

Beatrix chuckled to herself. "Oh, sure. This one, and all the women before her. Mr. Manning fancies himself quite the ladies' man. Lately, he's been coming in earlier than usual. I can't decide if he's actually working, or just up to something he can only do when the rest of us are not here. I'm just surprised this is the first pregnancy that has resulted from all of his extra-curricular activities."

"I spoke to Maureen, and she is having a hard time figuring out what to do."

Beatrix shook her head in disgust. "Let me guess. Lunchtime Romeo wants her to have an abortion? Well, I guess with his money and his connections, he could certainly find someone willing to do it."

I would be amazed if Dr. Henley had agreed to do the procedure, but maybe he gave them a name? Getting an abortion could be a dangerous thing, no matter how much money you might have. I worried for Maureen and what she might be subjecting herself to at the hands of an unregulated abortionist. "Yes, but I'm not sure that's what Maureen wants."

"Young women today haven't changed all that much from when I was your age. As far as I'm concerned, she should do what she wants, and if it means keeping the baby, so be it. 1962 isn't the dark ages. People aren't going to put an A on her forehead. Crossing Barb in this might be difficult, though. Now let's check out old Morty's hidey holes, shall we?"

It took Beatrix Crabtree mere seconds to find the missing police report stuffed behind some law books. She held it up and wiggled it through the air. "I think I'll go and put this on the judge's desk and tell him it was there in the file all along. Mr. Manning can't protest, because to do that he would have to implicate himself."

"You are wonderful." I hugged Beatrix.

She stiffened, apparently unaccustomed to being appreciated. "You don't have to get all sappy on me. I know my boss, that's all. This kind of thing is right up his alley. You know I love you like a daughter, Dot, and that is why I need to tell you to be careful. Mr. Manning can be vindictive and hold a grudge. The man has a class-a temper and feels like any action is justified if he's been wronged."

Her description of Morton unnerved me. You could say the same thing of a killer. I began to worry about my mother's old friend, Beatrix. "Won't he know you took it?"

"Probably, but trust me, I know where the bodies are buried. Mr. Manning wouldn't dare cross me."

"You're not going to believe this," Mom said when she called later that afternoon. "Your father just got off the phone, and they found the missing police report. Can you believe it? It turns out it was in the file all along. I knew he didn't misplace it!"

"I did too, which was why I visited Beatrix Crabtree, and we went on a treasure hunt in Morton Manning's office."

"You what?" There was a pause on the other end. "I thought you were at school."

"I didn't have to go today. Miss Robinson took a personal day after all the upheaval of being bested by a lowly student."

She didn't speak right away, making me flashback to high school, waiting for me to tell her what she needed to know. "It was hidden in Morton Manning's office. He purposely made Dad look bad to get him fired."

"That awful man..."

"Not to worry, the only way he can report us searching his office is to admit his wrongdoing. Has Dad pulled out of the campaign yet?"

"No, and now, thanks to you, he doesn't have to. If anything, it gives him more motivation to run, if only to get rid of bottom dwellers like our D.A. I can't believe Manning would stoop so low."

"Well, he did."

"Hold on a moment." Mom put the phone down and told my dad the story of searching Morton Manning's office.

"I'm going over there." I could hear him in the background. "I'm going to confront him at his office."

Mom got back on the phone. "He wants to confront Mr. Manning. Do you think that's wise?"

I glanced at my lady's Timex. "He might be still at home for another half hour, not that I think confronting him is a good idea. Beatrix told me he could be very unforgiving. Maybe it would be a better idea to lay low, right now."

I could hear my father still ranting behind her. "Getting a man fired because of a petty grievance..."

He was now full-on mumbling to himself and working his anger into a fever pitch. I had to de-escalate this before he did something foolish like punch our town's district attorney in the nose. Wouldn't Ben Dalton at the

Camden Courier love to put that one in the paper? "Mom, put Dad on the phone."

The sound of the receiver being jostled filled my ear.

"Hello, Dot," Dad said, sounding like he was half out the door.

"Please don't go over there. Manning has been stopped."

"This is between him and me, and I intend to end it once and for all."

I grabbed my purse. "Then, I'll meet you there. You'll need a witness when Manning starts lying."

When I got there, Dad was out of his car, pacing back and forth across the lawn.

"Dad, let's not do this. Get back in the car," I begged.

"I know. I must be crazy, but what Manning did to me is inexcusable."

"Dad," I repeated, hoping to get him to turn around.

He stopped pacing and then marched up to the door. I scrambled behind him, hoping I wasn't going to have to break up a fight. Instead of using the doorbell, he knocked on Morton Manning's door like the police about to raid a speakeasy. "Manning. I know you're in there. Come out and face me like a man." When Manning opened it, I could tell my father had to stop himself from pounding him in the face.

"Morgan. What is wrong with you?" Manning said in disgust as he looked out into the street.

"You tried to get me fired. You've done nothing but try to stop me, but I never thought you would do something like this."

Manning's thick eyebrows fused together. "I have no idea what you're talking about, but you can bet Barb has already called the police."

I glanced behind Manning's shoulder where Barb stood a little too calmly, observing my husband's behavior. From the slight curl of the corner of her lips, she looked to be enjoying the whole scene.

The sound of wheels came crunching up the driveway, but it wasn't the police. I was right. Ben Dalton was hot on the story. He jumped out with a small pad of paper and a pen in his hand.

"Ben, what are you doing here?" He wore a white short-sleeve shirt and a loosened pencil-thin tie, smiled wide enough to show his first molar angled slightly to the left.

"Got a call with a whopper of a tip, Morton. A big altercation between the district attorney and a city council candidate. Luckily, my office is only five minutes away. Do you have any comment?"

Morton's lips thinned. "No. Of course not. There is no altercation. Someone's been yanking your chain, Ben."

I wanted to know who that someone was. We had only decided to come over ten minutes ago, and the only person who had been near a phone was Barb. Did she call the press, then the police? Would it be to show the harassment Morton was receiving from Mike, or could it be revenge for a cheating husband? She had to have a little hatred stored up for her husband as well, seeing as he just impregnated his mistress. Maybe she hoped my father would punch him, so she didn't have to.

Not getting anywhere with Morton, Ben turned his attention to my father. "Mr. Morgan? What is your grievance with the D.A.? Are you on to something the voting public needs to know about? Here's your chance to show your voters your plans to root out corruption over in our city government."

"I beg your pardon?" Morton asked, looking insulted.

"You know what I mean," Ben said out of the side of his mouth. "This is a reporting technique I call priming the interviewer. Nothing personal, Mort."

All eyes were on my father as he gazed from Manning to Ben and finally to me. "No comment." Dad grabbed my hand and started for the cars. Relief flooded through me. I turned back, and Morton was staring at us as we made a hasty exit. I wasn't sure, but was that a look of gratitude?

Chapter Seventeen

"Manning is unbelievable," Dad said after we returned home. He had returned to the pacing, but this time, it was in the front room. "He orchestrated all of this. He thinks because of something that happened at your school, getting me fired is collateral damage? It's like I never left the army sometimes." I let my father's words sink in. I still felt it was my fault, and today, I was learning a valuable life lesson. This was why people didn't mess with individuals like Manning or Miss Robinson. With the power they possessed, the consequences of crossing them were enormous.

"I'm sorry. I know I should have just gone along with what Mr. Hudson decided."

Dad raised his hands in the air. "No! You did the right thing and exactly what I would've expected of you. I didn't raise you to back down when you've been cheated out of something. Please don't think I'm blaming you."

His words lifted some of the guilt I was feeling. "Well, there is one good side to all this. You don't have to give up your campaign."

He stopped pacing and let out a sigh. "I suppose you're right. I should be a shoo-in now that I'm running unopposed. That is if Manning doesn't try to find someone to run against me. I'm sure he would delight in finding another way to bring us down."

I hadn't thought of that, but I could see how he would feel like it would be the best way to get back at us. It started at the death of his brother, a man who messed up people's lives, and even after he was gone, it was still happening.

Mom stepped into the doorway, drying her hands on a towel. "I don't think he will," she said. "Come on. I have fresh-baked cookies in the kitchen."

My mother. Other people called the doctor, saved money, or committed the problem to prayer in a crisis. She made cookies.

I took his hand, leading him to the kitchen. "We can have milk and cookies and plan our next step in your campaign."

Once we were happily sinking our teeth into mouth-watering chocolate chip cookies, we listed on a piece of paper other functions he could appear at and what kind of promotional materials we would need.

"Some of this could get expensive. Besides, I don't think we need to overspend here. I don't even have an opponent to run against anymore," my father said.

"You're right, but we at least need a good sign. Maybe we could put it in our yard? Name recognition is very big, I hear."

"Dot. I'm the only one on the ballot. It doesn't matter if they see my name on a sign."

"Okay, but what about re-election? Have you thought of that?"

"Honey, the only thing I want you to concentrate on right now is finishing school. Your mother and I can take care of this."

What they didn't know was that I planned to pay them back every penny they spent for the school. Maybe I would even make as much money in my new job as my dad did in his. Probably wishful thinking on my part. Everyone knew men made more money than women. As to why a job was worth more in the hands of a man than a woman was beyond me.

My father placed a hand on my cheek. "You're amazing. Do you know that? How did I get lucky enough to have a daughter who is just stubborn enough to be a pain in everyone's side but mine?"

"I always called it bullheaded," Mom said.

"That too." He smiled. Now, completely recovered from his encounter with Manning, we were planning for the future and riding the high of sugar and freshly baked chocolate, everything seemed bright. We were putting this whole Manning thing behind us. I started to feel like I didn't need to know how Anson died, either by a freak accident or homicide. That's what the police were there for. Officer Sprague was on his own.

Dad was busy recording all our plans, and I was wallowing in a moment of joy. Then, a cloud started to drift onto the horizon, and the fringed umbrella I had seen in the photos of Anson Manning's death crept into my memory. How did it get bent like that? Could it have been used as a lever of some type to move the bookcase? As I looked off into the distance, my new resolve was already fading. As hard as I tried, I couldn't get Morton Manning and all the warnings I had been given about him out of my mind.

"Now, you be careful. Mr. Manning can be vindictive and hold a grudge. The man has a class-a temper and feels like any action is justified if he's been wronged."

"You don't know him. He has a way of making things happen."

War injury or not, Morton Manning was sitting at the top of my suspect list.

The next morning, I was feeling like I was finally getting back on track. I put my hair up in a bun and put on a crisp white blouse and grey skirt that hit right above my knees. It seemed like the skirts were getting a little shorter every year. Ellie, still glum trudged off to work with barely a word. Al still hadn't talked to her about what happened. I guessed if they waited five years to come to this decision, it might take a while for them to sort it out. When I headed down to the kitchen, I was stopped in the front room by Arlene.

"Dot, I'm glad you're here." Arlene's bottom lip quivered.

"What's the matter? Are you feeling okay?"

"It's not me. It's Clara. She's in the kitchen. I haven't been able to get her to settle down. It seems no one wants her to sing anymore. She was supposed to sing for the opening of the rodeo next week, and Bubba Simpson called and canceled. He was talking about getting the 4-H kids to do a skit. Little Clara is leagues above anything those farm kids could do when it comes to talent. Even the church choir put someone else on her solo. It's like she's been," she lowered her voice for dramatic effect, "blacklisted."

"Come on. You can't be serious. Why do you think that? Surely, this is just a run of bad luck. She's been singing at a lot of events around town. Maybe they want to give someone else a turn?"

Arlene harrumphed. "Bad luck, my foot. She's been blacklisted, and I know who's behind it all."

"Who?"

"It's that awful Barb Manning. Pay-back," she said, emphasizing each syllable. "The worst part is, I'm afraid Clara's sudden fall from grace is all my fault. I never should've told Anson Manning off at the Founder's Day banquet. My mother always said I didn't know how to hold my tongue. It's just when someone insults a member of my family, something happens inside of me, and I lose my head. I never had children of my own, and I love that little girl so much. I hate to see her like this."

Arlene's comments at the banquet hadn't been that bad in my judgment. She was making sure Barb called Clara by the right name. Then when Anson started making fun of her, she had to stand up for her. "You know, I probably would've done the same thing. After all, Clara is just a kid, and Anson Manning was an adult who should've known better. Heckling her was way out of line."

Arlene relaxed. "You would have?"

"Sure, I would," I said. "And don't forget you weren't the only one. My father got into a fight with Anson for leering at me."

"He did, didn't he?" A sigh escaped her lips. "Mike always was a good judge of character."

"I like to think so. Would you like for me to talk to Clara?"

"Would you? Maybe she'll listen to someone younger."

Arlene's bright and sunny kitchen was clean enough to be a two-page spread in the Ladies Home Journal. In the oven, there were cookies baking, and if my nose was correct, they were peanut butter. At the kitchen table, Clara, her brown hair pulled into pigtails was sobbing into a delicate handkerchief with pink roses embroidered on the corners. I had seen some of Arlene's handiwork and surmised she had made it for her. I pulled a chair out and sat down at the table. "Clara, your aunt told me about what's happened."

Clara's response was a blow into the hanky resembling the sound of a tuba.

"I'll never get to sing again. I'm a has-been at 16," she wailed.

I put my arm around her shoulders, intending to comfort her, but instead of calming her down, it brought on another rush of tears. I gave Arlene a desperate glance besieging her guidance, but she shrugged. She was out of ideas to help me ward off the tears of an adolescent. I continued my attempts, "Did you know when you sing, it's the purest sound I've ever heard? Your voice is so clear, almost like an instrument."

Her blue eyes brightened, and she took a breath. "It is?"

"Your voice is an instrument," Arlene repeated.

"You have a gift, Clara. You will be singing all through high school and in college. Any music department would be lucky to get you."

"Oh, I'm not going to college," Clara said matter of factly.

"Why not?" I asked. "With your voice, you might get a scholarship."

"My parents say girls don't go to college, but maybe I can marry a music teacher. He'll find me lots of opportunities to sing like Aunt Arlene does now."

The last thing I wanted to do was go against Clara's parents, but to not even consider college with a voice like hers was being unfair and frankly, old-fashioned. I patted her hand.

"What if you become the music teacher? You could find your own places to perform," I suggested.

"Me?" The proverbial lightbulb seemed to ignite over her head. "Really? I could do that?" Had she not even considered this possibility?

"Most certainly," Arlene gushed. "And I'll help you. Don't sell yourself short, my dear. Look at Dot, here. She's going to work to become a secretary, and maybe someday she'll run her own company."

I didn't know if I'd ever go that far, but Arlene's confidence in me was a boost to my spirit after my battles with Miss Robinson.

Clara blew into the hanky again. "Aren't the classes hard?"

"Pshaw," Arlene said, throwing her hands out. "You're a straight-A student. I think you could handle whatever they threw at you. Besides that, don't forget, you have talent."

And with the thought of a future that didn't include finding a music teacher to marry, but becoming one herself, the storm of tears subsided. The brightness of youth returned to her eyes. My neighbor Arlene, part-time manager, part-time guidance counselor, took over.

When she walked me to the door, she squeezed my arm. "I can't thank you enough. Sometimes it takes a young person to see things in a modern way. We all should have thought of this. Our little Clara is going to be a music teacher, or who knows? Maybe she'll become a professional singer? I can't wait to call my sister. She may not agree at first, but I think she'll want to see her daughter happy and successful."

"Clara will have to work hard, and there's the matter of tuition," I said.

"I know. An hour ago we felt like the situation was out of control, and people like Barb Manning held all the cards. Now, with your fresh perspective, we've got it back. Thanks for that."

Chapter Eighteen

I still had Clara on my mind when I strolled down the empty hallway at The Hudson Secretarial School, the sounds of my heels echoing against the walls. I was a little early and decided to sit down on a bench outside of the classroom to review my notes. I didn't want to give Miss Robinson any reason to find fault. Why was it ever since the Manning family had come into our lives there had been nothing but trouble? They barreled into a situation and then left victim after victim in their paths like Linda, Maureen, and now, little Clara.

There was a low rumbling from the next room. I leaned toward the door, trying to hear the conversation, and I was almost sure it was Morton Manning's voice, but the words were hard to make out.

Then I picked up on the staccato tones of Miss Robinson as her words snapped by me. "You can't let this get out of control, Morty."

Morty? The use of such an endearment caused me to confirm what I had been feeling all along about their friendship. Someone in her position should be calling him Morton. Morty was personal, intimate even. Had Miss Robinson been one of the former girlfriends Beatrix Crabtree mentioned? Could she still be seeing him? I tried to shut that mental picture out of my mind. He began to talk again, and then Miss Robinson responded as if soothing a small child, her words growing softer and harder to hear.

"Hey, you're back," a voice said from behind me. My heart jolted in my chest, surprised by the sudden appearance of one of my classmates. She styled her hair short in a pixie cut, and I could tell she had been struggling in class. I had been so focused on the conversation in the next room, that I hadn't heard her behind me.

"Miss Robinson said you were being demoted. I don't know what you did, but I've never heard of that happening before. You know, I don't always get stuff the first time and have to study real hard. I was sure they would make me repeat, but here I am with just a few days to go to graduate." She wasn't the only one who was amazed she was still with us. She had trouble with spelling and had to do her work with a giant black dictionary in the corner of her desk. She was doing okay with shorthand, but when she had to transcribe it into real words, it was a problem for her. I felt terrible for her some days, but I also admired her persistence.

"Yes, they changed their minds." As happy as I had been with the result of my complaint, I didn't want to elaborate on the details. Ironically, I felt it would be unprofessional, especially seeing as Mr. Hudson now knew the rest of the class cheated on the test.

"Wow, how did you do that?" She snapped her gum, making the echo ping off the walls.

"I'm not sure myself," I answered, hoping she wouldn't probe any further.

"Ladies, you may come in," Miss Robinson said from the door. Manning was no longer in the room, and it was my guess he escaped from the door at the other end of the classroom.

There was no missing the light red flush on Miss Robinson's cheeks. "Was that Mr. Manning I heard in here talking to you?" I asked in a light and I hoped a non-threatening tone.

She straightened her spine, and then she plopped a textbook on her metal teacher's desk at the front of the room. "Were you eavesdropping?"

"No, of course not. I just thought I recognized the sound of his voice coming through the door. He does have such a big voice." I slid into my desk which, if you know anything about defensive combat, was a mistake. She stood in front of the desk, towering over me.

"Why do you persist in snooping when it comes to Mr. Manning? What has he ever done to you?"

I started listing off things in my mind but seeing as I had just fought to return to this class, I kept my mouth shut.

Miss Robinson lowered her face to mine, her tone turning nasty. "Listen up, Little Missy." She softened her voice to keep it out of earshot of the other students. "You need to back off or get ready to pay the price. Do you understand, or do I need to spell it out for you?"

I understood what she was saying perfectly. She was more than absurdly loyal. She was in love with Morton Manning and would do anything to protect him, possibly even murder.

"Would that price you're referring to be getting my father fired because of a police report your Morty hid in his office?" Her eyes hardened. As she began to speak more students entered the classroom, making our confrontation easily heard. Could it be I knew information Miss Robinson hadn't counted on? She had a secret and hated it. I was the one she had to trust to keep it. Miss Robinson would have to be the one to back off or pay the price.

Chapter Nineteen

When Linda called the next morning, I was about to go out the door for class. With only weeks left, and after mouthing off to Miss Robinson yesterday, I didn't want to give the woman any reason to kick me out.

"I have all my forms ready. I took your advice and had them checked over," Linda said.

"By your brother-in-law?" I asked. She may not have liked him, but he was convenient. He might have also muscled his way back into dealing with Anson's final affairs.

"Are you kidding?" She laughed. "I'm not letting Morton near this stuff. I have my own lawyer now. I can't tell you how much comfort it is to have someone helping me look out for my interests. You showed me there is a world outside of the Mannings."

"Good deal. So why do you need me then? It sounds like your problem is solved."

"Moral support?" she answered. "Every time I go to the courthouse, I'm terrified I'll run into Morton. With you there, it provides a buffer."

A buffer where I'm getting all the bruises, I thought. Five minutes ago, I was thinking to lay low and try to finish my coursework. Showing up with Morton Manning's sister-in-law who chose to edge him out of his brother's affairs was not laying low. "I don't know. I have a class this morning."

"What about lunchtime? Surely they give you a lunch break at that school?" She asked.

I did have about an hour and a half between morning and afternoon sessions. If we were brief, I could do it. My father was back at his job so I would need to avoid him, especially after we discussed putting the Manning situation behind us.

"Please? You have to understand, the only people I've had to rely on are the Mannings. Some days it was like living in a snake pit. Please?" she asked. I couldn't stand it and gave in to her request.

"Okay, I'll meet you at the courthouse at noon. We'll march the papers into the probate office, drop them off..."

"And then I buy your lunch," Linda interrupted.

"Fine." I was willing to take any form of payment at this point.

Like so many days in early summer, a wet, sticky heat permeated the air causing straight hair to flatten and curly hair to frizz. Just as it felt like we were breathing cotton, a surprise thunderstorm announced itself.

We ran up the steps to the courthouse through the pouring rain and walked into the lobby, hoping to be unnoticed. That wasn't going to happen. Not only was Morton there, but the entire Camden Ladies' Club was holding a luncheon for the courthouse employees. Tables lined the cavernous space where lawyers, clerks, and judges were enjoying plates of sandwiches and sparkling lemonade. Yellow tablecloths festooned with tall green floral arrangements complimented the many dishes making this yet another Camden Ladies' Club success. In one corner was a picture of Constance Benedict with a fishbowl placed on the table in front of it. It was almost full of cash as the happy lunch guests deposited a goodwill offering for her hospital care. I grabbed a dollar from my purse.

"I need to put some money in for my newspaper boy's mother," I said.

"Oh, that was the woman who was hit by a car. I'll put some in, too. I still can't believe they haven't caught the guy yet," Linda said. In the back of my mind, I had only one person in mind who would be driving drunk at that time of day and in a green car. Anson Manning, her recently deceased husband. Was she worried about the same thing? If it were him, we would never know it now he was dead. If he drove drunk often, he might have quite a few dings on his car so that a new one wouldn't stick out.

After contributing her dollar to the fishbowl, Linda looked at the elegant spread and said, "I'm starved. Do you mind if we eat here?"

"I guess we could," I answered over the din of pleasant chatter. The offerings here looked better than we would have picked up at the new burger restaurant. I started feeling my stomach starting to grumble.

Linda grabbed a plate and took her place in the buffet line while Dad made his way toward me.

"What a lovely surprise," my father said, kissing me on the cheek. As he drew closer, he whispered in a little less fatherly tone. "What are you doing here?"

"Well, it's almost as if you aren't glad to see me," I whispered back.

"With everything that's happened, I'm a little on edge. I'm trying to go back to the quiet life I was leading before Anson Manning was killed."

"Then maybe this isn't the right time to tell you I came here with Linda Manning?" I said.

"With Linda Manning?" He asked. "I thought we decided…"

"I know what we decided, but she begged me. I'm the only friend she has, evidently. I couldn't say no."

He rubbed the scruff of his chin. "You are too nice, sometimes. Listen, I've got to get back to work." As he left, Ben Dalton wandered over.

"Boy. News of free food travels fast."

"You're not here on some deep dark story?" I asked.

"I wish I was. No, the only scoop I'm following today is Columbo's serving spoon. How is your cousin doing?"

"Uh, not good. She hasn't said much to me since that morning. I think she's embarrassed."

As Ben drew nearer, there was a light air of aftershave about him. "She shouldn't be. Five years is a long time to wait, and she deserved an answer."

"You don't think she was being too forward?"

"Sometimes, when the man doesn't, the woman has to make the first move."

"It sounds like you speak from experience?"

Ben grinned. "Who me? No. When I'm interested, you'll know it."

I blushed. Was he referring to me in particular?

Mary Oliva walked up, balancing a plate. "If it isn't my favorite junior detective. What a spread, huh? We got an invite over at the police station. Good ol' Officer Jerry didn't like it, but I stepped out for lunch for a change."

There were meatball sandwiches, pastrami sandwiches, and even a chicken Caprese combination on bread. "From all the Italian sandwiches, they must have had it catered from Columbo's," I said. "I'll bet Charlie's a happy man right now."

"Right up until he finds out what lousy tippers the Mannings are," Mary uttered under her breath.

I made a quick introduction. "Mary works for the police department."

"You're a policewoman?" Ben asked.

"Sort of. I mostly handle the paperwork," Mary answered. "I was helping Dot check on some information."

"That was nice of you," he said. "What kind of information?" He turned to me. "You were at the police station recently? Did you get arrested for something I don't know about?"

Mary's gaze darted from Ben to me, and I nodded, signaling it was okay to tell him.

She popped an olive into her mouth and then said, "On the Anson Manning death investigation."

Ben's right eyebrow rose, "And I thought it was a slow news day."

"It still is. I didn't find out anything important." I assured him.

"And if you did, you would tell me, right? I mean, freedom of the press and all that."

"Sure."

"Ben! You're here. Come take a picture of this wonderful food so you can put it in the Camden Courier." Barb Manning had spotted a photo opportunity and wasn't letting it go to waste.

Ben turned back, "Duty calls." His eyes warmed to mine. "Keep me in the loop, junior detective."

As Ben made his exit, Mary moved closer. "You have yourself a handsome guy."

"First of all, he's not my guy. Second, he's a reporter and a nosy one. If he

CHAPTER NINETEEN

thinks there's a story he is all over it."

"Hmmm. He's all over something," Mary said, a gleam in her eye.

My gaze drifted to the elaborate lunch, and the delicate yellow rose arrangement in the middle of the buffet. I wondered who the sap was stuck making that one? Jane, Barb Manning's number one lackey, stood next to a table holding the small of her back. Her pregnancy seemed to have advanced since the last time I had seen her, and the baby had grown significantly more substantial. She didn't look comfortable, and I noticed she was putting weight on one foot and then the other. I could only assume her feet hurt as well. From the slight swelling in her ankles, she shouldn't be trying to stand for so long. For a moment, I felt guilty thinking maybe she was the flower-arranging sap I had referred to earlier. As much as she hung on Barb's every word, she had to be willing to be her second in command. "Stay right here," I said to Mary. "There's something I have to do."

I picked up a chair and walked over to Jane. "Here, you should be sitting down."

She smiled and began lowering her bulk into the chair. "Thanks, Dot. You're a lifesaver. The doctor says I'm on my feet too much, but trying to help out Barb is a full-time job."

"You do so much for the ladies' club. Sometimes, you need to think about yourself."

Jane's eyes softened. "You're very sweet. Thank you."

I returned to Mary, who gave me a look of admiration. "That was a nice thing to do, Gidget."

"My name's not Gidget."

"You say that, but you look just like the girl in the beach movies. Like you're going to break out in song any minute."

I shot her a glance. She was saying I was the sappy Sandra Dee. "You can be assured that I'll leave all the singing up to our local talent. I'm here today to help someone with their probate filing. That's all."

"This is nice. The ladies' club sure puts on a good lunch," Mary said as she took a bite of her sandwich.

"Yes, I just quit the group."

161

"Why?" She looked at me as if I were addle-brained. "I thought they were the group women around here aspired to belong to. If you're in the ladies' club, you're in everywhere else."

"Let's just say I didn't fit in. I'm busy with school, and they spend a lot of time working on these events."

Mary looked around. "It shows. This lunch is nicer than the last wedding I went to. I do admire you for sticking to your studies. You probably made the right decision. Besides you are going to be working for them, not with them. Right?"

Linda came back with a plate piled high with a sandwich on thick slices of French bread and potato chips. "This is great. You better go get a plate before it's all gone."

"Are you sure it's okay?" I asked. "You don't work here, and neither do I."

"I'm Morton Manning's sister-in-law. I have an in, at least for a little while longer. You are the daughter of a courthouse employee. Relax. We belong here," Linda assured me.

Before I could get into the line, the lobby door opened, and a gust of rain blew around the tablecloths. The hot sticky day had broken into a rainstorm. I peered out at the clouds. Had they been that dark earlier? Maureen Johnson came into the gathering and headed straight for us even though I was standing with the wife of the man she had recently thrown herself at the Founder's Day Banquet. She was out of breath when she joined us.

"Maureen, this is a surprise," I said. Maureen clenched her fists by her sides. "I'm here to see Morton. Miss Robinson just called me to tell me they had set up an appointment with," she leaned closer, "an abortionist. She wasn't asking me to go. She was telling me. The nerve of that woman."

Both Mary and Linda gasped at the same time. I hoped the rest of the room didn't catch on to the conversation. "You're pregnant?" Linda asked. "You were only with my husband for one night. How can you know already?"

"That's easy. This isn't your husband's baby. Besides that, he was too drunk to make anything happen, let alone create a baby," Maureen said, her eyes scanning the room for her intended victim.

162

"So, you didn't have any reason to kill Anson?" Mary asked.

"No, she didn't," I answered quickly. Of course, I couldn't be entirely sure, and I was basing my vote for her innocence on our time together in the last few days.

"And how would you know this information?" Mary asked.

"I'm your junior detective, remember?" I reminded her.

"There he is…" Maureen made a beeline for Morton Manning, who was standing at the back chatting and laughing loudly with a group of men who looked like lawyers. He turned around, a look of surprise on his face. The laughter stopped immediately.

"Morton, can I have a word with you?" Even with the noise in the room, I could still hear Maureen's shrill voice. I was thankful for that because it would have looked awkward if I tried to move any closer. I noticed Mary and Linda were also listening to every syllable. It was a showdown at the courthouse, and none of us were going to miss it.

"I'm confused," Linda whispered. "Why would Maureen want to talk to Morton? Does he know who the father is?"

Mary moved closer to Linda and said in a hushed voice, "Maybe she knows who killed his brother."

"Mrs. Johnson," Morton said, his hand on his lapel. "How lovely to see you."

Observing the scene, I noticed Barb, who had been chatting with the mayor's wife, stopped to listen. Her lips formed into a thin line, but she made no movement toward her husband. Probably more than anyone else in the room, she knew exactly what was happening, and she was doing nothing to stop it.

Morton took Maureen by the elbow and attempted to usher her out of the lobby avoiding a scene, but Maureen pulled away and shouted, "I won't do it. You can't make me do it. I'm keeping it!"

The low chatter drew to a hush as the scene unfolded before the courthouse crowd. Maureen, suddenly aware of the crowd's interest in her, turned and pulled away from his grasp. Even though the onlookers only had a few details, Morton Manning's little secret had just blown wide open. He put on an act of looking shocked and laughed nervously.

"I'm sorry this is all very confusing. What was it you needed to speak to me about? I'm sure we've settled everything having to do with your last divorce. Number four, wasn't it?" he asked innocently.

"Don't even try it. You should know Dot over there knows all about us. She even knows who killed your brother."

Like a volley at a tennis match, the crowd's attention shifted to me, and if there ever was a moment when I wanted to melt into the wallpaper, this was one of them.

"Maureen, maybe this isn't the best time," I said, trying to calm her down. Making Morton this angry couldn't be good for her or her baby. All eyes were still on me. "And for the record, I don't know who killed Anson Manning. It was probably just an accident."

No one moved, and the eyes of the crowd were still on me. They were waiting for an answer. If I knew who killed Anson Manning, they wanted to know.

"I have no idea who killed Anson. Let's all settle down and enjoy this wonderful lunch the ladies' club has prepared for us. Can I get a round of applause for Barb Manning and her crew?"

Once I mentioned Barb's name, the stunned crowd obediently started clapping, and while they did, I grabbed Maureen and got her out the door. In another second, Linda came out.

"Are you alright?" Linda asked as we helped Maureen to her car.

"I won't go. Morton can't make me," she shouted into the rain.

"No, they can't," I assured her. "We won't let them. If you want to keep this baby, then you will."

"And damn the Mannings and their interference," Linda shouted, raising her fist to the heavens.

Chapter Twenty

"Well, that was interesting," Linda said as we ran through the rain to the courthouse lobby to get our things after walking Maureen to her car. I had offered to go home with her, but she wanted to be alone. "I had no idea that was going on. I never thought Morton would cheat on Barb. Did you know about this? From the sounds of it, you know a lot of things."

"Maybe." I didn't want to make it any worse for Maureen when the rest of the town put it together, that not only had they been having an affair, but a baby was on the way. "I'll take that hamburger now," I said, hoping to take the focus off me. "The sooner we leave here, the better." How long would it be until Officer Sprague came calling to ask me my theories on Anson Manning's grisly death?

Mary Oliva was throwing her napkin in the trash when we retrieved our belongings. Her focus was on Morton. "You know, once you got out the door, it was bizarre. Even with everyone at the luncheon watching him, Morton was acting as if his big fight with Maureen never happened. Barb too. She was back being hostess of the year, chatting it up with her lunch guests. Those two are like creepy windup dolls. They never stop smiling." Her head pitched up slightly. "You had better watch out. I think D. A. Manning seems to be coming for you next." Trying to look too busy to chat with Morton, I grabbed a plate and began piling food onto it.

Taking my cue, Linda went back to the dish she had put down before she ran out the door with me. Even though I looked like a starving woman at a buffet, he headed straight for me. What did Morton want to discuss? Was he going to continue to blame my father for his brother's death even though the police had cleared him? Did he have a new idea on how to get revenge for Miss Robinson's humiliation? I had three sandwiches piled on my plate when he began to talk.

"Miss Morgan, how lovely to see you. I'm afraid I must apologize for my little scene with Mrs. Johnson. You know redheads and their fiery tempers."

As he towered over me, a faint scent of minty aftershave reached my nose. Even though he had just been through the equivalent of a public brawl, his tie was straight, his shirt crisply pressed, and his appearance was impeccable. He looked so good that it was downright deceiving.

"I wouldn't know. Regardless of the color of her hair, Mrs. Johnson did seem very angry with you. I'm not Ben Dalton, but I would have to think there's a story there somewhere."

"Come, come now. It has not escaped my notice Maureen has confided in you, and now she tells me you have a person in mind who might be responsible for Anson's untimely death?"

His left eye twitched. It was killing him to say the word murder. "You're right. I do have a few ideas on the subject." I glanced around the room to see if anyone was listening. "I just didn't want everyone to know."

Morton let out a short gasp. "Was it Maureen? Did her temper finally get the best of her? With the way she was all over my brother at the Founder's Day Banquet, and then he spurned her at the debate, maybe she was mad enough to murder him." He clucked his tongue as if we were two wives talking over the fence. "I hate to say it, but it seems obvious to me she did it."

"As you say, redheads have been known to be dramatic, but I'm sure our capable police department is exploring all possibilities. Anson made many people angry in our community. That is if it wasn't just an act of an angry God settling some celestial scores."

A smile crept across Morton's face like Bella Lugosi opening the door to a beautiful maiden at Dracula's castle. "You are very bright, aren't you? Miss Robinson said you're too smart for your own good, and I'm beginning to believe her."

"Thank you. I guess." I wasn't sure if he had insulted me or complimented me. Morton Manning was one of the shrewdest men in town, and I tried to fight off my feelings of inferiority.

"You are welcome. You're the kind of daughter an up-and-coming city councilman needs to have." His words were confusing me. Was he saying something nice...about me?

Linda now stood across the room, avoiding Morton. I began to pray for her return, but she stood by the drinks table watching and waiting. She didn't want to encounter Morton any more than I did. I was on my own.

"I really should check on Linda."

His stubby fingers came down on my arm, a seemingly innocent gesture, yet from the tightness of his grip, I felt as if he had just put me in a wrestling hold.

"Before you go, I wanted to let you know I have an extraordinary surprise for you and your father. Barb and I discussed it, and we'd like to throw our favorite candidate a little barbecue on Friday." I looked at him curiously half expecting a punch line to come out of his mouth next. We were now his favorite candidate, as opposed to murdering scum who killed his brother? There was something very fishy about his newfound support of my father. Why would they want to throw a party for us? Were we the guests of honor or perhaps the main course?

"That's really not necessary, and frankly, I have no idea why you would offer to do such a thing," I said. Morton was the definition of running hot and cold. One minute he's getting me demoted at secretarial school and the next is offering to throw a party for my dad's campaign.

"I know it seems strange, what with our history, but to be perfectly honest, we had already booked the caterer for Anson's campaign, and the S.O.B. won't give us a refund." He laughed at that, the base of his voice booming against the walls. "Barb and I discussed it. That's an awful lot of brisket along with miles of white and blue bunting going to waste. We want to extend our hospitality to your campaign, and if you don't mind, we would also like to use the occasion to honor Anson. It only seems right, don't you agree?"

I searched the room for my father, hoping he had come back for a second helping of sandwiches. Would he want me to tell Morton yes? I could tell he wasn't going to leave without a decision. Was this really about not losing money on a catering bill? I doubted it. From what I'd seen so far, no one in this town angered the Mannings and stayed in business long.

"That is very kind of you, but..."

"It's settled then. Barb will call you and give you the details." He rubbed his hands together. "This is going to be fun."

As Morton walked away from me, he immediately started glad-handing another diner. Had I said yes? I felt myself being drawn into a trap and didn't know how to stop it.

When I returned to class that afternoon, I couldn't stop thinking about my conversation with Morton. It took everything in me to stay focused and out of the watchful eye of Miss Robinson.

I had to tell my parents about the barbecue. We were now the guests of honor of the town's most manipulative couple, and I wasn't sure how my dad would take it. I practiced a couple of speeches in my mind, but it always turned out the same. A couple who had done his reputation so much damage was now inviting us into their home. I felt like Dorothy heading into the witch's forest standing in front of a rickety wooden sign. Beware. Turn. Back. Now.

I went by the library where I found my mother helping a man use the leather-bound set of encyclopedias. Once she was free, I told her about Morton's invitation.

"Are you serious? He wants to have a party for us?"

"That's what he said. I don't know how I'm going to tell Dad. When I ran into him at the luncheon, he didn't want to do anything that would make other people think he wasn't doing his job."

"The chance of losing that job scared him to death. We're not that far from retirement, and if we lost our government pension, it would be disastrous. Ironically, we had planned to cook out on the grill tonight. Why don't you come by and we'll tell him together."

When I arrived a couple of hours later intending to help my mother with the preparations, she pointed to a bag of charcoal and told me to start the grill. I had never actually made a fire using charcoal, but I'd seen her do it, and it didn't look that difficult. After opening the bag, I threw the dusty cubes in and then threw a match at it. The match hit the black chunks, and to my delight, there was a tiny fire, and then it dwindled. I attempted it a couple more times, but the match couldn't last long enough to start the fire. Why did it look so easy when someone else did it?

My mother was working in the kitchen, and I hated to bother her, but I knew I needed help if we were going to have enough time for the charcoals to white.

At first, she laughed, not at all what you want to hear when seeking help, but then she gave me her best reference librarian answer. "You need to stack the charcoal in a pyramid shape. You have to make it ideal for the flame to catch."

"Seriously, a pyramid? Is this an Egyptian thing? It won't catch with the briquettes lining the bottom?"

"No, dear, you have to have all of the elements side-by-side and perfectly aligned. By putting them in formation, your chances are greater one of those little charcoals will catch a spark and be close enough to another one to double the heat. You have to trick them into lighting."

My mother had an excellent way of describing things. A few minutes later, as I watched my charcoal now stacked to rival the pharaoh's tomb catch a spark and then ignite, I couldn't help but compare it to catching a killer. Things had to be lined up just right for the spark to catch. The killer had to feel the heat spreading from one problem to the next. I only worried I would set myself on fire in the process.

"What do I smell?" Dad said when he came to the door. "Steak? On a weeknight? My, my Mrs. Rockefeller, you spoil me. What's the occasion?"

"I just wanted to celebrate you getting your job back," she said. "And we have Dot here to help us commemorate the occasion."

"That's wonderful. What a treat." He kissed my cheek. I felt guilty for partly telling the truth but telling him we were buttering him up to announce we were about to endure another social occasion driven by the Mannings wasn't going to be easy. He looked so happy. Maybe breaking the news to him would not be that bad?

"Are you sure that's all this is?" He questioned as his glance pivoted from me to Mom. "You two look...too happy."

"That's all," I answered quickly.

"...I'm on to you when you're holding something back." He put a finger under my chin, lifting it. "What is the real purpose of this extravagant dinner?"

"Well...I did have a little something to discuss with you."

"I thought so."

I drew in a breath and smiled like a door-to-door salesman with a new case of samples. "Morton and Barb Manning are throwing a barbecue for your campaign Friday night."

"The Mannings? Why would they do that? I thought they hated me. He practically accused me of his brother's murder, and then he tried to get me fired. Are you sure?"

"I agree it sounds crazy, but Morton told me they had already planned this party for Anson and now they felt it was only right to give your campaign the party. Maybe they're trying to extend an olive branch to make up for everything that's happened?"

He cocked his head to the side. "And you believed him?"

"I don't know what to believe. I tried to tell him it wasn't necessary, but he wouldn't take no for an answer."

"He's up to something. People like the Mannings don't throw a party for you unless there's something in it for them. I don't trust Manning. Why should I trust him? He hid evidence to get me fired. He'll do anything if he thinks it will benefit him. Maybe he's setting me up to take the fall for Anson's death? He couldn't get rid of me at the courthouse, so maybe he has something planned at this party to get his revenge."

My father voiced everything I'd been thinking. I wasn't quite sure what Morton could do at the barbecue, but a trap was not out of character for him. Then I added the worst part. "They also want to use it as sort of a memorial for Anson."

He snapped his fingers. "Of course! Because, even though his brother is dead, he still wants to have him there when he takes me down. I can't win for losing on this one. If I don't humbly accept his offer, he can tell the whole town I'm uncooperative and not suitable to work in such a close-knit city government. If I do accept, he has me right where he wants me to spring whatever trap he has planned." He grunted, staring down at the table.

After that, we ate our steak quietly, lost in thought. I couldn't stop thinking of the investigation as I ticked off all the suspects in Anson Manning's murder. Linda, Maureen, but at the top of the list was his brother, Morton. The man who wanted to give my father his support, just like he did his dead brother.

Chapter Twenty-One

N
ow that my parents had agreed to the barbecue, I decided I should visit Ellie's dress shop. I needed something new for the occasion, and it also allowed me to talk to her before she could run away.

My cousin Ellie's dress shop was located on the main street of Camden and over the years had acquired quite a reputation for fashionable clothes and original designs. Ellie had always made her own clothes, anxiously awaiting the new patterns each season, and then knocking out outfits that were the envy of even Camden's elite. Her work was so good that they started asking her to make the same outfits for them. She could change the material, do wonders with the fit, and create an original they wouldn't find anywhere else. It made perfect sense when she opened Bluebonnet Fashions, her dress shop, named after the delicate blue Texas state flower. She not only sewed custom orders but carried the latest fashions from New York and Los Angeles. People drove from miles around to shop in her store. It was ironic really because almost all of her friends from high school were married, but she was the girl who never got asked to dances or parties. Now she made more money than many of her girlfriend's husbands and loved every minute of it.

When I entered, I checked the dressing rooms and established there was no one else in the store but the two of us.

"Can I help you?" Ellie asked, treating me as if I was any customer who came in off the street.

"Yes. I need a dress for a barbecue the Mannings are throwing for my parents on Friday."

"Oh, yes. I heard about that. Several of the ladies' club ladies have been in looking for outfits. I should have known you'd be doing the same."

"That's not the only reason I'm here. You still haven't talked to me about what's going on with you and Al."

"Yes, I have. Nothing is going on. I offered, and he didn't respond."

"Did you ever think he's as nervous about all of this as you are?"

She put a hand over her heart and leaned up against a display case filled with hats and scarves. "Why would Al be nervous? He's the man."

"He may have different hardware, but he's a human being just like you. What would you have done if he showed up at your door wearing revealing pajamas?"

Ellie laughed. "Revealing pajamas? I don't think they make such a thing."

"Well, maybe they should. Have you ever stopped to think that the two of you are a lot alike? You're nervous about going to the next step, and so is he."

"I don't think so. Men always want to have sex."

"Yes, and so do women, but it's how you get there that's the tough part."

"And how do you, my young cousin, know so much about this matter? Are you leading a secret life I don't know about?"

"Not hardly. I may not have experienced what you're going through, but I'm observant, and well, Al and I had a little talk. He's scared to death."

"He is?"

"Yep. Just like you were."

"That would explain the deer in the headlights look," she revealed.

"I'll tell you one thing. You wanted to shake things up between you, and maybe you have."

Ellie laughed again. "I guess I did. I just hope I didn't...mess it all up. Maybe I was too forward, and he'll write me off as being desperate."

"Don't say that about yourself. You were trying to change things. People don't like change. Look at Morton and Maureen. He doesn't want to change their relationship by having a baby, but she does."

"And that's the kind of thing that can lead to fighting in the courthouse."

"Or murder."

"Okay. I don't know quite how I will fix this, but I'll try to talk to Al."

"It couldn't hurt. So about my dress?" As I finished my sentence, Arlene stepped in with Clara.

"Fancy meeting you here! We need a new dress for Clara's next singing appearance."

"Me too. Well, not singing, but I need something that looks modern." I eyed the endless hangers. "Any suggestions?"

"So, you want the latest thing off the rack to wear to a barbecue? Hmmm. To be honest, every dress complements your figure." Ellie started scraping hangers across display racks in search of the perfect outfit. Once I knew we were going to the Mannings, I began to worry about what to wear. Barb Manning always looked immaculate, and this time, I wanted to be as close to that as I could get.

"I think she's beautiful in everything she wears. Oh, to be young again," Arlene said. "And maybe you can help me out picking something suitable for Clara. Teenagers today wear such wild things, but for the barbecue, our little Clara needs something proper. It also has to be washable. Her mother, bless her heart, doesn't ever read labels, so a garment that requires dry cleaning is ruined after the first wearing."

"Now, let's see what we have on the rack destined to stun the den of snakes we like to call the ladies' club around here." She began going through the racks of dresses, sliding the hangers by with an efficient click.

"This might work." She held up a bright pink gingham sleeveless dress with a full waist and a fitted bodice.

The bell on the door rang behind us.

I scrunched my nose at the dress. It looked like something Debbie Reynolds would wear in one of those sappy Tammy movies. "No, too pink."

"Too pink," Arlene repeated agreeing with me. Disappointment showed on Ellie's face and shook her head.

"That looks like something a third-grader would wear," Clara said.

Ellie bit her bottom lip and nodded. "I get your point. You want to go in there armed for bear. You're a woman, not a child. Grrrr. How about this one?" She held up a red dress with a revealing neckline, making my thoughts switch from Debbie Reynolds to Liz Taylor. Not only could I not pull off her sultry air, but I didn't have the necessary elements to fill out the bodice. "I know, it's daring, but this color ought to make you look like a successful candidate's daughter."

"Oh no, my dear. That will never do for a candidate's daughter. You need to look like a sophisticated, well-raised child," the new customer's gaze shifted to me, "they will judge him by what they see in you. How you have turned out is a reflection on what they think their government will be."

The new customer was a woman in her fifties who stood next to a young man in a dark suit, a white shirt, thin tie, and a razor-sharp crewcut. Following behind them came a girl about Clara's age and another suit-wearing man that could have been a twin to the first one.

"Don't mind my escort, ladies. He's a necessity, I'm afraid," she said.

"Oh, my stars," Arlene gasped, clutching at her chest. "Mrs. Lyndon Johnson. Right here in Ellie's dress shop. As I live and breathe." Arlene curtsied as if in the presence of royalty.

"No need for that, my dear, and you can call me Lady Bird," she said. "When I'm back in Texas, I like to lose a little of the pretension of being the vice president's wife."

Ellie stepped forward. "I'm Ellie Monroe, Mrs. Johnson...Lady Bird...we are so honored to have you in Bluebonnet Fashions."

"With a name like that, how can I resist? You know, I love flowers."

Lady Bird Johnson was well known for her efforts to beautify Texas with wildflowers. In a state filled with smelly cows and oil wells, her efforts to bring color and fragrance were a welcome change. Even though she was the wife of the vice president of the United States, she seemed very friendly and unassuming.

"Mother," the young girl with her pointed to a rack of dresses.

Lady Bird put her hands on the girl's shoulders. "And let me introduce you to my daughter, Luci."

Luci smiled and rolled off an automatic, "how do you do."

"Go have a look," Lady Bird told Luci, her introductions out of the way. "I'm afraid your reputation precedes you, Miss Ellie. Some of your custom work has been showing up at the balls and events in Dallas and Austin. Little Luci here has to attend several functions in the next few months, both here and in Washington, and we hope we might be able to find something exceptional. We can't have her looking like some senator's child, now can we?"

Lady Bird's gaze returned to me as Luci began her search through Ellie's offerings. "So, you are the daughter of a local candidate? Forgive me for eavesdropping, but dressing a young lady whose father is in political office is an area I am well trained in."

I blushed and stepped forward, fighting the insane impulse to curtsy as well. "I'm Dot Morgan, and it is wonderful to meet you. My father is running for City Council. Nothing on the grand scale of vice president."

She chuckled softly. "Ah yes, but that's where it starts. Each election is a stepping stone to the next one. How about something like this?" She held up a white tailored jacket and under it a sky-blue shift.

I hadn't even considered a suit jacket. I loved the way it dressed up the elegant but simple blue dress underneath. I reached for the price tag and then stepped back.

"I'm afraid that's out of my budget. I'm still a student, studying to be a secretary."

A warmth came into Ladybird's eyes. "Ah, those were the days. Did you know I financed my husband's first campaign? Money isn't always plentiful, is it? Why don't you just try it on? What could it hurt?"

Ellie nodded and pushed me to the dressing room. When I emerged a few minutes later, Clara and Arlene were pulling out dresses on the same rack as Ladybird who was helping her daughter read a tag.

"Read it again, slowly," she said, her head bent close, as Luci held the tag closer to her eyes. "Oh, it's taffeta. I should have caught that."

Ladybird looked up and smiled. "Luci has what they used to call an eye ailment, but it is more than that. She is dyslexic."

I pursed my lips together. I was unaware Lady Bird's daughter had anything wrong with her eyes. I read the newspaper daily, but this was something they must have kept out of the press.

Luci interrupted, "I can't read."

"That's not true. She reads just fine, but it takes a little longer."

176

"The words jump around the page," Luci explained. "It's hard to understand if you've never seen it."

"Oh, I know someone who reads like you do at school. It takes him a long time to finish," Clara said. "I just thought he was lazy."

Luci shook her head. "That's what everybody thinks. I'm sick of it."

"Sorry," Clara said in a whisper.

"It's not your fault, young lady," Lady Bird said. "It's a common mistake. Is there a subject you have trouble in at school?"

"Math," Clara answered.

"And I'm sure there are times when the rest of the class finishes something, and you are still struggling with it," Lady Bird said.

"Sometimes."

"You'd hate it if someone called you lazy because you couldn't figure it out as fast as everyone else, would you? That's what my dear Luci has had to deal with, especially before we understood her learning style."

"Yeah, I'm not dumb. I just have trouble reading." She let out a sigh, clearly tired of a conversation she'd had before with countless others. Luci held up a dress. "How about this one?"

Lady Bird smiled and began to examine the garment, but her eye caught me standing in the blue dress. "Well, that's a whamo. I love it on you. All you need is a string of pearls, and you'll be the best-looking candidate's daughter at your banquet."

I put my hand to my neck and turned to look in the mirror. "You think so?"

"I know so. Trust me. I do a lot of events both as the wife of the Vice President and for Mrs. Kennedy with that dear new baby. I spend plenty of time planning my outfits, and that one is a stunner."

I took in a breath and turned to the side. It fit me perfectly.

"Let me buy it for you," Lady Bird said coming forward.

"Oh, no. I couldn't ask you to do something like that."

"It's my gift to you. You remind me a lot of myself at your age. You're a real go-getter studying to be a secretary, and I'll bet you're getting some negative opinions on that. Women should stay at home and not work, some people still insist on saying, even though the idea is antiquated. Women should take care of the children and mind the husband, they say. Did you know I have two college degrees and I'm here in Texas checking on my radio station KTBC? Sometimes you have to stretch as a woman, even beyond what others expect of you. Let me buy this for you, as one candidate's family to another."

"Do it," Ellie whispered her eyes wide. I guess getting a gift from the vice president's wife was pretty amazing.

"Well," I said, "I'm honored by your gift, Mrs. Johnson."

"Lady Bird," she corrected me.

"Of course, Lady Bird," I repeated awkwardly.

"I'm not making any promises, but I'll try to keep track of your father's campaign. Lyndon and I have plenty of commitments, but I love to watch politics on the grassroots level. That's where all the fun is." Luci came up with an armload full of dresses. "And as you can see, my daughter has a few ideas to fill up my time as well."

Clara came out of the dressing room wearing a dress with a big bow at the collar. Arlene started nodding approvingly. "Perfect," she said.

Luci Johnson, dressed in black slacks and a white and black striped top leaned over to Clara. "Big bows are for kids. Dress older, not younger."

"Luci," Lady Bird scolded. She turned her attention to Clara. "You look lovely, dear."

Clara smiled at Luci and nodded, taking her suggestion. "Dress older. Thanks. I'll look around some more."

Arlene rolled her eyes at her niece.

Lady Bird apologized. "Sorry. These young people get these ideas in their heads, and then there's no stopping them. I thought the outfit was lovely myself. They're all in such a hurry to grow up, aren't they?"

Arlene puffed up slightly, as Lady Bird commiserated with her over the frustrations of teenagers. It was like they were old friends comparing notes. "Yes, your Maj...Lady Bird," she answered, star-struck.

Lady Bird turned back to her daughter and pointed to one of the dresses she was holding. "Start with that one." She turned to one of the crew cuts who had been quietly observing the scene. "How much time do we have?"

CHAPTER TWENTY-ONE

He consulted his watch. "About forty-five minutes, ma'am."

"Then we shall have to make the most of it. Miss Ellie, I would be obliged if you would put Miss Morgan's dress on our bill, and then we'd like to talk about some of your original designs for Luci."

"Yes, ma'am." Ellie returned to the register with efficiency.

"Thank you," I said.

"My pleasure," she answered warmly.

Chapter Twenty-Two

W hen Friday finally rolled around, I couldn't get it out of my head it felt like I was going to a funeral, not a party to support my father's run for city council. Something didn't feel right. With the Mannings in charge, so much could go wrong.

During the week, Arlene had kept up her daily vigil to Constance who continued to sleep. The police still didn't have the hit-and-run driver. How long would it take for Officer Sprague to write it off to a dead man they couldn't prosecute? It had to have been Anson just days before his own death.

When we arrived at the Manning's home, I struggled to pick up a heavy metal sign one of my mother's library patrons had made for my father. We didn't need to spend money when he was the only candidate in the race, but at least we had something we could put up at the barbecue. My father's picture was encircled in red and underneath were the words

Mike Morgan. He's your man.

Vote for Mike for City Council.

"Here, let me do that," Dad said when he saw me trying to lift a bulky sign. "It's not that heavy," I said even though my arms were beginning to ache.

"I just wish our benefactor had provided a way for the darn thing to stand up," he said. Trying to make the sign waterproof, he had fashioned it out of a steel square that would typically be a part of a furnace or air conditioning unit. Unfortunately, he couldn't find any kind of support beam strong enough to hold it up. We would need to get a sturdy easel for it eventually. Hopefully, we could prop it up somewhere at the party.

As we loaded the car, the blue sky and puffy clouds of earlier were being replaced by lines of angry grey layers. A gust of wind blew around us, making me wish I had put a scarf on when I was in the house. I decided to wear my hair down today, and strands of it were already blowing in my face. At least I had remembered my umbrella. I wasn't completely sure Aqua Net was as waterproof as the can said.

"This may be a very short barbecue," I said, sounding more hopeful than wary. The shorter, the better as far as I was concerned. I wondered if my father was having second thoughts about running for office. I know I was. I thought back to my meeting Lady Bird Johnson at the dress shop. Were there days when she wanted to throw the whole idea of her husband's campaign away and live life like an average person? Being the vice president to John F. Kennedy had to be as far from ordinary as one could get. I couldn't believe I had actually met someone I'd seen on television. Not only that, but her teenage daughter, Luci. Just like the Johnsons, our entire family was in this campaign, and now we had to make the best of it.

"It would be even better if they canceled the party because of the weather. According to the forecast, we're supposed to have a whopper of a storm," my mother said.

"This whole thing is awkward enough," Dad agreed. "Whoever heard of a wake combined with a campaign event? Of course, you have to take into account the Manning's are throwing it. I've lived in the same town and worked in the same building as Morton Manning and was happily going along not knowing anything about him or his screwy family. Ignorance is bliss, I guess. I'm beginning to think I'm not cut out to be a politician."

My dad had always been a get-it-done kind of guy, but now I could see his resolve was faltering. "And that's where you're making a mistake. You have misgivings about holding office because you have a good heart. The thing that's different about you is you don't want to be on the city council to gain power. You want to help people."

"I suppose." He didn't sound convinced. "It does seem to help me rationalize putting up with people like the Mannings if it means I can get something positive done for the community. Even with that in mind, I'm still not sure I'm the right man for the job."

My father's attitude, no matter how much I tried to keep him positive, was still the same as we stood among the crowd gathering at the Mannings. Morton, along with Officer Sprague, came over and patted him boisterously on the back, causing him to grimace. I just hoped he could hold it together and not get overwhelmed with the social side of all this until we could get this over with.

As they walked away swooping my father up with them, Ellie came over to where we were standing, her white gloves perfectly matching the clutch bag she carried. "Have you seen Al?" she whispered into my ear.

I glanced around the luscious backyard. "Not yet...wait. There he is."

Al awkwardly held a glass of punch about ten feet from us. His hair looked different. He had slicked it back with something. Of all the times I had ever seen Al, this time he looked nervous. He spotted Ellie in the crowd and pulled at his collar and straightened his tie. I had never seen Al look so... neat.

Just as I was about to comment on that fact, I noticed Ellie smoothing down the front of her dress. "What is going on with you two? You both look like you're going out on a first date."

"Who's going out on a date?" A voice boomed from behind me. Ben Dalton had on a yellow cotton shirt with two broad vertical stripes on either side of the buttons. He didn't look like a crumpled reporter today, and I gulped in a little air when I saw him.

"I think I am," Ellie answered, her eyes still fixed on Al.

Ben followed the direction of Ellie's eyes, and a look of recognition came to his features. "Oh. I see."

I touched her hand. "You should go over and talk to him, Ellie."

She nodded and took in a breath. "After our talk in the dress shop, I decided to call him. I told him I was coming to this shindig, and well, there he is."

"With that hair, I think he's interested. Very interested," Ben said.

Ellie's blue eyes looked large. "Do you really think so?"

"You'll never know if you don't ask," I gave her a little push. Before she could take another step, Al started walking over to us.

"Ellie. What a nice surprise." His tone was formal.

"I told you I'd be here."

He cleared his throat. "Uh. Yes. Yes, you did. Would you like lemonade?" He raised his glass, sloshing a small amount on the grass.

"I guess so."

"Good. I wanted to get the chance to talk to you about something."

"Sure."

As they walked away, I worried about my cousin. Had he decided to go through with her proposition, or could he be breaking up with her? I felt an arm around my shoulder.

"Don't worry. I'm an observer of people, and he likes her too much to hurt her," Ben reassured me. I know his words were meant to give me peace, but his arm around my shoulder was stirring up a whole new batch of emotions inside of me. I looked into his eyes, and he looked back, then Morton Manning's laugh broke the spell. The small group of men had wandered back to where we were standing. Ben immediately scrounged for a notebook in his pocket.

Barb popped out from behind Morton, holding an assortment of cigars in front of my father. "I have a fresh box of Cuban cigars. How about coming into the house and telling us about your plans for the city council? I'm sure you've been up nights hatching all of your ideas to make our town a better place."

"And God bless America for that. Don't you love our political system?" Morton said. He gestured to the men collecting around them. "Besides, you'll be surprised to learn you have competition."

"Who?" Dad asked. "I thought I was the only one running after..."

"Hello, Mike." Charlie Columbo, with a cigar already in hand, butted in between the two men. He was much shorter than the two of them and took a quick puff from his cigar. "I hope you don't mind me throwing in my hat, but after what happened to Constance Benedict, I can't sleep at night. I have to fix this. I went to the council meeting for years telling them how dangerous that corner was, and nobody would listen to me. They looked at me and thought who am I but the guy who owns the diner. Maybe if I'm on the council, they'll finally listen."

"Can I quote you on that, Charlie?" Ben asked.

"I don't see why you need to print it in that paper of yours. I've been saying it every day in the diner to anyone who will listen."

Officer Sprague nodded, "You're a good man, Charlie. We're working on running down the green car. I have my men checking out anything that's ever been remotely green in three counties. Too bad it was such a popular color in the last few years."

"That's good. Do it for those poor kids who need their mama back," Charlie said.

"Yes. We will find the culprit. Anyone who would leave an injured person by the side of the road could be capable of much more. Even murder."

"I know you were upset about the hit-and-run, but I didn't know you had an interest in running. I think it's great." My father smiled at Charlie and then reached out and shook his hand. For a man who just found out he had a new opponent, he didn't seem all that upset.

Morton continued, "Charlie's the squeaky wheel around here rambling on about that stoplight. Too bad about the Benedict woman, of course. I suppose if she survives, she'll be hitting the welfare rolls so we can pay the bills for that family out of our tax dollars." He laughed at what he thought was a joke, and those around him smiled uncomfortably. Morton once again had displayed how insensitive he could be. When no one else laughed, he put on a serious face and quickly changed the subject. "I thought it might be a good chance for both of you to state your platforms. We tried to do this when Anson was around, but sadly we couldn't. I think he would have enjoyed our little barbecue tonight and the way the campaign has changed again with the entrance of Charlie into the competition. I have to say, gentlemen, this is turning out to be quite the horse race."

Dad nodded and followed Morton and Charlie into the house, looking back at us in quiet desperation.

"I'll go with him," Mom said. "He might need me if for nothing else, moral support." She followed quietly along with Ben, who was furiously writing as he tried to navigate the lawn. Barb refocused her attention on a tray of appetizers a waiter was bringing out and immediately began barking orders.

CHAPTER TWENTY-TWO

Once again, this event would be a tightly run ship.

Arlene, who had been standing close to the whole scene with Clara, shook her head. "Poor Mike. He's going to have to start shaking hands and kissing babies."

"He feels this whole barbecue idea is weird, that and making it a memorial for Anson," I said.

"Well, I do find it strange Mr. Manning is throwing this shindig for a man he accused of murder."

Barb was flitting from group to group her black polka dot shirtwaist with a full pleated skirt swishing around her legs. She wore large white pearls in her ears, and even though there was a warm, humid breeze, she never even broke a sweat. I noticed Jane over by a table, her swollen form parked in a folding chair. She looked exhausted, and the Texas heat couldn't be helping a woman that late in her pregnancy. Even though it was overcast, the pre-storm humidity was thick. Looking at her I worried the next thing we'd be doing was boiling water and getting towels.

Arlene gave me a warm smile. "I just wanted to thank you for asking to let Clara sing today. I know it will put her back on the map, no matter what. That woman," Arlene's gaze shifted back to Barb, "tries to do."

"Aunt Arlene," Clara's eyes widened at her aunt's potential interference, "please don't talk about Mrs. Manning like that." Like my father, she didn't want to stir up trouble. Clara looked like a different girl at today's event. Instead of the blue pinafore she had been wearing at the Founder's Day banquet, she had on a simple black shift, black patent leather shoes, and a white beaded necklace. The cute little girl pigtails were gone. Clara had pulled her hair back in a bun at the nape of her neck. She looked years older. I thought I even spied a little lipstick. "I know you love me, but I can handle this on my own."

Arlene's lips thinned and then she promised, "I'll be good." She followed my gaze. "I see you're noticing Clara's new look. I thought the blue dress would have looked not so...severe, but this is what Clara wanted."

"I highly approve," I said, making Clara beam. I was beginning to see the strong, confident woman she would one day become.

It looked like almost everyone in town was here as they milled around the graceful slope of Barb and Morton's landscaped back yard. The wind picked up again, causing summer dresses to flutter and our campaign sign that was leaned against a table leg, fell face down. "Let me get that." I turned to Clara. "Good luck on the song."

"Thanks, Dot," she said with a grateful smile. "I'm a little nervous. Mrs. Manning wants me to sing before the candidates give their speeches." She turned to her aunt, "Is it okay if I go inside and look at the Mannings' grand piano?"

Arlene nodded, adoration in her eyes. "Of course, it is. Just don't touch it."

I wasn't sure how a person who loved music as much as she did could resist touching a Steinway, but with her aunt's permission, Clara skipped off in search of the instrument. I returned to my task of righting the sign.

"Do you want me to help you lift that?" Arlene asked.

"It's pretty heavy. I can get it, though," I said.

"Are you afraid this old lady can't lift a sign? Please. I'm stronger than I look," Arlene boasted.

I attempted to prop the sign up again, but at ground level, no one could see it. Most people walked right by it, their attention on the food. Now that Dad had competition, the placement of this sign was more important. Picking it up by the corners, I pulled it to a less-traveled area, but there was nothing to lean it against. Finally, I hit on sticking the point of my umbrella into the ground and leaning the sign against it. A minute later, as I precariously propped it up, Barb Manning began to speak from behind me.

"Darling, that will never do. Umbrellas bend too easily. Let me see if I can get you something from the house."

"You would think I'd know that after seeing that bent umbrella when the bookcase fell at the debate."

"I didn't recall seeing that. How strange. You're very observant."

"You know, it was the one with fringe on it. I know this sounds crazy, but I thought it might have been used as a lever to turn over the bookcase. That was why it was bent in half like that."

"Oh my, you do have quite an imagination. And I suppose you know just

186

who it was that wielded this fringed umbrella?"

"I, uh…" I stumbled over my words. I wasn't so sure it be a good idea to tell her that someone might have had to do with her husband. My dad was still inside campaigning and if I spoke up now, it could ruin everything.

"I see. You youngsters and your penchant for mysteries where there are none," she remarked with a condescending tone. She glanced at my father's photo on the board that had been giving me so much trouble. "Such a cute little sign. Did you make it yourself? I have an idea. Let me go see if I can find it, and I'll be right back." The sky continued to cloud over and having my umbrella back would come in handy at this point.

A few feet from me, Maureen was having an intense conversation with Morton. She must have pulled him out of the cigar-smoking politics talk. I hadn't even seen her arrive at the party. Although I couldn't hear a word, it was apparent they were still fighting over the baby. It was as if he thought he could make all the decisions concerning the pregnancy, and she had no rights at all. If she wanted to keep it, then she should be able to keep it. I was about to go over and offer support when Linda Manning stepped up, linking her arm through Maureen's. Morton stopped speaking, looking shocked at the alliance between the two women. Outnumbered, he snorted and walked off. It gave me a particular delight to see him silenced by the teaming up of two women he probably had felt were under his thumb.

"That was great," I said to them after placing Dad's sign on the grass. "You shut him up."

Linda gave me a knowing look. "For now, anyway. You know how it is with Morton. Nothing is really ever over until he gets his way."

Maureen smiled. "I decided I'm keeping the baby for sure, and he can't stop me. It's my body and my baby. I don't expect him to do a thing for it, as a matter of fact, even though I was desperate to keep Morton, now that I have a little Morty, my ideas are changing on how much I need his father around as well."

"Sounds like a good idea to me but do us all a favor and don't name him little Morty," I said.

"Especially if it's a girl," Linda added.

"Let's get some banana pudding before it melts in this heat," Maureen said. "I'm famished, and I now have permission and a duty to eat fattening desserts."

They laughed and started walking to the refreshment table near the house. Another gust of wind came through, and I struggled to keep my full skirt from sailing up like Marilyn Monroe over the subway vent. At least that would get Ben Dalton scrambling for his camera.

Barb returned lugging a spindly-looking easel. "Here, this was a leftover from my artistic days. I don't know how long it will hold, but at least it has three legs instead of one," Barb said.

"Thank you." We lifted the sign onto the easel. "And thank you for all of this." I waved my hand to point out the food and drink-laden tables.

"It is quite a spread, isn't it?" She surveyed the crowd and spotted Linda, who was happily eating banana pudding with Maureen. "My, my I didn't expect to see my sister-in-law grazing the dessert table with...that woman. Once you lose your figure, it's all over." Then she whispered, "your father is much more deserving of it than that wastrel of a brother-in-law I had. He would have been a terrible city councilman."

I was amazed at her sudden revelation. She had always seemed so protective of the Manning name and reputation. Had the whole nasty affair finally broken down her defenses? Was she finally beginning to see her family for what it really was? A lying, power-hungry manipulative group of people?

She must have picked up on my shocked expression. "Don't look at me that way. Everyone in town knew what a failure he was. Anson was impossible, and in spite of our best efforts, let's face it darling, people can smell a loser." Her gaze continued to watch the crowd enjoying themselves. "Oh, that's the judge's wife. We like to keep in good graces with our judge. You never know how it will help in the future when Morton decides to run for judge himself. I think your father is going to be learning all about getting to know the right people and keeping them happy." She waved at a heavyset woman wearing a light blue dress that was too small for her and a hat decorated with purple forget-me-nots.

After Barb left, I had no one to talk to and glanced around the lawn. Ellie and Al were standing on the patio near the house. He reached out and pushed a strand of hair from her face, and she gave a gentle smile. Maybe they were finally on the journey Ellie had hoped for. Whatever was going on, I needed to let them be alone. Maureen and Linda were moving from the banana pudding to a selection of small frosted cakes. I had to admit that when I first laid eyes on the voluptuous redhead, I didn't like her, or maybe, to be honest, I didn't like her type. Any woman who thinks all men are available to supply their needs be it financial or physical was not the type of person I would choose to be friends with. I also doubted that kind of girl would want to pal up with me. What would I have to offer her? But when I learned her real story, she was just like me, trying to figure out how to get through life. Maureen had thrown herself at Anson because she was in trouble, in more ways than one. She had to get Morton's attention and why not encourage some sibling rivalry? It's one thing to flirt with a man's brother, but she was had flirted with a brother that man hated. She had provided yet another reason to make Morton angry enough to kill his brother. To her, the seduction of Anson made perfect sense, as so many things do in hindsight. She could not have known the damage it would do.

Working the heels of my pumps across the moist grass, I started making my way to Maureen and Linda again. I had just passed Arlene who was scribbling down a recipe she was getting from the caterer when a tremendous clap of thunder rang out above us. The wind picked up significantly, and plates and cups started flying off the tables. I clamped onto my skirt, losing the battle of keeping it in place.

"It's another tornado," someone shouted from the patio at the top of the hill. "Everyone to the house."

After what had happened to Anson Manning, people were playing it safe and getting out of the storm. Really safe. The crowd rushed onto the veranda and through the French doors not wiping their feet. That wouldn't make Barb happy. I wondered if she cleaned her own carpets the same way she took care of her roses, feeling she could do a better job than anyone she could hire? As the tables filled with food were abandoned to the wind, a solitary scream rang out from behind me. Arlene lay on the ground holding onto her ankle, the contents of her purse scattered across the grass. The caterer was long gone.

"I was just putting the recipe in my purse, and I turned wrong. I think I sprained my ankle." One of Arlene's shoes was off, and she rubbed at the tender joint.

The wind had become deafening. I shouted, "Here, let me help you up and into the house." I placed my hands under her arms and attempted to pull her up, but Arlene was too heavy. I made a second effort from the front but was afraid I would injure her ankle further if I got her to standing and then dropped her.

"I can't do it. Let me go get help in the house," I yelled against the wind.

"Okay, I'll keep trying to stand up. I'm sorry for being such a bother. It's hell being old."

I grabbed Dad's campaign sign off the easel. After trying to lift Arlene, it felt light. "Here, this will keep the rain off. I'll be right back."

She gave me a weak smile as she balanced the board on her head. I started pushing through the stinging rain up the hill to the house. The Mannings' yard didn't look this big before the rain started. My heels were sinking into the mud, and I found I could balance better, grabbing onto the tree branches on the edge of the lawn. As I scrambled for an oak branch, I was suddenly pulled off the path into the thickness of the trees.

Barb squeezed a tight grip on my arm. Did she think this was safer than trying to make it to the house? "Barb? Thank God, Arlene fell and sprained her ankle," I shouted. "Can you help me get her to her feet?"

Barb looked strange, and I noted in the downpour the top of her head was now flat with what looked like a piece of scalp hanging from a bobby pin. As many times as I had seen her, I never realized Barb Manning wore a clip-on hairpiece. Her hair was thin, barely covering the top of her head. I tried to focus on something else. Her eyes were hard, and I sensed a wildness about her. A fierceness. Could she be this upset the rain had spoiled the party? She scowled at my words.

"Fat pig. Maybe she needs to lighten up on all those high-calorie casseroles.

If there is one thing I hate, it's a woman who doesn't maintain her figure. How does that look to others? How will she ever keep a man..."

As Barb rattled on about Arlene's extra pounds, I realized she was clutching something in the hand that wasn't squeezing my arm. It was a rock the size of a softball.

"Barb?" I broke into her endless insults about Arlene. "Are you okay?"

She nodded her head up and down rapidly, the hairpiece flipping in a macabre rhythm. The head of the Camden Ladies' Club was looking more like a person with a mental health condition than a local matriarch. "What do you think? Of course, I'm not okay, thanks to you. Time and time again, it always comes back to you, Dot Morgan. That perky little blonde who wants to be a secretary. She's so excited about it she even helps grieving widows figure out their husband's probate. All hail the blessed Dot." She rolled off my name as if it left a bad taste in her mouth. This was the real, uncensored Barb. No more passive aggression. No more little digs. She had bared the ugliness of her soul, and it scared me.

"What kind of name is that? Dot? Dot? Dot?" She repeated my name several times, changing her tone slightly as if she were trying it out every outlandish way she could think of.

I tried to get her to move past her fit of temper. "Just a name." I wasn't sure what was going on with her, but I still had to get help for Arlene. How safe could it be holding a metal sign over your head in a thunderstorm? "Can you help me with Arlene? I was on my way to get help..."

"On your way to get your daddy...Mike Morgan... He's your man. Isn't that what your sorry little homemade sign says? It shows what amateurs you are. Babes in the woods, who don't have any idea how over their heads they are. You know, I so enjoyed telling that reporter about your father getting caught at the cathouse. Our city council candidate engaging in carnal acts with a prostitute? He was so excited to get some juicy news to report. Can you believe he asked me if I was sure I wanted to have him publish it? A reporter with a conscience. That was a shock. Let me tell you, I reveled in the fact your daddy got caught with his pants down! I loved what a stink it caused." She laughed, pitching her head up into the rain. "I'm amazed at how

191

stupid you all are. You, your father, that reporter, Morton, Anson. Just plain stupid."

I'd heard enough. I wasn't going to stand out in the rain with a madwoman while she insulted my father. "Okay. That's enough. I'm getting help on my own. You can rant and rave in a tornado all you like." I turned to leave, but with a powerful tug, she yanked me back again. This time she forced my head down to her soaked shoulder. Was she trying to be some sort of twisted mother to me?

"I know you know," she whispered in my ear, her hot breath on my cheek. Her words were quiet, almost a whisper but they caused me to tremble. She wasn't just crazy, but dangerous.

My neck began to ache in the position she was holding me. I had to get away from her. I tried to free myself, but she tightened her grip. Finally, I gave in and responded to her. "Okay, Barb. What do I know?"

"Don't ever make the mistake of underestimating me, darling. Others have and it never worked out well for them."

The tornado siren joined the chorus of thunder startling her. Her grip loosened for a second, and I made another attempt to free myself from her grasp. She pulled me back before I could get any ground.

"Let me go, Barb," I begged. "I don't know why you're acting like this, but I have to help Arlene. If things start flying around, she could get hurt."

"Honestly, how bad would it be? It would be an end to that old busybody and the whining toddler she drags around. She had the nerve to correct me. Nobody cares what that kid's name is. All these idiots care about is the food. Arlene can sit there and be a lightning rod, for all I care." She held up the rock with her free hand. "Flying debris. You know, I'll say that's what happened to you, my snooping little friend. For the record—Anson never even saw it coming."

I had been so sure it was Morton who had murdered Anson. It had been Barb, all along. Just like pruning her own roses, she took care of the weed who was her husband's embarrassing brother. "You killed Anson? Your own brother-in-law? Why?"

She laughed. "He was a wastrel. He'd be there every month to borrow money and write out some I.O.U. on a piece of paper. Like that was going to make a difference. He thought he could invest in some get rich quick scheme and when one after another flopped, he couldn't even tell that hayseed of a wife he took and risk losing her. She was the biggest payout, and no matter how much he wanted to be with other women, he had to keep that little country bumpkin. He never intended to pay us back, not one cent. Other people have no-account lazy people in their families, but not the Mannings."

"How did you get the bookcase over on top of him?" I asked, trying to stall for time. If I could keep her talking, the chances were greater that someone would come out to find us. I was sure my parents would be looking for me when I didn't come in with everyone else.

"I'm capable of much more than you think, and for your information, I knew all about Morton and that little slut Maureen Johnson. Oh, you were so righteous in telling me. Such a noble thing to do. Did you know he spent the night with her last week? I stayed in my car at the curb watching her house. He was in there with her. Doing...whatever it is he did with her. The nerve of the man, but that's okay. I can handle it. You know how I do it? I decided I would act as if it hadn't happened. If it didn't happen, I didn't have a problem. Do you see how simple that is? When the sun started coming up, I drove home without a care in the world. It would have stayed that way, except for that idiot woman. Who goes for a walk around town before dawn? It was her fault. She didn't even look before she started to cross the street."

My mouth dropped open. "Are you saying, you're the one who hit Constance Benedict?"

"So? What of it? Sprague is hot on the trail of a green car. He'll think he has it figured out soon enough and put the blame on Anson. Green car, drunk driver, someone who runs from responsibility, Anson did it all. That stupid woman doesn't even know her colors. I know it was early, and the sun might have been in her eyes, but turquoise. My car is turquoise. I could find an easy target in my drunk brother-in-law for someone else hitting the Benedict woman, but it wouldn't be as easy to cover up crushing Anson with the bookcase. I used Maureen's cheap umbrella to do it. The one with the ghastly fringe on it. She'd forgotten it when she ran off. Ironic, huh? I was kind of hoping it would make the police look at her. Silly, me for hoping they were smart enough to figure it out, but you, my darling, not only knew Anson was murdered, but that I was his killer."

I had been so focused on Morton that I hadn't seen it. His arms were weak, and I had assumed, he had been the one to tip the bookcase with the umbrella. I even considered him having Miss Robinson do it for him, but it had been Barb. As scheming and conniving as Morton was, his wife was even more so.

She continued, "I can't have that. You understand, don't you? I want to say it's been marvelous getting to know you, but the truth is, you are nothing more than a little fly to shoo away. As they say in Italy, *Ciao*, darling."

She raised the rock to clobber me, but before her arm could deliver the blow, I saw my father's smiling face come down on her, knocking Barb off her feet and sending her rolling down the sodden hill.

Arlene, her face red and looking winded, stood precariously on her ankle with the sign still in her hand.

"I guess Mike Morgan is our man," she yelled down the embankment to Barb. "That's what you get for calling me fat!"

I watched for a second and Barb didn't move. The weight of the sign must have temporarily knocked her out and I had to hope she wouldn't come back up the hill toward us. "I can't believe you did that!" I called to Arlene in the rain.

"I can't believe I did it either," she said, balancing on one foot. "I started trying to make my way to the house on my own and saw Barb holding you with one hand and holding a great big rock in the other. One more minute you would have been as dead as Anson. Who knew she wore a wig?"

I had to laugh that this was the takeaway Arlene was talking about instead of Barb's attempt at murdering me.

"If you can stand here, I'll get help," I said.

Arlene held onto the sign. "That's what you said the last time. If she comes at me, she knows what she's going to get."

As I fought the rain and made my way to the house, I heard Arlene shout in the distance, "Don't even try to get up. I'll hit you with the sign and then sit on you. A few extra pounds are pretty damn useful when you have to take down a murderer!"

Chapter Twenty-Three

"A toast to Mike Morgan. He's our man," Ellie said, raising her glass. It had been three weeks since the terrible scene of the Manning's barbecue, and we were celebrating at Columbo's.

"And a toast to our new city councilman, Charlie Columbo," Dad said, raising a glass of port. Yes, he had lost the election, but for a loser, he couldn't be happier.

"And a toast to the newest graduate of The Hudson Secretarial School," Mother added, beaming.

"That's right," Ellie said, her arm linked into Al's. "This is so exciting. Tell me, what will you do now?"

I smiled and sat back in the booth. "I don't know. Whatever it will be, I'm sure it won't be as much of an adventure as the last few weeks."

My father leaned his head over to me. "Whatever you embark upon, Miss Morgan, I can assure you it will be an adventure."

Al took a spoon and gently tapped a glass making a tinkling sound. "Uh, Ellie and I have an announcement."

Ellie grinned widely and then took the spoon out of Al's hand. "Yes, we do. After some pretty rocky times this last month…"

"I'll say," Al said, wiping his forehead with a handkerchief he pulled from his pocket.

"Al and I have…changed our friendship a little bit…"

Now Al blushed, and he patted his forehead again. "I'll say," he repeated.

"Oh, what the hell. We're getting hitched!" Ellie announced with a chirp in her voice.

I couldn't have been happier for her. I reached over to hug her and whispered, "So you finally got to the next step with Al."

She whispered back, "I'll say."

Columbo's Diner was packed, with every table filled, Dean Martin and Frank Sinatra over the loudspeaker and pasta on every plate.

As word spread throughout the diner, congratulations continued to the newly engaged couple, I squeezed Dad's arm and said, "I'm so proud of you."

"Why, because I lost?"

"No. Because you tried, you had a desire to do something, and instead of just thinking about it, you did it. I know you didn't win, but you tried. I love you for that," I said and kissed him on the cheek.

"Ah, isn't that sweet," Linda Manning stepped up to our table with Maureen at her side. "A girl can never go wrong with her daddy. I just wanted to say thank you to Dot before I leave town."

"Leaving town, so soon?" Ellie asked.

"Not soon enough, if you ask me. I'm headed back to the ranch. I want to be there when they bring in the alfalfa for the livestock, and now that Morton is practicing law in Dallas and Barb is in jail awaiting trial, this place feels like somebody else's town. A better town, for sure, but it's time I get back to where I belong. You know, after I left Anson at the debate that day, I began to realize what I'd left behind. Like a crazy woman, I drove around in the storm for an hour. I missed my home full of wide-open spaces, bossy brothers, and needy cattle. Living there was a whole lot easier than living with the social-climbing elite of Camden, Texas."

Maureen stood by her side, a little quieter than I'd first seen her. Instead of flirting with every man in the room, she seemed happy to be a part of our group. She had so many things in front of her with the baby. Maybe after four husbands she was finding another place to give her love.

Linda also looked different from the first time I saw her on the night of her husband's death. She was happy now and seemed to be at peace with her decision. Gone were the designer clothes and carefully applied makeup. She now wore a simple blue skirt with a floral blouse. She was already a natural beauty and had augmented it with only mascara and some lipstick. Yes, I liked the look of the new Linda, and I had a feeling I was finally seeing the real person she had always been. I stood up and gave her a warm hug.

"You be happy," I whispered.

She pulled away, a tear in her eyes. "You know, I think that's the nicest thing anyone has ever said to me here in Camden. I will certainly try."

"I'm going to miss you," Maureen said, hugging her next.

Linda wagged her finger. "You better call me when you have that baby."

As Linda left, Charlie stepped up to the microphone in a makeshift stage area near the front of the diner. "Hello everybody. Welcome to Charlie's election celebration party."

The crowd clapped and cheered. "I promise I'm going to work hard to get a big beautiful stoplight put in. There will be no more needless accidents on Charlie Columbo's watch, but now, we will be treated to the song stylings of our beautiful little Clara Clark. I'm also honored to announce she's agreed to let me accompany her on the accordion."

As the restaurant diners clapped, Clara stepped up in the black dress with pearls. She took the microphone to begin to sing, but then stopped as the door to the diner opened.

Bertram Benedict wheeled his mother into the restaurant, and on her lap was Mr. Sammy with his new handmade green sweater. Constance looked pale, and a little shaky, but her smile outweighed everything else. Charlie took the microphone from Clara and said, "Everyone, stand up and clap for Mrs. Benedict. It's a miracle she's back with us and with her precious bambinos!"

We stood and clapped while Bertram awkwardly rolled his mother's wheelchair to a table where Arlene sat waiting. There were tears in her eyes, and she gave Constance a hug and then Bertram.

Constance waved a hand at the crowd. "Thank you, everyone. I'm sorry Sylvia couldn't be here, but she's getting stronger every day. Thank you all for your help and support through all of this. Camden, Texas is more than a town. It's a big family."

When the crowd quieted down, Clara said, "I would like to dedicate this song to Bertram Benedict...and Bertram, if you want to do some of your ventriloquist act after me, I'd be honored."

Collective hearts of the room melted when he held up Mr. Sammy and waved at Clara and said in his high Sammy voice, "Sure, beautiful." Bertram's lips barely moved.

As Clara began to sing Arlene sidled in next to me in the booth. "I hope you don't mind, but I can see better from over here."

"Hello, Arlene," my mother whispered. "How is your ankle?"

"Fine, just fine," she said.

Clara began to sing, her clear voice now accompanied by the soft tones from the accordion. Charlie beamed at her as she sang "La Vien Rose" to the assembled group.

"She really is talented," I whispered.

With her eyes never leaving Clara, Arlene whispered back. "She told her parents she's applying to Julliard when she gets a little older."

"Good for her," Ellie said. "You can't let a talent like hers go to waste."

When Clara finished, and after much applause, Charlie announced, "thank you, and I'm happy to announce our little Clara here has agreed to sing for us an hour each Saturday night, so please come to Columbo's!"

As Arlene left to congratulate her niece, Mary Oliva came in with her husband holding hands with an adorable little boy and a shy little girl.

"Dot, this is my husband John, and our children, Marisol and Joey." Her children were small, maybe three and four. John reached out and shook my dad's hand.

"Sorry, you didn't win. I voted for you," John said.

"Thanks, but you know I think Charlie is the right man for the job." Dad was humble. I gave him that. He was also vastly relieved as evident from the smile on his face.

"So, now that you're done with school, I thought I'd mention there's plenty of filing to do over at the police station," Mary said.

"Maybe I'll apply. It may be the only offer I get," I answered. "I think Officer Sprague was pretty impressed with me, and of course I'm a big favorite of Officer Jerry. Now that Miss Robinson has lost her champion in Morton Manning, she doesn't have a lead on any jobs at the courthouse. I guess I'm on my own."

"You know she was in love with him, right?" Maureen said. "There were rumors that when she was younger, they had an affair."

"I thought so. What happened?"

Maureen leaned on one hand. "He dumped her when someone younger and prettier came along. Who knows where I was in the long line of women. And here's an interesting piece of information...I hear Miss Daisy had to shut down a room after he left."

I laughed at the irony of it. Barb blackmailed me because my father walked in the door at Miss Daisy's one night to help a friend hold onto his marriage, and her husband was a regular.

Maureen looked wistful as she let out a sigh. "The thing is, Miss Robinson never stopped loving him. Now that he's practicing law in Dallas, I wonder if she'll try and follow him?"

"And that would be sad," I said.

"So, when do we start the Camden Working Ladies' Club?" Mary asked.

"It probably would be good if I was actually working."

"Okay, but I already have an idea for our first service project."

I cringed as I started to see shades of Barb in Mary. What would I be doing? More flower arrangements?

"A scholarship fund for young women," she said. "Let's support our Camden ladies who are going to college."

"What an excellent idea," I said.

"Don't get her started," John said jokingly. "My Mary loves to help people."

I remembered how she had helped me get answers to my questions when Officer Jerry shut me out. She was going to be a great founding member of the club.

"I think it's the best idea to help the women in our town in decades." Jane, Barb's gopher, stood behind us, holding a tiny baby swaddled in a pink blanket. "With Barb out of the picture, I've been asked to take over running the ladies' club, but you know, I just don't feel like it fits me anymore. This is our third child, and our finances are pretty stretched. I don't think we're going to fit into the country club set much longer. If you'll have me, I'd love to be a part of the working women's club."

"That would be wonderful, but you don't work outside the home, do you?" Mary asked.

"I work day and night taking care of my family. No days off, no sick days. Trust me, I work," Jane said as the baby cooed, making us all smile.

"Indeed, you do," Mary said.

"Great, now we have three members," I said.

"And scholarship money to raise for little women like this one," Jane said.

"Exactly," I agreed. "We have a lot of money to raise. I hear tuition is up to 1200 dollars a year at public college."

"And that's what makes it fun!" Mary replied.

It seemed we were all starting new chapters in our lives, and as Ben Dalton walked in and caught my eye, I had to wonder what my next adventure would be?

I smiled back and then felt Ellie squeeze my arm. As he started over, I thought to myself, I think I'm beginning to like the swinging sixties.

Acknowledgements

I would like to thank Dawn Dowdle, my agent who believed in me when I told her I wanted to write a historical mystery. Being a writer with big ideas is easy, but having someone else believe in them is an entirely different matter. Also, thank you to Level Best Books for your support and encouragement!

About the Author

Teresa Trent writes historical mysteries, cozy mysteries, romance and short stories. She lives in South Texas with her husband and son with Down syndrome and splits her time between writing and caretaking.

SOCIAL MEDIA HANDLES:
  Facebook - www.facebook.com/teresatrentmysterywriter
  Twitter@ttrent_cozymys

AUTHOR WEBSITE:
  https://teresatrent.com

Also by Teresa Trent

Camel Press

The Piney Woods Series
    Murder of a Good Man
    A Sneeze to Die For
    Die Die Blackbird

Self-Published

The Pecan Bayou Series
    A Dash of Murder
    Overdue for Murder
    Doggone Dead
    Buzzkill
    Burnout
    Murder for a Rainy Day
    Oh Holy Fright
    Till Dirt do Us Part

CPSIA information can be obtained
at www.ICGtesting.com
Printed in the USA
BVHW072230040122
625441BV00006B/130